Ian: A Scottish Outlaw

Highland Outlaws, Volume 6

Lily Baldwin

Published by Lily Baldwin, 2021.

To my readers with love.

Chapter One

Haddington Abbey, Scottish Highlands 1306

A full moon shone high in the sky as Ian raced up the steps of Haddington Abbey and pounded his fist on the chapel door. "Open up! I need to speak with the abbot!" Hearing the sudden shuffling of feet and muffled voices coming from inside, he ceased his knocking. Moments later, the door swung wide. Two monks filled the entrance, one holding a candle high over his head, illuminating his deeply furrowed brow, which eased an instant later. "Master Ian, what are ye doing here at this hour? 'Tis nearly Matins."

"I need to see the abbot," he barked. "Step aside...please," he added, remembering himself, but that was the only courtesy his fury would allow. He didn't have time for niceties. "I will show myself to his room," he boomed, barreling past the monks, their mouths gaping open in surprise.

"But he's sleeping!"

"I'll wake him up," he called back, then hastened down the aisle, making the sign of the cross as he passed a side altarpiece with Jesus and the Virgin Mary at its center, flanked by the naked figures of Adam and Eve. Hurrying down a columned hallway, he broke into a run when he reached the cloisters. Then, he cut across the courtyard and raced into the monks' dormitory.

"Abbot," he called before his knuckles had even made contact with the slatted door. Not waiting for permission to enter, he swung the door wide and stepped inside, his gaze immediately settling on the narrow platform bed in the corner, but it was empty. Surprised, he scanned the room, finding the abbot sitting in one of the rough-hewn, wooden chairs in front of the blazing hearth.

Abbot Matthew met Ian's gaze. "I wondered how long it would take ye to beat down my door."

"Then ye've heard?"

The abbot nodded, his face impassive.

Ian raked his hand through his hair. "Ye know what I must do, then."

"Ye needn't do anything," the abbot said calmly.

Ian's eyes flashed wide. "Bishop Lamberton has been arrested for the role he played in bringing about the Bruce's coronation!"

Abbot Matthew nodded. "I ken."

"Then why do ye sit there when ye should be assembling the agents? We have to break him out!"

To Ian's dismay, the abbot did not lunge to his feet. He merely raised his brows, seemingly not alarmed by Ian's impassioned plea. "That would be most foolhardy. Whatever put such an idea into yer head?"

Ian's mouth fell open, but he pushed through his confusion. "Did ye fall and hit yer head or something, Abbot? Mayhap, ye didn't hear me right. The bishop is being charged with treason and is locked away in the Tower of London. Ramsay's arrival is imminent. Then we ride to London and—"

"And what?" The abbot arched his brow. "And get yerselves and the bishop killed?"

"How can ye say that? Do ye doubt our skills?" Ian whirled around and stormed back toward the door. "We're breaking him out, with or without yer support."

"Steady, Ian. The bishop does not require yer assistance."

Ian froze, his fingers gripping the latch. "Have ye more news?"

The abbot walked toward him and outstretched a placating hand. "Listen to me. Ye're upset, and I ken why, but ye must try and calm down."

"Calm down! Do ye not ken what will happen to him if he's found guilty? He'll be drawn and quartered. We have to save him!"

"Breathe, Ian. No one is going to rip the man apart. He's a bishop. His Holy Orders, and only his Holy Orders, will save him. If ye and Ramsay interfere, ye're bound to get yerselves and the bishop killed."

Ian backed away from the door and started pacing, raw fury coursing through him, clouding his thoughts. He fought to understand the abbot's reasoning when all he wanted to do was start building the plan that would free the bishop and bring him home to Scotland. He whirled around, looking the abbot hard in the eye. "Ye cannot expect me to stand by and do nothing."

"Ye're right, not when there's work to be done. Scotland's army was decimated at Methven, and our king has fled to the Hebrides where he hides in a cave like a common outlaw. Ye'd best not stand around—not when we've an army to rebuild."

Ian stopped pacing, but still his heart pounded. "I thought we had finally done it," he growled, venting his fury. "I stood with the bishop at Scone and watched the Countess of Buchan place Scotland's crown on the Bruce's head, and now..."

"I ken," the abbot said, his tone placating. "We're facing more setbacks. We cannot change what has transpired, but we keep going. We keep fighting."

Ian turned away, his anger still red-hot.

"Listen to me. Ye and Ramsay are two of my finest agents. Ye can't go after the bishop—it would be suicide. Scotland needs ye. I need ye." The abbot moved to stand alongside him. "Come on, lad. Do not let yer temper be yer guide, no matter what color hair ye have."

Ian closed his eyes and pictured the waves lapping the shores of Colonsay, a small island in the Hebrides where his family—all outlaws to the crown—hid away from the brutal reaches of Longshanks. Conjuring the pungent scent of the sea air, he began to feel his rage dissipate. When his calm returned, a smile tugged at his lips, and he glanced sidelong at the abbot. "Rose is always telling me that I've a temper to match my hair."

The abbot chuckled, looking rather relieved, owing, no doubt, to Ian's newfound calm. "I'm not certain yer elder sister has the right to that particular judgment, not with her piles of red hair and her fiery soul to match."

Ian released a long breath, the last of his hot air. "That's true," he said before collapsing in one of the chairs by the hearth, his legs outstretched. Accepting a mug of ale from the abbot, he took a long swig. "All right," he conceded. "I defer to yer wisdom. We won't go after the bishop."

The abbot took the seat beside him and gave Ian a fatherly pat on the hand. "Rest tonight, son of Scotland, for come the morrow, ye'll be so busy, ye won't have blinked and we'll be welcoming the bishop home."

Ian rested his head against the back of his chair, but then he jerked upright. There was one thing he needed to make clear. "I'm just telling ye now, Abbot. If ye're ever arrested, there's nothing anyone could do or say that would prevent me from saving ye."

"Glad I am to hear it," the abbot declared. "I'm no bishop. King Edward would string me up with little worry for his soul."

"I'd never let that happen," Ian vowed. Then he held his cup high. "*Alba gu bràth*." Scotland Forever.

Abbot Matthew raised his cup. "*Alba gu bràth*," he said, repeating the secret password of their cause.

Chapter Two

Castle Toonan, Scottish Lowlands, 1306
Laird Malcom Fergusson's head pounded, and his heart raced. He paced in front of the hearth in his chamber, glancing every few seconds at the door through which his steward should arrive at any moment.

"Where is he?" Malcom growled aloud.

An instant later, Thane threw open the door, his chest heaving, sweat beading down the silver hair at his temples. His round face, boyish despite his forty years, was crimson, his cheeks puffing as he fought to catch his breath. "My...my laird, Captain William has just arrived."

"What has he to report?"

"Laird Stewart continues his advance."

"Blast," Malcom cursed, clenching his fists. "And Baron Wharncliffe?"

Thane shook his head grimly. "He still leads the march."

Malcom raked his hand through his hair. "How much time do we have?"

"William witnessed the enemy crest Toonan Hill before he raced back to the keep to warn us of their proximity."

Malcom closed his eyes against the news and turned away, not wanting his clansman to see his despair. Taking a deep breath, he turned back, locking eyes once more with his most trusted adviser. "We have one hour before they reach our gates, maybe less."

"There's more," Thane blurted.

Malcom took a deep breath, bracing himself for further ill tidings.

"William also reported that Baron Wharncliffe's cavalry is fully armored."

"But why?" Malcom exclaimed, unable to contain his fury. "What have we done to incur his wrath?"

"I'm not certain, my laird, but ye did refuse Laird Stewart's offer to betroth Josselyn to his eldest son."

Malcom shook his head. "I cannot believe the Stewart marches on Toonan Castle now for something that happened more than a year ago. And what concern is the alliance of two lowland clans to an English lord?"

"I do not ken, my laird."

Malcom renewed his pacing. "We are a humble clan, brought lower still by our poor harvest this season. Baron Wharncliffe can have no reason to march against us. Unless..." He stopped in his tracks, his heart suddenly racing. Turning his back on Thane, he pressed his fist to his lips. "Could it be?" he muttered under his breath.

"I did not hear ye, my laird."

"'Tis nothing," Malcom snapped, again turning to face his steward. "There must be something we've missed."

Thane's cheeks puffed out before he released his breath in a long stream. At length he said, "Laird Stewart has rejected the Bruce, aligning himself with King Edward. The English have made gains throughout our region. Mayhap yer continued loyalty to the Scottish king draws them to Toonan."

Malcom shook his head. "Then why did Wharncliffe's men pass through Ross territory on their way to Stewart castle without incident? Ross is still loyal to the Bruce."

Thane ran his hand through his thinning hair. "I know not why they march on Toonan, my laird."

Malcom's nostrils flared. He pressed his lips into a grim line. "Damnation," he whispered, turning back to gaze into the hearth at the hungry flames. Again, he searched his mind for answers, struggling to find another explanation, anything but what he feared most.

"We have but one certitude. Neither Laird Stewart nor Baron Wharncliffe are after our coffers."

"Certainly, the West Lowlands boast far wealthier clans than ours," Thane agreed.

"Not that we're destitute," Malcom said, quick to defend his own. "None among our number have ever gone hungry. My people are content, this I do not doubt."

"They are, indeed, my laird. If not our coffers, then mayhap the temptation is our fine borders?" Thane suggested.

Malcom drummed his fingers on the mantle while he considered this. Fergusson territory abutted Stewart territory to the east, but to the west, Fergusson land stretched clear to the coast. Certainly, Lorne, the self-serving leader of Clan Stewart, would not turn his nose up at expanding his territory, but Malcom shook his head.

"If Lorne acted alone, then ye might be right, but Fergusson territory could never tempt a lord as powerful as Baron Wharncliffe."

Malcom could deny the truth no longer.

He turned and locked eyes with Thane. "There is only one reason an army led by one of King Edward's most trusted advisers marches this way."

"What are ye suggesting, my laird?"

Malcom gripped the mantle, his knuckles whitening under the strain. "I've been betrayed," he hissed before pushing away from the hearth and storming from his chamber.

Torch fire blurred into orange streaks as Malcom barreled through the corridor to his solar. Throwing open the door with Thane following just behind, he crossed to the table laden with maps, missives, and accounting records and sat down, scrubbing a hand over his face.

Looking bewildered, Thane moved to stand in front of him, his arms hanging limp at his sides. "What has happened, my laird?"

"They must know," Malcom hissed, his fist coming down hard on the table.

"Know what?" Thane asked, but then his eyes widened, and Malcom knew his steward had put the pieces together for himself. "They couldn't...why...that's impossible!"

"Trust me," Malcom growled, fighting to maintain control. He took a steadying breath. "Baron Wharncliffe leads his army with the support of the treacherous Stewart onto Fergusson soil for one purpose alone...to reclaim the king's treasure."

Two years ago, Bishop Lamberton, Scotland's great defender, had entrusted Malcom with secreting away a vast treasure, a portion of which had been stolen from Westminster Abbey by Scottish rebels.

Thane moved closer. "How do they know ye're the keeper?"

Malcom shook his head. "I ken not." He stood up and crossed to the chess set on a table near the fireplace. Idly picking up the queen, he tossed it in his hand. "I confided my possession of the treasure to so few," he muttered.

Then he set the queen down and began to pace. "I took Laird Munroe and Captain Angus Grant into my confidence, but neither man would have betrayed me, or Scotland for that matter. Laird Monroe fought by my side at Dunbar after the sacking of Berwick, and Angus was godfather to my daughter. For pity's sake, they both died this summer at Methven. Men do not betray their country, then willingly die for it."

Thane nodded resolutely. "I do not doubt their loyalty, my laird, but..." His voice trailed off.

Malcom stared impatiently at his servant. "But what, man? Speak up!"

"'Tis possible that they each might have confided the knowledge to someone they trusted wholeheartedly who, in turn, told someone else and so on."

Malcom fisted his hands, his nails biting into his palms. "The folly of men," he growled. Expelling a long breath, he dropped his arms to his sides and hung his head. "And my own folly. I never should have spoken of it." He circled around his table and sat down before continuing, "but when Bishop Lamberton was arrested, I feared what might happen to the treasure if I, too, was imprisoned or died in battle."

"Ye only meant to do what was right for yer people and for Scotland," Thane offered.

"Do not placate me. Save yer comfort for the families who may be hurt by my actions." Fury once more coursed through him. He couldn't let his people suffer. "Damnation," he roared, dragging his arms across the table, sending the contents crashing to the floor.

Chest heaving, he sat back in his chair and gazed at the tapestries lining the walls as he fought for calm. Each one told the story of a Scottish king from the very first to be crowned on the Stone of Destiny, Kenneth MacAlpin, to the last, Alexander the third.

What would the great kings of ol' do in his stead?

It was not the first time Malcom had wished the deceased leaders could step down from the wall hangings to advise him, but as always, the weight of his next move rested on his shoulders alone. At least, he had prepared for the worst, although he had prayed he'd never have to carry out his plans.

Inhaling deeply, he pressed his hands on the table and stood up, looking Thane hard in the eye. "'Tis done. We cannot change the past."

Malcolm circled around the table and hastened across the room to an ornately carved chest. Opening it with a key he kept loosely tied around his neck, he seized one of three bags of coin.

"If I may be so bold, my laird, mayhap take just a small portion of the treasure—"

Malcom whirled around. "An army breathes down my neck. The hour for building our defenses or replenishing our stores has passed. And even if we did have time, as I've told ye before, we cannot use the treasure."

"Indeed, the hour is late for preparations, but mayhap ye could use a portion to bribe our enemies—"

"For the last time, Thane, the treasure cannot be used, not by my hand. Enough talk. We must act before we run out of time. Tell the captain to stand down all defenses."

Thane's eyes widened. "But, my laird, our enemy will certainly take the keep."

"They will take Toonan no matter what we do. Our warriors are no match for such a force, nor can our stores outlast theirs."

"But...but..." Thane stammered. "Ye cannot mean to open the gates and invite him into slaughter yer people."

"They will not attack if we do not fight. They're not after Toonan. They're after me."

"If they take ye prisoner, what will ye tell them?"

"Nothing. The men who march here may know that the treasure is in my possession, but no man knows where I've hidden it."

"They'll hurt ye, my laird!"

"I understood the risks when I agreed to conceal the treasure for the bishop."

Thane, drawing his stomach in and puffing his chest out, declared, "Ye cannot do this, my laird. Do not surrender!"

"What would ye have me do? If I don't surrender myself, blood will be spilled."

"Yer people have the right to defend their laird!"

Malcom shook his head. "These are dark enough times as it is. The Bruce has been defeated. Even now he hides in the Hebrides, not only from the English King, but from his Scottish enemies, too. 'Tis only a matter of time before Edward's fury is felt this far north. I would rather surrender myself so that my people might live to fight another day."

"What other day?" Thane snapped before quickly bowing his head. "Forgive me, my laird, but what day do ye speak of? This might be the last fight."

Malcom shook his head. "The Bruce will rise to power again. Scotland's fight is not over." He expelled a long breath.

"But mine is." Handing the bag of coin to Thane, he said, "Take my family far from here. I entrust them into yer care."

Thane refused to take the coin. "Surely, Lady Clara and Lady Josselyn will be safer at Toonan. Ye just said that ye intend to surrender yerself."

Malcom pushed the bag into his steward's chest. "Take the coin," he hissed. "Lead them west to the Hebrides or east to the Orkney Isles, some place far from the greedy reaches of King Edward."

Thane clutched the bag, tears glistening in his eyes. "Does such a haven exist?" Shaking his head furiously, he set the coin on a table. "Send someone else, my laird. Do not ask me to abandon ye now, in this yer darkest hour."

Malcom shook his head. "Do this for me, old friend. There is no one else I can trust. Vow to me now that ye'll keep my family safe."

Thane cast his gaze to the ground. "This I vow, my laird."

"Come," Malcom urged. "We have to move quickly."

Chapter Three

"**I**s it not the most beautiful tunic ye've ever seen?" Lady Josselyn asked, spinning in a quick circle in front of her maid Ruby.

Ruby's emerald gaze shone with admiration. "Indeed, it is. Yer mother has a fine eye and hand. No one weaves such beautiful cloth as Lady Fergusson."

"'Twas a gift for my birthday," Josselyn said, holding her head higher. "Do I look older?"

"Ye look every bit of yer ten and five years," Ruby declared. "Yer mother will be so proud."

Josselyn looked expectantly toward the door. "Where is she? She was supposed to join us. I hope she's all right. Her cough has returned. Mayhap she's taken to her bed again."

"Nay, I saw her sitting with her needlework in the solar not two hours ago. She must have been detained." Ruby's voice dropped, taking on a conspiratorial tone. "Something is going on. I'm certain of it."

Josselyn leaned close, awaiting the latest gossip with bated breath. "Did she discover who's been looting the stores?"

"Aye, but that was yesterday's news. It was Jacob's sons, those good-for-nothing lay-abouts. They were stealing sacks of grain from the clan stores to pass off as their own. Can ye imagine? And with the poor harvest we've had so far," Ruby said, clucking her tongue with disapproval. "Of course, when their father did the rounds and saw their oat fields still in need of harvesting, he caught on right quick to what had happened.

Set them to work straight away, he did, and has commanded that they finish the harvest for the rest of the cottars on the Eastern slope. He's even making them work the Sabbath."

Josselyn gasped. "He didn't?"

"Aye, he did. He told them they could add breaking the sacrament to their list of sins when next they sought confession, and then Cook said she saw them filing into the chapel this morning, faces scrubbed clean and in their finest tunics. She said she'd never seen a more pathetic or repentant lot."

"Oh my," Josselyn exclaimed. "Well, that is one mystery solved, but what is now afoot? A lover's tryst in the pantry? Or mayhap an unplanned handfasting?"

"I ken not," Ruby said eagerly. "Although, wouldn't that be grand, so romantic." She drew closer. "All I can tell ye is that before dawn I saw the captain and a band of ten warriors leave through the gate at a gallop. And as I was leaving the kitchens just now, on my way to yer chamber, I spied the steward racing through the Great Hall!"

A tightness settled in Josselyn's chest at this news. "Oh dear! But why?"

Ruby lifted her shoulders. "I asked Cook and she told me to mind what was mine and to stop asking her so many questions."

Josselyn smoothed her hands down her tunic, once more admiring the colors, deep green and wine red, both of which her mother had chosen to complement Josselyn's chestnut hair and creamy complexion. "Whatever has happened, it can't be too worrisome or dangerous or else the alarm would have sounded."

Suddenly, the door swung wide. Josselyn whirled around and clapped her hands together in excitement as her parents hurried into the room. "Ye're both just in time." She spun in a circle. "Ye've out done yerself, Mama! Thank ye—"

"Josselyn, we have to go," her mother said abruptly before crossing the room to the wardrobe against the far wall.

Josselyn made a careless gesture with her hand. "My lessons can wait." She fanned out her skirt. "Look at how the colors blend when I spin."

"Ye look beautiful," her father offered.

She turned, ready to rush into his arms but faltered when she glimpsed his drawn brow. "What has happened? Ye look so sad."

"I told ye," Lady Clara said, draping Josselyn's heavy wool cloak around her shoulders. "We must go."

Eyes wide, Josselyn took in the hard set to her mother's features. "But...I don't understand. Why must we go?"

Her father drew closer. "There's no time to explain," he said before pulling her into his arms.

Josselyn's heart pounded. There was a finality and a desperation in her father's embrace that frightened her to her core. She pulled away, her own gaze seeking her father's for reassurance. Like her, he had one golden brown eye and one pale blue—both were heavy with sorrow.

"Da, please, ye're scaring me. We've always confided in each other. Tell me what's happened."

Once again, he crushed her against his chest, his warm, familiar scent surrounding her. "Hush, sweetling. Ye're going to be fine, but 'tis time to go."

"But ye've not told me where?"

"That is not important now," he said in a calm voice that did nothing to mask his worried expression.

Her gaze darted around the room. Thane stood in the doorway, his face red and his eyes wide. He was wearing his cloak and had a bulging satchel clutched in his fist. Ruby stood in the center of the room, wringing her hands, her face stricken.

Josselyn whirled around to face her father. "But Ruby hasn't readied my trunks. She's coming, too, is she not? I've never traveled anywhere without Ruby and my trunks."

"Look at me," her mother said firmly, seizing Josselyn's face between her hands. "We need ye to be strong."

Tears flooded Josselyn's eyes, blurring her mother's determined face. She nodded, unable to speak.

"'Tis time," Thane urged, half out the door.

Panicking, she sought her father's gaze. "Da!"

He pulled her close once more. "Everything will be all right. Just mind yer mother and Thane."

She gasped, gripping his tunic in her fists. "Ye're not coming with us?"

His face softened. "All will be well in the end, my sweet lass, ye'll see."

"Ye didn't answer me!"

Thane drew close. "I promise ye, my lady, I will protect ye with my life if need be."

She looked away from him, shaking her head furiously at her father. "I won't leave ye."

A sad smile curved Malcom's lips. "We are never truly apart, daughter."

A sob tore from her throat. She threw her arms around his neck. "I will never let ye go."

"Ye must trust me, lass," he whispered in her ear. Despite how she struggled, he forced her arms down. "Go with Thane and yer mother," he said firmly.

Lady Clara drew close and looked her hard in the eye. "Ye're made of stronger stuff than ye realize."

Josselyn had never seen her mother look so unyielding. She ceased her protests, although she could not quell the tears rushing down her cheeks. Hearing a stifled sob, Josselyn looked over at Ruby who was crying into her hands.

She rushed to her maid's side. "I love ye, Ruby," she blurted, throwing her arms around Ruby's neck.

"And I ye, my lady!"

A moment later, Lady Clara clasped Josselyn's hand, pulling her toward the door. "Come now."

"Wait," Malcom burst out, storming after them. He took her mother into his arms and kissed her long and hard. Josselyn's chest tightened. She could hardly draw breath as she watched her parents embrace as if for the last time.

Then her father turned to her and crushed her against his chest. "I love ye," he whispered before he pulled away and reached again for his wife. "Clara, ye unlocked my passion and taught me love. Ye're my queen. Remember that," he declared. Then his gaze shifted to Josselyn. He cupped her cheek. "Mind what I've always told ye—the greatest gift ye can give someone is time."

"But Da," she cried, clinging to him. "I want more time."

A bittersweet smile suddenly curved his lips. His gaze raked over her face as if memorizing every detail. "I'm so proud of my wee lass. I love my wee lass." Then he thrust her away from him. "Go now! Before it's too late!"

Her mother seized her arm and yanked her through the door. Crying, Josselyn stumbled forward, down flights of stairs, through the Great Hall, then into the courtyard. Tears blurred her vision. Her mind raced. Tremors of fear coursed through her. She thought her knees would give way, but, suddenly, strong hands seized her waist, lifting her into the air and setting her astride a horse.

She sat, numbly, her chest tight, her breathing shallow. She couldn't feel her limbs.

"My lady, ye must grip the reins," a man's voice said, the sound muffled by the din of her heart blasting in her ears.

"We must ride, Josselyn," she heard her mother call out, although her voice sounded distant. "Take up the reins!"

"Mama," she cried, fumbling with the leather straps, searching the hazy faces around her for warm, brown eyes and a heart-shaped face.

"I'm here," her mother said, bringing her horse alongside Josselyn's. "Take a deep breath, lass."

Josselyn nodded and did as her mother bade.

"Good. Now, take another."

Josselyn inhaled deeply and then again, and soon her heartbeat stopped drumming in her ears. For the first time, she looked clearly at the warriors and horses surrounding them. There were ten guards altogether, plus Thane and her mother.

"Let's ride," Thane shouted, his mount thundering forward.

Josselyn gripped the reins as she set out, but she shifted in her saddle to look back. Her father stood on the battlements, and once more, deep, soul-wrenching sobs claimed her. It was all she could do to keep her seat as Toonan and her father faded in the distance. Even when the tallest tower could no longer be seen, she continued to gaze back. Finally, she closed her eyes, leaned over in her saddle, clung to her mount's neck, and prayed it was all just a nightmare from which she would wake.

"This isn't real," she told herself.

It couldn't be.

Soon, the terrorizing dream would all be over. She would rise from sleep and join her family in the great room to break their fast, and after that, she would work for a while at her needlepoint before going to visit Cook and Ruby in the kitchens. Then, her father would send for her, and they would pass the afternoon together playing chess as was their habit.

Aye, it was all a dream.

She swallowed hard, squeezing her eyes tighter, wishing to deny the moment, but she could not ignore the pain shooting through her thighs and hands from gripping her mount so tightly. Wincing, she opened her eyes, seeing the world streak past in a fury.

And she knew it was no dream.

When their pace suddenly slowed, she sat up straight for the first time since Toonan had passed from view. A chill crept up her spine as the warriors leading their party entered the narrow path through Craobh Forest.

Turning in her saddle, she gazed back longingly at the Eastern slope, dotted with stone cottages basking in the late morning sunshine. Facing forward once again, she glanced up at the leafy branches tangled overhead, blotting out the light. Her shoulders hugged her ears as shadow closed in around them. Why had they journeyed into the forest? Why not keep to the main road where it was sunny and easy to traverse?

She sat straighter, her nostrils flared. Why were they fleeing Toonan in the first place? Still, no one had bothered to tell her what was going on.

Turning to look back, she sought her mother's gaze. Lady Clara sat alert in her saddle, her back straight, her jaw set.

"Mother," Josselyn began, "please tell me why—"

"Not now," Lady Clara hissed. "We are in danger. Be quiet and ever vigilant."

Josselyn drew a sharp breath, then jerked forward, mimicking her mother's intent pose. She became aware of the natural choir of the forest—birds chirping, leaves rustling, branches snapping. Breathless, her gaze was pulled in all directions. Then suddenly a loud screech sounded deep in the wood. Josselyn gasped, her heart renewing its thunderous pounding. Then a blur of shadow shot out between two trees, streaking toward her. She screamed and ducked.

"I'm coming, my lady," Thane called.

Through the gap between her arms covering her face, she saw Thane circle around and ride back to her side.

"'Twas only a bird." He reached out and squeezed her hand. "Have courage, my lady. I will keep ye safe."

Gulping for air, Josselyn nodded, wanting to believe him. Slowly, she eased her shoulders down and straightened her back. "I will be brave, Thane. I will try."

But no sooner had she spoken the vow than a pained gargle rent the air and the lead Fergusson guard fell back off his horse, landing with a hard thud on the ground. She screamed, eyes bulging at the sight of the arrow protruding from his chest. A breath later, the forest erupted around her.

Stewart clansmen poured out from between the trees. Her horse reared up on its hind legs. She clung to her mount desperately. When her mare's hooves touched back down, her heart quaked at the sight of clashing warriors, their swords slashing and their faces twisted with ugly rage. She closed her eyes to block out the bloodshed.

"Ride!" Thane shouted at her.

But she couldn't move. She squeezed her horse tightly around the neck, her body frozen with terror. Strangled cries of the dying blasted her ears, forcing fearful sobs from her lips.

"Josselyn," Thane shouted.

Her eyes flew open. She gaped in horror at an enemy warrior charging at her, his face menacing. He raised his blade to strike. She crossed her arms in front of her face. She squeezed her eyes shut, but the agony of death never came. The clash of metal stung her ears. She opened her eyes to see Thane parrying the warrior's next blow.

"Josselyn!"

"Mama," she cried at the sound of her mother's voice. Sitting straight, her gaze darted in all directions, but panic blurred her vision, catapulting her fear to depths she'd never known. Her mother charged past her, seizing her reins, veering them off the path into a thicket.

"Take yer reins," her mother cried, tossing them back.

Josselyn fumbled with the leather straps, then bent low in the saddle, weaving through the thick trees after Lady Clara. An agonizing cry forced her to glance back at the forest path where a Stewart warrior was yanking his blade free from her fallen clansman's chest. She gasped, realizing Thane was the only Fergusson left standing.

"Run, Thane," she cried, though he was too far away to hear her plea.

Like all Fergusson men, Thane could wield a sword, but he had the small stature of a clerk. She knew he would never survive against so many. She prayed he would surrender himself, but her heart sank as she watched the Fergusson steward ready his stance, sword raised high.

"Mama, Thane fights alone! We must do something!"

But Lady Clara did not look back. She charged ahead, winding around trees. Branches tore at Josselyn's hair and cloak as she followed, but still she strained to keep her gaze trained on her beloved clansman.

It happened in a flash.

A Stewart warrior charged. Thane swung his blade. The warrior ducked, then seized Thane's wrist and twisted his arm, until he cried out, dropping his sword. Still, he struggled, swinging his fists, but to no avail. Within moments, breaths, the warrior had tied Thane's wrists, tossed him over the back of his horse and rode off with him.

"Spread out! They can't be far!" another warrior shouted.

"Mama, they're coming!" Josselyn cried.

"Just stay low and keep silent," her mother snapped.

Josselyn bent over in the saddle. Winding, jumping, surging forward. Her horse jerked left, then right, then left again. Her stomach heaved. Her chest ached. She buried her face in her mount's mane, closed her eyes tight against her terror, and held her breath.

After what felt like hours, although Josselyn couldn't say for sure, her mother's voice broke through her terror. "'Tis all right, Josselyn. We've lost them."

She didn't look up or release her grip on her horse's neck. She dared not move or speak.

"Josselyn," her mother said, sharply. "Sit up!"

The hardness of her mother's tone forced Josselyn to jerk upright, realizing for the first time that they were no longer racing for their lives.

Lady Clara's face was pale and strained, her eyes stricken. "I need ye to be strong, lass."

"But I'm not like ye," Josselyn cried. "Ye're scared of nothing."

"Ye could not be more wrong, lass, for I am a mother. Ye've never known fear until ye've had to pray for yer child's life to be spared. But we are Fergusson women. We are made of stronger stuff than ye know." Her voice was firm. "Now sit straighter. Take some deep breaths."

Josselyn did as her mother bade her. She breathed deep and prayed for courage, then breathed out and prayed for strength. At length she opened her eyes. "I will be brave," she promised, infusing her tone with greater confidence than she truly felt, but that was how faith happened: one had to leap.

They rode until the woods thinned, and rolling moorland once more spread out before them. In the distance, torch fire from a small village beckoned them with flickering light and the promise of food and rest.

"'Tis the village of Beag. We'll be able to purchase supplies. That is if…" Her mother's words trailed off as she swung down from her horse to search through her saddle bags.

"Blast!"

"What is it?" Josselyn asked.

"Thane was in possession of our only coin." Brows drawn, Lady Clara again fumbled through her bags, her movements becoming increasingly frantic. For the first time, since her mother had rushed into her chambers, Josselyn glimpsed fear in her eyes.

"Damnation," her mother cursed again. "We'll never make it to the Orkney Islands now."

"The Orkney Islands! But that is so far. Oh, what are we going to do?" Josselyn sobbed, tears streaming down her cheeks.

Her mother turned, giving her a fierce look. "We haven't time for tears."

Josselyn swallowed hard. "But...but ye just said that we've no coin. Where will we go? How will we survive?"

"I do not ken, child, but whatever we do, I promise ye, it will be hard and dangerous."

"Nay, mama!"

Lady Clara cupped her cheeks. "But ye can do this, love," she hissed fervently.

Josselyn trembled, shaking her head. "I can't." She jerked away from her mother's touch.

"Josselyn, look at me."

She opened her eyes and obediently met her mother's gaze. "I believe in ye!"

Within Lady Clara's eyes, Josselyn saw truth. She took a deep breath. "I believe in ye, too, Mama."

Lady Clara crushed her close. "We can do this."

Mirroring her mother's stance, Josselyn straightened her spine and threw her shoulders back. "I am ready. What now? Where will we go?"

Her mother turned resolutely, her gaze transfixed beyond the village to the distant horizon. "We will go where no one will think to look for us—south, to England. Straight into the lion's den."

Chapter Four

Two years later...
Durham, England 1308

Jo was racing against a deadline. For days and days now, she had sat at her loom from dawn until dusk, weaving an intricately designed fabric, inlaid with small beads, that was destined to be made into the surcoat worn by Lady Ashton at her eldest son's wedding. Jeremiah, a tailor favored by the nobles in the north west of England, had commissioned Jo to create the piece because of his appreciation for, in his words, her 'impeccable standards' and 'care for detail'.

Jo had accepted the commission despite the rushed deadline, owing to the generous size of Jeremiah's promised payment. However, to ensure she finished on time, she'd had to turn down other offers for work, which meant that she was entirely reliant on this one piece to meet all her upcoming financial obligations, and today was the due date.

A quiet whine forced Jo to look up from her loom at her dog Ruby, stretched out on the floor in front of the door, giving Jo a pointed look.

"I know you're hungry. But it is still early, and I have so much to do—"

Jo's own stomach growled, interrupting her. She cast Ruby a guilty glance. "All right, we'll go to market, but remember what I told you last night, I only have coin enough for bread."

Ruby jumped to her feet, wagging her tail, and padded over to where Jo sat.

Jo wove her fingers through Ruby's thick fur. "You look excited, girl, but when I give you a crusty bun, instead of the meat pie I know you think you're getting right now, you won't be so happy with me. But worry not. After Jeremiah pays me this eventide, we'll be knee deep in meat pies!"

Jo stood and stretched her arms high, working the kink out of her back. Then she seized her cloak and fastened Ruby's leash. "Remember," she whispered as they stepped outside. "We must be vigilant."

Pulling the hood of her cloak over her head, despite the warmth of the day, she plowed ahead, leaving Tivoli Street behind, setting out toward Durham's market square with her trusted companion at her side. Thinking of the several inches of length still left to weave, her chest tightened, and for a moment, she regretted having abandoned her loom. But then she took a deep breath to calm her nerves. Without doubt, she knew her goal would be met with perseverance...and a little nourishment.

Durham's crowded market square was full of bustling activity, stalls laden with goods, vendors crying out to passersby, eager to sell their wares. Throngs of shoppers, performers, and beggars wove through the narrow-cobbled streets, some impatiently pushing through the crowds as they hurried to reach their destinations, but Jo was not one of those people.

She never had to push her way through any crowd, not since she and Ruby had found each other.

A year ago, Jo had been at market, searching the stalls of yarn for the perfect shade of blue to complete her mother's latest commission...

After purchasing several skeins, Jo turned to hasten back to their workshop when she heard the most mournful cry coming from behind the neighboring stall, where costly skeins of silk thread were for sale. Jo glanced at the merchant who seemed oblivious to the pained cries.

"Here," he said, thrusting a skein of yellow silk at a young woman. "Feel how soft. You will find no softer silk in all of Durham, and the color will make your flaxen tresses shine."

The young woman blushed, tucking a lock of blonde hair behind her ear. "It is not for me, but for my lady."

"If your lady is half as beautiful as you, then..."

Taking advantage of the merchant's simpering preoccupation with his lovely young customer, Jo darted through the billowing sheets of silk lining the sides of the merchant's stall and circled around back, following the soft whimpers. Gasping, her hand flew to cover her mouth. Tied to the side handle of a large chest was an animal curled on the ground with straggly tufts of fur circling bald patches dotted with angry sores down the boney ridges of its back. At first glance, she couldn't discern what type of animal had been so cruelly abused, but then she drew closer and softly, she clicked her tongue. Its head lifted, and sorrowful yellow eyes locked with hers. The neglected creature was a dog, and in its gaze, Jo felt its plea.

Save me.

She didn't hesitate. Scurrying around the side of the stall, she made sure the merchant was still occupied. The young maid was now examining a purple skein of thread, her cheeks pink while the merchant peppered her with compliments. Quickly, Jo circled around to the back and untied the dog. For a moment, it just looked at her lamely, it's yellow gaze holding naught but despair.

"Come on," Jo whispered.

With a heart-breaking whine, the suffering beast dropped its head on its front paws, releasing a puff of air. Jo scanned the animal, her gaze checking for any visible injuries, bone protruding through flesh or places of blood letting.

"Can ye walk, girl?"

Chewing her bottom lip, Jo reflected on how best to proceed while the animal continued to look at her with pleading, woeful eyes but still did not budge.

"Be sure to tell your mistress who sold you such fine silk," she heard the merchant say.

Sucking in a sharp breath, Jo looked the dog hard in the eye. "We have to go now. Come on." Jo backed away, patting her hands on her thighs. "You can do this. Come on. If you want freedom, you must have courage."

Slowly, the dog climbed to her feet and limped toward Jo, barely setting weight on one of her hind legs.

"Good dog!" She continued to back up, calling softly, urging the wounded creature to keep going. Soon, they were both beyond the confines of the merchant's stall and had crossed the aisle into the next row of vendors.

"Let's have a look at you then," Jo murmured, examining the dog under the bright sunshine. "My, but you're a large one, aren't you and a girl." Her back nearly came up to Jo's waist. "You're almost as tall as me and, as you may have noticed, I'm not a small woman." Squatting down, she gently petted the dog's head. "You poor dear."

The idea of forcing the suffering animal to walk any farther on her painfully thin and unstable legs broke Jo's heart. "I hate to push you, girl, but you aren't safe here."

Hobbling slowly beside her, the dog managed to follow Jo through the narrow market pathways to the side of the busy cobbled road abutting the square.

"You did it, girl," Jo praised her; however, the triumph of the moment was short lived. Her mother's workshop wasn't far for those in possession of vitality, but for her new-found companion, Jo may as well have asked her to walk to London. "Don't worry," Jo reassured her. "I will think of another way."

Just then a wagon came into view, driven by a young man with a friendly countenance. He had wheat-colored hair, a freshly scrubbed face, and he smiled, dipping his head in greeting to those he passed.

Jo called out to him as he drew near. "Boy!"

"Whoa," the young man said, his smile faltering as he pulled tight on the reins, bringing his work horse to a halt next to her. "Who are you calling boy? I'm nearly fifteen."

Jo bit her cheek to keep from smiling at the young man now scowling at her. "Thank you for stopping," she said as she hurried to peer over the side of the wagon. There were trays of cakes and hand pies and baskets piled high with crusty loaves.

"Are you a baker?"

"My father is the baker. I'm his assistant," he replied, puffing out his chest and sitting straighter in his seat.

She smiled up at him warmly. "I dare say you've room for a couple of passengers. Will you not take pity on this poor beast and drive us to Tivoli Street? I dare not make her walk the whole way."

The boy slowly scanned her from head to toe. Despite him being nearly three years her junior, he looked disapprovingly at her threadbare tunic. She held her chin high, refusing his assessment. Then his gaze settled on her weary and neglected companion. "She'd never make it," the boy observed, his scowl deepening. "If you cannot care for your dog properly, then you shouldn't keep her."

Jo's eyes flashed wide at the boy's assumption. "She's not mine, or at least she wasn't until a few moments ago. I've just stolen her away from her undeserving owner." Her face softened, remembering she was asking for help. "Please," she beseeched him. "Help me save her."

The boy jumped down and bowed at the waist. "My name is Joseph."

She smiled. "What a coincidence. My name is Jo."

He gave her a quizzical look. "Allow me to guess...Jo is short for...Josephina?"

She shook her head.

"Then it must be Johanna?"

"I am simply Jo—nothing more, nothing less."

He cocked his brow at her. "It must be short for something. I've never heard of a girl called Jo before."

She lifted her shoulders, giving him a mischievous grin. "Are you going to powder me with questions like I'm one of your cakes, or are you going to help me save this dog?"

"Dog?" he blurted before turning his gaze to the large animal standing at her side. "She is no mere dog."

"What do you mean?"

"She's part wolf. You can tell by the markings around her eyes and the length of her snout, but her size exceeds even that of a wolf. I think she must also have some Mastiff in her." Joseph jumped down. "It will take us both to get her into the wagon." He stepped toward them, but suddenly the dog growled, baring her teeth at him."

Eyes wide, Joseph scurried back.

Jo frowned and crouched down, petting the animal's bristled head. "Hush, now," she crooned. "He's a friend and means to help us." She looked up at the young man. "Try again."

Flashing Jo a dubious look, Joseph stepped toward the dog, but again she snarled, only this time, she snapped her jaws at his outstretched fingers.

Joseph held his hands up in surrender. "I won't be much of a baker with only one hand to knead my bread. I'm afraid the task of getting her in the wagon is up to you, but you must hurry. I am due at my next stop."

Jo nodded. "All right, girl," she said, patting the back of the wagon. "You'll have to jump."

The dog looked at her with pathetic eyes.

"None of that," Jo admonished, looking the frail beast hard in the eye. "If you can draw breath, you can fight." She cupped her under the chin. "You can do this, love" she said fervently. Then, smiling at the intent animal, Jo climbed into the wagon and sat down, then patted the seat next to hers. "Come on, girl," she encouraged. "Keep fighting!"

The dog eyed the spot.

"I believe in you, girl," Jo urged. Then suddenly, she leapt off her hind legs, landing in the wagon. Jo would have sworn she glimpsed pride in the dog's eyes, but the look was fleeting, replaced with desperation as she collapsed on her side, panting from the painful effort.

"I knew you could do it, girl," Jo crooned, gently snuggling her new friend. Panting and whimpering, the dog licked at a sore on her hind leg, then rested her head in Jo's lap.

"She belongs to you now, heart and soul," Joseph declared. "See the way she's looking at you? True love, that's for certain."

Jo smiled. "I love you, too, and I'll make you well," she promised softly, meeting adoring yellow eyes. "Here." She pulled a pigeon pie she had bought at market from her satchel. The dog sniffed at it but did not take it. Jo set it on the wagon in front of the poor animal. "You need it more than I do. We need not stand on formalities. Go ahead." Finally, the dog took the pie between its paws and in two bites, finished it off.

Jo laughed. "There's more where that came from. Stick with me and you'll be better in no time at all."

"What will you call her?" Joseph asked after giving the reins a gentle snap. As the wagon rolled forward, Jo considered his question. She gently stroked her newfound companion's patchy fur. "What shall I call you, girl?" she murmured.

Yellow eyes held hers. "Oh, you lovely beast." Jo wrapped her arms around the dog's neck. "We shall be the best of friends." With a soft gasp she pulled away. "Ruby! I shall call you Ruby." For a moment, sorrow, heavy and threatening, seeped into Jo's heart. Her beloved maid Ruby, like everyone and everything she had ever loved, had been lost to her.

"No," Jo whispered, chiding herself. Pushing her shoulders back, she shook her head, chasing away the memories. "It does no one any good to dwell on the past." She gave her new Ruby a hard look. "And I don't want you lamenting what brought you low either. You're safe now, and that's what matters."

Jo smiled and scratched her companion behind the ear, earning a sigh from the weary animal, who laid her head on Jo's lap and fell asleep.

Now, robust and healthy, Ruby was enormous with thick, tawny fur—tufted with darker streaks—and big, pointed ears. And she loved Jo with her whole heart but...despised absolutely everyone else.

To say that Ruby was protective of Jo would be an understatement, which did mean Jo had to keep her on a short leash or else she might bite anyone who even tried to speak to her. Ruby's loyalty meant the world to Jo, who traversed the streets of Durham with her cloak drawn and her head down, always vigilant and watchful for those who hunted for Clan Fergusson's missing ladies.

A memory flashed in Jo's mind, of the first night she and her mother had crossed the border into England. Using a small gem Lady Clara had pried loose from her wedding band as payment, they had taken a room at an inn. Most of that night, Jo had spent in tears, crying for her father and the comforts of home while fleas bit at her skin and the raucous din of drunken men rose up from the common room below them.

Lying beside her, her mother stroked her back. "Your name is Jo now," she insisted in an accent that had fooled the innkeeper into believing they were English. "We are English peasants, weavers by trade."

Jo gulped. "But we've no loom," she cried.

"We will," her mother said firmly. "We will sell—" Her mother's words were interrupted by a deep cough that racked her shoulders.

"Oh Mama, ye're not well."

Lady Clara shook her head while she continued to cough. At length, she cleared her throat. "I am fine. As I was saying, we will sell the remaining gems from my ring and our fine clothes to purchase a loom and find a room to rent."

"In this place?" Jo asked as her shoulders shot up around her ears, frightened of the wild noises below.

"No. We are still too close to the border for my comfort. We could be recognized. We shall venture farther south."

"Nay," Jo cried. "I want to go home. I want to return to Da. Don't ye?"

"There is no point wishing for what cannot be. Right now, we have no choice but to accept our fate and do what we must to survive. And make no mistake, daughter, you are fighting for your life. From now on, you keep your head down and trust no one."

Jo swallowed hard. "I will try," she answered in her best English accent. But despite her attempt to be brave, her tears renewed, streaming down her cheeks.

"Cry all you want tonight," Lady Clara soothed, her voice softening for a moment. "But come the morrow, you must dry your eyes for good. You can't see who's coming with tears flooding your eyes."

"Who is after us, Mama?"

"Anyone...Everyone!"

Jo buried her face in the crook of her arms and sobbed.

By the next day, however, Jo had done as her mother bade her. She stopped crying and had not shed another tear since—not when they arrived in Durham and found their small, shabby room to rent; not when she had to start weaving from sun up until sun down, day after day, to earn enough coin just to survive one day to the next; not even when her mother grew so ill that she insisted Jo bring her to the Durham Abbey to live out her last days in God's house.

Jo had become hard.

Jo had become vigilant.

Why *anyone* and *everyone* would wish to hunt down a modest lady from a humble lowland clan was beyond Jo's ability to comprehend, nor did her mother ever fully explain the matter, even when pressed.

And so, Jo simply had to accept her fate. She was Lady Josselyn no longer. Now, she was a simple English peasant, fighting everyday to survive.

Reflecting on her mother made Jo pick up her pace.

"Come, Ruby. We must hurry!"

Today, of all days, Jo was even more grateful for the wide berth people gave her fierce friend—she had fabric to weave, rent to pay, and payment for her mother's care was due.

As they approached the baker's table, the scents of flaky piecrust and fresh baked bread reached her nose, making her stomach rumble again and Ruby whine with excitement.

"Good day, Jo," the baker's assistant said in greeting as they approached his stand.

"Good day to you, Joseph."

Joseph beamed at her. "Will today be the day you tell me what Jo is short for?"

"Not Joseph," she replied with a cheeky grin.

"I believe we had already established that."

"I'll never tell," she teased. "So you may as well stop asking."

"Where's the fun in that?" Joseph asked with a wink before shifting his gaze to Ruby. "Well, if I can't win you over, mayhap Ruby will warm up to me today." Meat pie in hand, Joseph circled around to the front of the stall and started toward the hungry animal. "What do you say, girl," he crooned softly. Slowly squatting, Joseph started to reach out his hand to Ruby, but Jo stopped him.

"No meat pies today," she blurted, trying to ignore its succulent scent. "Two rolls will suffice."

Joseph cocked a brow at her. "Do you honestly believe a roll is going to satiate a wolf's hunger?" He held out the pie to Jo. "It's still warm."

Resisting the urge to snatch up the handful and shove it into her mouth, Jo put her hands on her hips. "I was explaining to my landlord just last week that despite Ruby's lineage, she is still just a dog."

"All right, all right," Joseph conceded. "But whether wolf, dog, or young woman, a single roll is still not enough."

Of course it's not, Jo wanted to scream, but it was all she could afford. Forcing a smile to her lips, she said, "Just the bread please."

Again, Joseph outstretched his hand. "'Tis a gift."

Jo stood her ground. "I appreciate your kindness, but I cannot accept your charity."

Giving her a dismissive look, he turned to Ruby. "This has nothing to do with you, Jo. The matter of pie versus roll is between me and Ruby." He outstretched his hand toward her dog. Despite his savory offering, Ruby's lips curled in a fierce snarl. "Come on, girl," Joseph pleaded, his voice low and soothing. "Come and get it. It's been nearly a full year since we first met. Show your mistress how you truly feel about me."

In response, Ruby's low growl deepened. Despite the dog's clear warning, Joseph reached his hand out further and lifted his foot to step closer, but Ruby lunged. Poised and ready, Jo pulled Ruby back, ensuring her snapping jaws clamped down on air instead of the baker's hand.

"I'm sorry she refused your offering, Joseph, but it's nothing you did wrong. She doesn't like anyone; you know that."

Joseph shrugged good-naturedly. "She doesn't like me yet, but there's always tomorrow." He tossed the pie at Ruby's feet.

"Joseph!"

A partial smile curved the baker's lips. "What? It slipped out of my hand."

She cocked her brow at the young man but allowed her smile to break through her disapproval. "Thank you, Joseph, but we must be off. The tailor is expecting me before the day's end."

"Good luck, fair Jo."

She waved, flashing her young friend a smile before pulling her hood low over her brow and dropping her gaze to the ground. Lengthening her strides, she hastened back toward home, her mind fixed completely on her work.

Turning onto Tivoli, she froze. Two massive men dressed in simple homespun woolen tunics and hose tucked inside tall boots, stood outside her neighbor's house. One of the men had blond hair, which was woven into a single plait that skimmed his lower back. His shoulders were broad, bulging with muscles that strained the fabric of his tunic, and judging by the mighty hammer strapped to his back and his thick arms, she guessed he was a blacksmith by trade. His companion had red hair, bright as fire in the sunshine, which fell in disarray down his broad back. He was even taller than the blacksmith, although his build was slightly leaner. Strapped to his back was a broad sword so massive, she doubted she would have the strength to wield it.

She tightened her grip on Ruby's leash and narrowed her eyes on the strangers' wide, sinewy backs. What did such daunting men want with her quiet neighbor anyway?

Drummond was an older man, slight of build. The top of his head barely came up to her chin. He was thick around the middle and had a rim of snow-white hair wrapped around his otherwise bald head. A man of few words, he left home only to attend Mass, and except for the odd delivery, he never had visitors.

As if the red-haired man sensed her gaze, he jerked around, and they locked eyes.

Jo stiffened and Ruby growled, moving to stand protectively in front of her.

The man's gaze dropped to Ruby for a moment, but then he looked up and once again locked eyes with her. She swallowed hard as she took in his powerful body and his strong features. Even at a distance, she could see the radiant blue of his eyes, like the sky in August, bright and clear. A shiver shot up her spine when he suddenly smiled at her, his whole face softening. So struck was she by his gentle handsomeness that she almost forgot herself...almost. Just as her lips began to upturn, she dropped her gaze.

On another day, she would have just turned on her heel and walked back the way she'd come, but today was too important.

"Hush, girl," she soothed, stroking her hand down Ruby's erect hackles. "If they were after me, we would know it by now."

She chanced another glance in their direction. The red-haired man was still staring at her, but there was no recognition or malice in his gaze...only admiration.

"Blast," she cursed under her breath. It mattered naught how blue his eyes were or gentle his smile. She didn't have time for this.

Just go away, you big lugs, she wanted to scream. The fabric in her loom was not going to weave itself.

"Thank you, God," she murmured when at last, the blond giant opened Drummond's door and passed inside. The red-haired man dipped his head to her. His lips curved in a sensual smile that, on another day, would have made her heart race. Then, he turned and followed his friend.

Relieved, Jo hastened toward her door and swung it wide. Immediately, she untied Ruby's leash, then crossed to her loom, sat down, and got to work.

Chapter Five

"Which one is it?" Ian asked his companion as he considered the row of one and two-story wood and thatch buildings.

"This is Tivoli street, and Abbot Matthew said it was across from a tavern, but I do not see a sign for a drinking house," Ramsey answered absently as he, too, scanned the road in both directions.

Suddenly, a door farther up the thoroughfare swung open, and a man rolled onto the street. Behind him a buxom woman with unnaturally orange hair stomped onto the road, her heaving bosom threatening to burst free from her plunging neckline. "And stay out, you louse," she shouted before turning to go back inside.

Ian winced when the door slammed. "That is one woman I hope never to cross."

Ramsay nodded vigorously. "I don't think that fool ever will again," he said, his gaze following the stooped shouldered man, stumbling drunkenly down the road.

Ian lifted his shoulders. "Well, at least we know where the tavern is." He scanned the buildings on the opposite side of the road. "That means the bishop's man must be there."

Skirting around passersby, horses, steaming piles of dung, and a young boy pushing a wheelbarrow piled high with firewood, Ian crossed to the other side of the road and knocked on the door. After several silent moments passed, Ramsay tried, knocking louder than Ian had. Still, no one came to usher them inside.

"The abbot was confident that he would be here," Ramsay said, his voice agitated.

"He also said that Drummond was an old man," Ian reminded the blacksmith. "Give him time."

Just then, movement caught Ian's eye. He glanced over his shoulder, spotting a young woman holding tight to the leash of a fierce-looking dog. Or was it a wolf? Ian's interest in the animal diminished the moment he and the lass locked eyes. Even beneath the hood of her tattered cloak, he could see that she was beautiful, tall, and slim.

And her eyes...

Ian had never seen eyes like hers. She had one pale blue eye and one golden brown.

He smiled at her to ease the look of wary suspicion on her face, but her expression did not soften. A moment later, she dropped her gaze to the ground. Her stance widened. Like her growling companion, she looked ready to fight.

"I'm going to try the door," the blacksmith said in a low voice.

Ian grunted his approval, unwilling to tear his gaze away from the lass's tall, slender curves and her uncanny, yet striking gaze that peeked up at him every few moments.

"'Tis unlocked," Ramsay whispered before easing the door open and stepping inside.

More than anything, Ian wanted to walk straight up to the beautiful lass and introduce himself, but when he considered her stony gaze and the dog's raised hackles, he knew neither would welcome his attention. Taking one last look, Ian dipped his head to the lass before following Ramsay inside.

The ground floor was simply furnished with a small square table and two chairs near the blazing hearth. A pot bubbled over the fire, issuing coils of herb-scented steam. A quick scan of the room told Ian the owner was either upstairs or not at home.

"Drummond," he called up to the second story.

"If I wanted company, I would have answered the door," a tremulous yet agitated voice called down. "Who are ye? What do ye want?"

"Abbot Matthew sent us," Ian called up the stairs.

A rustling sounded from above, and a few moments later, a short, stout old man appeared at the top of the stairwell. His bushy, silver brows furrowed above his narrow eyes. "Who are ye?"

Ian bowed his head. "*Alba gu bràth*," Scotland forever, he said quietly.

The older man's displeasure vanished from his face, replaced by a welcoming, albeit toothless smile. "*Alba gu bràth*," Drummond said, repeating the secret password of their cause. "Scotland's agents are always welcome here," he said, gripping the rail while he slowly descended the narrow wooden stairs.

When at last he stood before them, the old man scrutinized both Ian and Ramsay from head to toe. After several moments, a smile spread slowly across his lips. "I should have known ye were both sons of Scotland." The older man had to crane his neck back to look up at Ian. "Yer both as tall and mighty as the Argyle mountains. What are yer names?"

Ian bowed his head. "My name is Ian MacVie, and this here is Ramsay MacTavish."

Drummond raised his brows, and his smile widened. "Neither of ye are strangers to me, for I know ye by reputation. The bishop has told me all about the MacVie brothers who used to ride under the guise of the Saints."

When Ian was only nineteen years old, he joined ranks with his brothers, and, with the help of Bishop Lamberton, formed the Saints—a gang of highwaymen who robbed English nobles on the road north into Scotland. But Ian and his brothers had not been hell bent on riches. Every coin and jewel they stole went towards building Scotland's army and caring for orphans and exiles whose families had been crushed beneath Longshank's cruel hammer.

"To hear the bishop tell it, ye'd believe no other family has done more to advance the cause." Drummond beamed, smiling up at Ian with admiration. Then he turned to Ramsay. "I've also heard of ye, blacksmith. Ye've done more than yer share for the cause." A glint of mischief entered the old man's eyes. "I also heard ye serve a fine ale in yer hidden tavern beneath the floor of yer smithy."

"Aye, that I do. Ye'll have to join us for a meeting of Scotland's secret rebels sometime and try a cup for yerself."

"If ever the bishop is granted freedom to leave this city, then I might take ye up on yer offer, but until that day, I will stay here to serve His Excellency. Now, with that in mind, there can only be one reason Abbot Matthew would send two of his best agents to my doorstep—ye've come to see the bishop."

Ian nodded. "Since his arrest, 'tis not as easy to gain an audience with him as it once was. In fact, we've waited two long years for this meeting. The last time I saw the bishop was at the Bruce's coronation."

After spending two years imprisoned in the Tower of London, the bishop was tried for treason and found guilty. Thankfully, his life was spared solely because of his Orders. He was released from the tower, but his freedom was not fully restored. The Bishop had been sentenced to city arrest. He was not allowed to leave Durham by order of the English king.

"Ye can see the bishop on Thursday when he hears confession," Drummond informed them.

Ian furrowed his brow. "But that is four days from now."

Drummond nodded. "Regrettably, there is no other way. Ye'll have to wait until then."

Ramsay rubbed the back of his neck, his brow pinched with concern. "A lot can happen in four days."

Ian nodded. "A lot can go wrong."

Drummond's gaze journeyed down the length of Ian and then Ramsay. "Ye're not the most inconspicuous agents? Giants, both of ye." Drummond shuffled to his window and pulled back the thick leather curtain. "Did anyone see ye enter?"

"Aye," Ian confirmed. "A young woman. She had a beast of a dog with her."

Drummond's features relaxed. "That's just Jo. She lives next door." Drummond released the hide and turned back to face the men. "Edward has spies all over the city. He watches me to make sure I don't arrange to have the bishop smuggled out of Durham." He motioned to the chairs at the table. "Sit and tell me what Abbot Matthew is up to now, and I'll get ye something to wash the dust from yer mouths."

Ian and Ramsay did as the old man bade them. The chairs creaked in protest under their weight.

"Ye needn't trouble yerself," Ian told Drummond as the old man shuffled over to the hearth and ladled some of the contents of the bubbling caldron into small clay mugs.

"'Tis no trouble at all, only some broth." Drummond set the steaming cups on the table before claiming the rocking chair near the hearth.

"Now then," Drummond began. "Ye were going to tell me about the abbot. How does he intend to set Scotland back on course for victory?"

"Our aim is singular. Always we are working to rebuild Scotland's army."

Drummond blew out a long breath of air and rocked back in his chair. His expression held a note of concern. "If 'tis coin ye're after, ye'll have to look elsewhere. The bishop's wealth was confiscated. He lives as humbly as any monk."

Ramsay shook his head. "We aren't after the bishop's coin; 'tis information we seek."

"With the Bruce still in hiding, many of Scotland's nobles have renewed their pledges of loyalty to England," Ian explained. "We are hoping the bishop can help us discern who is still loyal to Scotland."

"A-ha," Drummond blurted, a glint of eagerness in his eyes. "Ye need to know who's betrayed us, so that ye can empty their coffers when they're not looking."

Ian smiled at Ramsay, then back to Drummond. "Our reputation precedes us. Aye, we are planning on bleeding the disloyal nobles dry for their betrayal, but we also want to know who to reach out to for aid. Those who are still loyal to

Scotland will no doubt want to donate what they can spare in terms of warriors and weaponry."

"Well, with any luck, the bishop will have the answers ye seek," Drummond said. A shadow fell across his face. "Despite how King Edward tried, he never could break Bishop Lamberton's spirit. Ye'll find him little changed, except for the plainness of his garb and the—"

"Open this door!"

Ian jumped to his feet, seized his blade from the scabbard strapped to his back and crossed to stand in front of the door, creaking beneath the might of the fist pounding on the other side.

"Damnation," Drummond cursed under his breath. "Someone must have seen ye." He motioned for the stairs and hissed quietly. "Go. Hurry!"

Ian shook his head and whispered, "Ye just said they must have seen us already. If we run, how will ye explain our presence?"

Drummond's gaze darted around the room, but then his eyes widened and glinted brightly. "Remember, lads, the bishop hears confession on Thursday. Now, run! Up the stairs with ye both!"

Ian was about to repeat his question—how did Drummond intend to explain what Ian and Ramsay had been doing in his home, when the old man suddenly called out, "Help! Thieves!"

A smile upturned one corner of Ian's lips. "I've been called worse." Then he turned to Ramsay. "Pray we fit through the upstairs window. Ta for yer help," he whispered to their host before he turned and raced upstairs, hastening across the plainly furnished bedroom to the window. Throwing open the shutters, he motioned for Ramsay. "Ye first."

"Hurry, they're getting away!" Drummond's words reached them from below. Then they heard a rumble of heavy footsteps.

"They're inside," Ramsay hissed as he tried to squeeze through the narrow frame. "Damn it," the blacksmith cursed before seizing his hammer. With a few well-placed blows, he expanded the opening to freedom and climbed onto the roof of the neighboring home with Ian following after.

"Do not slip from the crossbeam. 'Tis the only thing strong enough to bear our weight," Ian cautioned. Hearing heavy footsteps thundering up Drummond's stairs, he hissed, "Hurry! They're coming!"

The wood creaked. "The beam is going to break," Ramsay exclaimed.

"Step lively and it won't!"

"Get back here," a voice growled from behind Ian.

Ian glanced back at the window just in time to see an English soldier take aim with a crossbow.

"Duck!" Ian shouted, but he was too late. Ramsay grunted in pain, an arrow now protruding from his shoulder. The blacksmith teetered to one side, then the other. Ian reached out but caught naught but air as Ramsay lost his balance and crashed through the thatch. A breath later the sound of splintering wood rent the air, followed by a piercing scream and vicious barking.

"Don't move, Scotsman!"

Ian glanced back at the soldier staring at him down the sight of his bow. "I arrest you in the name of the king!"

"Bloody hell," Ian muttered before leaping through the hole Ramsay had made in the roof. He landed with a hard thud on a tangled mess of splintered wood and yard. A sharp pain shot through his hand and the back of his thigh.

"Get out of my house," a shrill voice shouted.

Ian jumped to his feet, ignoring the sliver of wood sticking out of his palm as a woman charged at him, swinging a broom like a broad sword. He backed into Ramsay who was fending off her massive dog, holding a table like a shield.

Shouts from the soldiers above combined with the beast's snarling and the woman's continuous shrieks.

Ian met her mismatched gaze. "Ye must be Jo," he gritted out, trying to sound pleasant as he grabbed a chair to keep the dog's jaw from gnashing on his calf. "We're friends of Drummond. We're not going to hurt—"

His attempt to calm the woman down was cut short by a loud yell as one of the soldiers plummeted from above, landing as Ian had on the pile of splintered wooden rods, yarn, and fabric.

"My loom," Jo cried.

"My arse," the soldier groaned.

Ian grimaced, guessing where he'd received his splinters.

The arrival of the English guard drew the dog's fury. He lunged for the soldier. Now that their way to the door was no longer blocked by fierce, biting jaws, Ramsay threw the table aside. "Come on," he shouted back at Ian.

"Look what you've done," the distraught woman cried, her eyes scanning the damage to her home.

"I'm truly sorry," Ian began to say.

"No time," Ramsay shouted at Ian before disappearing out the door.

"Blast," Ian swore, hearing the English soldiers shouting from above. "We'll pay ye for the damage," he promised the woman before racing after Ramsay.

Chapter Six

Jo seized Ruby, throwing both arms around her thick, furry neck to keep her from attacking the soldier, who hobbled down the street behind the small band of soldiers giving chase after the two giant Scotsmen, who had just ruined her life.

"Come on, girl, back inside." Jo shut the door behind her. At once, a whimper of desperation fled her lips as she slumped to her knees in front of her shattered loom, her arms hanging in limp defeat at her side.

"I don't understand," she croaked, taking in the surrounding destruction. Hand shaking, she picked up the shuttle, the only wooden piece to have survived the trauma of being crushed beneath the weight of no less than three men, two of whom had been massive in size. The piece slid from her fingertips back on top of the rubble that had once been her livelihood. Tears flooded her eyes, but she shook them away.

Raising her eyes heavenward, she gasped. A vast, jagged hole in the thatch revealed a patch of cheery blue sky, which mocked her with its brightness.

"Blast them all," she muttered, burying her face in her hands once more.

Her one consolation was that she hadn't been sitting at her loom when the first of the giant men rained down from the cloudless sky. Mere seconds before he plummeted into her life, she had crossed the room to fetch some water; however, when her landlord saw the state of his property, she might just wish she had suffered the same fate as her loom.

With a sigh, she knelt and stroked her hand across a piece of the soft fabric tangled amid the wood and yarn.

"If, in your wisdom," she began to pray aloud, "you saw fit for men to drop through my roof like gigantic and loutish rain drops, could they not have held off long enough for me to finish this one job?"

Ruby whimpered, placing her big head on Jo's lap. "What am I to do?" she muttered, stroking Ruby's thick fur. Staring at her broken loom, emotion knotted in her throat, but she leapt to her feet, defiant. "No crying," she gritted, then looked down at Ruby. "And that goes for you, too. If we can breathe, we can fight, remember?"

I believe in ye.

Her mother's words echoed in her mind, fueling her spirit and courage to new heights. Again, she ran her hand across the intricately designed fabric. It was beautiful, her best yet. Mayhap the tailor wouldn't notice that it was short by a hand's length.

She took a deep breath. "Ruby," she declared. "We carry on as planned."

Now, she had to untangle the mess of splintered wood. "Join me in praying that the cloth is undamaged."

When the sky above her was painted with streaks of pinks and golds, she finished examining the fabric, freed from the remains of her loom. Her heart swelled as she took in the exquisite detail and rich colors. Not a single hole marred its beauty, and although there were several snags, she felt they did little to diminish the overall quality.

"With any luck, the tailor will share our opinion," she said to Ruby while she folded the length of cloth and placed it carefully in her leather satchel.

Feeling confident, she slid her slippers on, seized Ruby's leash, and threw open the door, ready to sprint to the tailor's shop before he left for the day.

But just as she stepped outside, she locked eyes with her lecherous landlord.

Quickly shutting the door behind her to conceal the damage, she glanced up at the roof. The side that showed was free of man-sized holes. With relief, she smiled at her landlord in greeting. As long as he did not venture to the back side of his property, he shouldn't be able to tell anything was amiss. And if she could still get the promised sum from the tailor, she might be able to pay someone to fix the roof before MacLemore was any wiser.

"How is my favorite little weaver?" The scent of stale beer assailed her nostrils.

"Late," she said in a clipped tone. "If you'll excuse me, Master MacLemore, I must be off."

"Not so fast," he said, blocking her path. "I have yet to drink in your beauty."

"I think you've had enough to drink," she said under her breath.

His eyes narrowed on her. "What did you say?"

"I said that I think I'm hardly a vision at the moment," she lied, pushing her disheveled hair from her eyes. "I've been working all day. I'm sweaty. My tunic is filthy."

"Let me be the judge of that." With a leering smile, he leaned closer, but Ruby growled, baring her teeth.

MacLemore's eyes darkened for a moment, but then a smile, dripping with insincerity, curved his lips. "How's Ruby this eventide?"

"She's fine," Jo blurted. "Now, if you will only let me pass. I really must be going."

Still, MacLemore didn't budge. Jo swallowed a shriek of frustration. Before Ruby had come into her life, she might have been nervous. Her landlord used to be all hands, touching her waist, her lower back, grazing his greasy fingers down her cheek. But Ruby's bared teeth had put an end to his continuous pawing. Still, there was little she could do to fend off his spoken advances. It wasn't as if Jo could sic Ruby on her landlord, not unless she wanted to lose the roof over her head—or what little roof there was left.

"Master MacLemore, I really am in a hurry."

His leering smile stretched wider, revealing yellow, crooked teeth. "I appreciate you have somewhere else to be, but we've our own account to settle. Have you forgotten what day it is?"

She swallowed the knot that rushed up her throat. "I've not forgotten. You will have your rent, but I must take this to Jeremiah before he closes the shop."

He gave her a knowing smile. "Your coffers need filling then?" He started to step toward her, but, once again, Ruby's low growl changed his mind. He scowled at her dog before turning falsely kind eyes on her. "I can make it easier for you, Jo. I know how hard you struggle, supporting your sick mother and yourself. What you need is a man to take care of you, a man like me."

"Your wife might disagree with you," she said pointedly.

He gave a grunt of disapproval.

Giving her chin a lift, she dipped in a curtsy before saying, "If you will excuse me, I'll bring you the money owed on the morrow."

He considered her for a moment. "How is your mother?"

"She is well enough," Jo lied.

"With more coin ye could pay for a surgeon," he rasped. "I can help make her well again."

Jo's chest tightened. Nothing could make her mother well again. Her health had been failing even before they'd been forced to flee Toonan, but seven months ago Clara's condition had worsened. She'd lost her ability to walk and hadn't the strength to even hold a cup of water. Just the mention of her mother brought Jo back to the urgency of the day. Her rent was not the only payment due; the Prioress would be expecting the promised coin for her mother's care.

Get out of my way, you lecher, she longed to scream.

If she didn't make it to the tailor, all would be lost—she would no doubt face debtors' prison and then what would happen to her mother?

The golds and pinks slashing the sky above were darkening, taking on a violet hue. The hour for Vespers was upon them. She stepped sideways, pulled her hood over her head, and clutched the folds of her cloak together with her free hand to give nothing for MacLemore's roving gaze to look upon. "I'll just be going."

Again, he shifted to block her way.

"Don't fret if your purse is short this month." Licking his lips, his gaze traveled the length of her body, despite her effort to shield herself with her cloak. "We can always come to an agreement."

"No need," she bit out, resisting the urge to smack the salacious grin off his face. "I will pay in full."

He dared to step closer, despite Ruby's warning growl. "Let me taste those sweet lips and you can forget this month's rent."

With the state of his roof as it was, she swallowed the line of insults aching to burst free from her so-called sweet lips. She pushed against his chest. "Come along, Ruby," she said, then turned on her heel and hastened down the dirt street in the opposite direction, deciding it would be quicker to take the long way than to escape her landlord's stubborn advances.

Chapter Seven

Jo raced through Durham's narrow, bustling streets. Her heart pounded and her breaths came in great heaves from her exertions, but thanks to Ruby, she did not need to push her way through the crowds. As always, people scurried out of the way of her wild-looking pet.

When she hastened around a corner and spied the over-sized wooden sheers denoting the Tailor's shop, her heart leapt, but then the door swung wide. Jeremiah stepped out, his cloak covering his shoulders, and he carried a large parcel.

"Wait, Jeremiah," she shouted as she saw him turn to face the door, key in hand. Again, she called his name, heedless of the stares of passersby. Finally, the tailor turned. She smiled and waved, receiving only a frown in return.

Breathless, she came to an abrupt halt when she reached his side. "I'm sorry," she panted. "Late...loom broke." She held out the folded fabric. "But I have it."

He held her gaze for several moments before sighing. "All right, you can come in, but we must be quick. I will get an earful from the wife if I'm late for supper again."

Jo started inside. "Bless you," she breathed as relief poured over her.

"Hold." Jeremiah held out his hand to stop her. "You know that beast is not welcome here."

"Of course," Jo said quickly. "Forgive me, I was hurrying so, that I forgot." She walked Ruby to the nearest hitching post. "Sorry, girl," Jo crooned as she tied off Ruby's leash. The impatient expression on the tailor's face urged Jo not to linger. "I'm coming," she called and hastened back, following Jeremiah inside his shop. After setting his parcel on the rough-hewn table near the cold hearth, Jeremiah lit a candle and sat down, awaiting her presentation.

"The pattern is beautiful." His brow furrowed as he inspected her work. "Truly, you've outdone yourself."

Her heart swelled at his praise, but when he stood and retrieved his yardstick, her heart started to race. He spread her hard work out on the large cutting table. She held her breath as he swept his hand over the soft fabric. "It truly is stunning. Lady Ashton will be..." His voice trailed off. Her heart sank when his smile faded. "There are snags, Jo, and I don't have to measure to know it is shorter than we discussed."

"Only by a few inches," she insisted.

He slowly shook his head. "I'm surprised. You are usually so careful, which is why I chose you for this commission."

She swallowed, knowing he was right. "I told you, my loom broke as I was finishing."

His lips pressed in a grim line. "This piece is for the tunic Lady Ashton will wear at her son's wedding. My expectations were clear, Jo."

She ran her hand across the myriad colors. "Look at the bead work, and the pattern is exceptional."

"But it is marred, and the bead work is incomplete, and there is still the matter of the missing length."

Her face grew warm as her temper surged. "You remarked on its beauty just now. Why should anything else matter?"

"Those missing inches will matter to Lady Ashton."

"But how will she even know?"

"She always insists on inspecting the fabric before I begin sewing."

Jo sank into a nearby chair and expelled a slow breath.

Sighing, the tailor sat in the chair beside hers. "I'm sorry, but you know I cannot pay you the four marks as promised."

Refusing to give up, she scooted to the edge of her seat, looking the tailor hard in the eye. "Please, reconsider," she said, seizing his hand. "There is enough there to make two tunics."

Frowning, he shook his head and pulled his hand free from hers. "If I show this to my lady, she will expect me to lower my commission considerably on her tunic. You know how eccentric the noble class is. She may see it as being flawed and no longer wish to use it all together. I'm sorry, Jo, but two marks is all I can offer."

"But I paid nearly a mark to buy the thread!" Her mind raced while she considered his offer. With the profit, she would have enough to pay her rent and for her mother's care but there wouldn't be enough to purchase a new loom. She could sell the piece independently for more, but the next big market was two days away.

But then what about food? What about the state of her home? MacLemore was not the most understanding of men. She knew how he would suggest she work off the damages, satisfying his salacious needs.

At that moment, she remembered the promise made by the red-haired giant before he raced from her life as quickly as he'd entered it. He had vowed to pay for the damages. She leaned forward and dropped her head in her hands. But what was his promise worth—the word of a stranger, one clearly embroiled in his own troubles. She did not doubt that he had already forgotten about the girl whose life he ruined.

Not that it hadn't been ruined already, but at least with a loom, she could keep going. She could eat and have a roof over her head. Without it, she was nothing, just another penniless, unconnected young woman facing starvation or worse...accepting her landlord's so-called help.

"Jo," Jeremiah said, drawing her gaze. "I need your answer."

Shaking off her despair, she sat straight. She would find a way. Ignoring the voice in her head reminding her that she had to start again but, this time, without her mother's guidance and strength or their costly jewels, she looked Jeremiah hard in the eye and held out her hand. "I accept."

Night had descended, cloaking Durham in shadow. Jo gazed heavenward, her own future as cloudy and bleak as the starless sky overhead.

"How will I ever afford a new loom?" she asked Ruby who looked up at her with adoration in her yellow eyes, but whose only answer was to nuzzle her head into Jo's waist. "Thank the good Lord for you," Jo murmured, wrapping her arms around her beloved pet. "Come on. Let us return home. We'll think of something."

Opening the door, she stepped inside and sucked in a sharp breath as she locked eyes with her landlord. Ruby lunged, barking ferociously. Yanked forward, Jo dug her heels into the ground and strained with all her might to hold her massive protector at bay.

Seizing one of her chairs, MacLemore held it high like a sword at the ready. "Let the bitch come!"

"You shouldn't be in here," Jo gritted.

"You are in no position to tell me what I should not do," he snarled, motioning to the gaping hole above their heads. "What the hell happened?"

"I hardly know myself," Jo blurted. "Men crashed down from the heavens nearly upon my head." She gestured angrily toward the bits of wood scattered about the floor. "Look at what they did to my loom!"

He stopped and stared at her, his wide eyes slowly narrowing into mean slits. "Men?"

She nodded. "Yes, three in all, two of them as big as mountains."

His face nearly purple, he made a grab for her arm, but Ruby snapped at him. He jerked away, barely escaping the animal's fierce jaws.

"Try to put your hands on me again and I will let her go!"

He backed away, shaking his head at her, his eyes flashing with fury. "So, is that what it takes to get beneath your skirts? You like big men, do you?"

Her eyes widened. Shaking her head furiously, she blurted, "I never said that. I said that men—"

"How were they here, if you didn't welcome them inside?"

"I just told ye, they fell from the very sky." Realizing what her landlord was implying, she gasped. "You cannot possibly think I would—How dare you suggest—"

"How did they get inside?" he boomed.

"I've already told you," she snapped. "I was working at my loom. I stood and crossed the room for a drink. Before I knew what was happening, the first man fell through the roof, landing directly on my loom. Seconds later, another man fell, then another."

"That's absurd. You're lying!"

"I swear I'm not."

"They were your lovers, no doubt. Let me guess, you were entertaining one man when another walked in and then another, and in a jealous rage over you, a fight broke out, destroying my property."

"No! You're wrong! I've never taken a lover!"

His lips twisted in an ugly sneer. "All this while you have turned your nose at my advances. Now, I know why. It is not your chaste heart but me you've rejected." He leaned close. "So, you think you're better than me? You who are as common as the dirt on my boots."

"I am no more common than you," she snapped.

"You're a whore," he growled. "Yes, that's right—a whore! Mayhap, they weren't fighting over you at all. Mayhap, you were entertaining all three men at once, and they humped their way right through my roof!"

She put her hands on her hips. "That's ridiculous! You're accusing me of entertaining men on your roof."

"I don't know what sick appetites your lovers have."

She gasped. "How dare you?"

"How dare I? You've damaged my property, and you will pay." He held out his hand. "Give me your purse."

"Nay," she cried, backing away, pulling hard on Ruby who was still growling and snapping her jaws. "It is all I have, and I've no loom now to earn more."

"Give it to me now or I'll fetch the constable and have him drag you off to debtors prison." His voice dropped deadly quiet. "Who will look after your mother and your precious dog then?"

Her nostrils flared. "Damn you." But what choice did she have? She tossed the purse on the ground.

He seized it and gave it a shake, clinking the handful of coin. "This won't cover it all."

"I told you, it's all I have."

He glowered at her. "You're lucky I don't make you work for the rest." His gaze scanned the length of her, his lip curling with disgust. "But I don't buy cheap goods." He pointed to the door. "Get your things and get out of my house!"

Her eyes widened with fear. "But you cannot take it all. Some of that coin is for my mother."

He snatched an open missive off her table. "A messenger from the abbey came while I was awaiting your return." He shoved it at her. "Your mother doesn't need more coin. She needs a miracle, but God does not smile on whores."

Glaring at him, her heart pounding, she seized the missive...*Dearest Jo,*

Your mother has taken a turn for the worse...

"Oh God," Jo gasped. "She's dying. Please Master MacLemore, leave me some coin to—."

"Get out of my sight!" he bellowed.

Clutching Ruby's leash, she turned on her heel and raced out into the night toward Durham Abbey. "Keep breathing, Mama! Keep fighting!"

Chapter Eight

Ian towered above the heads of pilgrims trudging in a line like a slow-moving river down the cobbled pathway to the north entrance of Durham Cathedral. They came from far and wide to kneel at the shrine of Saint Cuthbert and pray for a cure to whatever affliction had laid claim to their bodies or loved ones. Just ahead of him, he could see a young man who should have been walking on able, strong legs but, instead, was lying on a stretcher, his limbs rail thin and bowed. He was but one of so many who suffered and sought relief from their pain.

Moving forward through the crowd, Ian came alongside a woman walking alone, head bowed, her long, straggly, gray hair hiding her face. As though sensing his gaze, she looked up. He was struck by the paleness of her blue eyes, which glistened with tears amid her creased and dirty face. Dipping his head, he saw that her bare feet were wrapped in grimy bandages, dotted red by her blood. Still, she shuffled ever onward, toward the beacon of hope housed within the hallowed walls that were now so very close.

"I will pray for ye," he promised, wanting to give her what comfort he may.

She met his gaze. "Bless you," she croaked through her dried and cracked lips. "But pray not for me, for I have walked here from Bath on legs that may now be tired but are strong. I have bled and nigh starved over these last weeks, but my suffering has cleansed my soul. I have repented my sins and cast away my worldly belongings. Now, I am ready to lay my heart bare to Saint Cuthbert and pray that he might cure my granddaughter."

Ian bowed his head to her. "Yer courage and hope are an inspiration to me. I, too, vow to beseech Saint Cuthbert's mercy on behalf of yer granddaughter." Then he withdrew the costrel from his satchel and offered her a drink. She accepted and took a long swig before she handed it back to him. Her face brightened, a slight smile curving her lips. Straightening her back, she stood taller, then she dipped in a low curtsey, and in that moment, Ian glimpsed a fineness in her bearing that only came with instruction.

"Ye're of noble birth," Ian observed with surprise.

"I *was* of noble birth," she corrected. "I am Lady Thynne no longer. I've relinquished my title and wealth. With humility and gratitude, I have suffered." Her smile widened. "Do you know the Latin word for suffering."

Unlike his educated brother, Quinn, Ian's understanding of Latin began and ended with the Mass. He shook his head in answer.

"*Patientia.*"

Ian puzzled over why she had shared this, but then it dawned on him. "Patience," he blurted.

Her eyes glinted brightly. "Patience will allow even the weakest of God's creatures to weather any storm. Life demands suffering, and by that, I mean to say, life demands patience." She smiled. "Just keep breathing and carry on; God will take care of the rest."

He looked down with amazement at the diminutive, shabbily dressed woman carrying herself like a queen. "True nobility is something earned," he said, then dropped to one knee. "It would be my honor to carry ye the rest of the way to Saint Cuthbert's tomb."

Tears filled her eyes. "You see," she said, her voice breaking. "One only needs to be patient and prayers will be answered. Now, who am I to include in my prayers for the remainder of my days?"

Standing, he swept her into his arms. "Ian MacVie, and may I know the pleasure of yer name?"

"Susanna."

His heart as light as the tiny woman in his arms, he walked the rest of the pathway and carried her through the threshold of the cathedral. Stepping into the aisle, he continued on between two wide columns, one carved with a lattice pattern and the other a spiral, into the vast and crowded Nave.

"Are you ready, Susanna? Yer journey is nearly at an end."

She smiled, deep crinkles forming around her eyes. "In truth, it has only just begun. Please set me down here, Ian."

"Are ye certain?"

She took a deep breath. "Don't you see? I'm still breathing."

"And so, ye must carry on," he said knowingly as he gently put her down.

Dipping once more into an elegant curtsy, Susanna bade him farewell.

He watched her shuffle away, swallowed by the great sea of pilgrims moving towards Saint Cuthbert's tomb. After she disappeared from view, he turned in a circle, taking in the majesty of the cathedral. Vast columns lined the nave on either side, each carved with a different pattern and painted in myriad colors. His gaze followed the colors to the high, arched ceilings, and then along the opposite wall where he spied the confessionals. Eager to see his old friend, he crossed the busy nave and ducked into one of the booths. Kneeling, he made the sign of the cross and said, "Bless me, Father, for I have sinned. It has been one month since my last confession."

The small curtain on the priest's side of the confessional slid to the side. "What sins have you to confess?"

Ian did not recognize the voice.

"Forgive me, Father," he murmured.

"What sins, my child?" the priest insisted, but Ian had already made the sign of the cross and stepped back into the aisle, then darted along to the next booth.

"Bless me, Father, for I have sinned it has been one month since my last confession."

"What sins have you to confess?"

Ian smiled. "My sins are many, Bishop, but then ye already knew that."

The bishop's face appeared in the small opening, his eyes crinkling in a smile. "Ian MacVie, you're a wonderful sight for these old eyes."

"How are ye, dear friend?" Ian whispered.

"I'm no longer locked away in the Tower of London; I find, suddenly, I have precious little to complain about."

Ian scowled. "When they first arrested ye after the Bruce's coronation, Ramsay and I pledged to ride to London and break ye out, but the Abbot forbade us, arguing we would only get ye and ourselves killed for our effort. He assured us that yer Orders would save ye."

"And so they did. I was, after all, found guilty of treason, but even King Edward fears God enough not to hang a bishop.

Had I been a monk, priest, or even an abbot, I do not doubt I would have been drawn and quartered. But enough of that. I'm free now."

"But ye're not," Ian hissed, fury building within him. "Ye've been forbidden to leave the city."

The bishop waved his hand, dismissing Ian's concern. "Calm yourself. Neither of us will benefit if you release that temper of yours here. I do not object to being imprisoned within a city with such a fine cathedral, and I assure you that I am treated with every honor due my station. I did, after all, swear fealty to England, and so I am under King Edward's protection now."

Ian remembered when word had reached him that Bishop Lamberton had kneeled before the English king. "I won't lie—when I first heard ye'd sworn fealty to that bastard, I nearly lost all hope." Ian cocked a brow at him, lacing his voice with mock disapproval. "But I didn't realize that bishops could lie."

A smile curved the old man's lips. "Trust me," he began, "I went to confession with a very contrite heart."

"Are ye certain ye're being treated properly?"

"Do not fash yerself," he said, good-humoredly mimicking Ian's accent. "There is little by way of restraint to hinder my involvement with Scotland's fight for freedom, and that is all that truly matters. Now, enough of that. I'm certain you came here with another purpose in mind than fussing over an old man."

Ian nodded. "The abbot seeks yer advice. Our king remains in hiding, as I'm sure ye know. He needs an army, but

Scotland's coffers remain bare. The good abbot doesn't have yer knack for persuading our nobles to open their purses."

"Say no more," the bishop interjected. "Tell the abbot that *I* will reach out to those nobles still loyal to Scotland and eke from their coffers all that I may." A hint of mischief glinted in the old man's eyes as he continued. "Now, tell me about the cause's secret rebels. What are my agents up to these days?"

"Spies are in place from Cape Wrath to Dover, but we must do more to rekindle the spirit of rebellion."

"And I know how best to begin," the bishop said, a conspiratorial tone to his voice.

Intrigued, Ian leaned closer. "What do ye have in mind?"

The old man smiled. "'Tis time to call on the Saints."

Once upon a time, Ian and his four brothers, with the help of the good bishop, formed a gang of secret Scottish rebels. Bishop Lamberton gave the MacVie brothers masks and called them each by a different saints name to conceal their true identities.

"But those days are over. My brothers are all wanted men. Ye risk exposing the identity of other agents by involving known outlaws."

"Jack, Quinn, Rory, and Alec have sacrificed enough for Scotland." A slow smile spread across the bishop's face. "'Tis time to canonize new saints."

Ian's lips curved in a sideways smile. "Ramsay would make one hell of a Saint. Forgive my blasphemy."

Bishop Lamberton made the sign of the cross. "Say two Hail Mary's when you go. Now, who else do you have in mind?"

"David, Nick, and Paul, with me that brings our number to five."

The bishop nodded. "Word will soon spread of the Saints return and everyone will know Scotland's fight continues."

Ian stood. A thrill shot through him at the prospect of reforming the gang of honorable thieves. "We'll replenish Scotland's coffers one English noble at a time."

"Your king is counting on it. Scotland is counting on it," the bishop declared. "Go now, my friend, and may the Lord God keep you and watch over you."

Ian dipped his head and started to turn away.

"Ian."

"Aye, Bishop."

"Don't forget to say two Hail Mary's."

Ian smiled before he threw back the curtain and hurried down the aisle, his new purpose driving his feet forward at a quick pace. But he only took a few strides before he was forced to slow down and pick his way through the crowded nave. Avoiding a cluster of nuns, he skirted around one of the ornately carved columns and ran headlong into a cloaked figure.

Small hands darted to the hood and threw it back.

"'Tis ye," he exclaimed, recognizing the heart-shaped face and flashing, mismatched eyes.

THE MASSIVE MAN WITH wild red hair and sky-blue eyes was someone she had hoped never to see again. If it were not for him and his friend, she wouldn't be homeless and penniless.

If it were not for him, she would have had the coin to pay for a proper burial for her mother.

Gripped by desperation and despair, she spun away from him only to feel his hand close around her arm.

Scowling, she glanced back. "How dare you!"

His red brows pinched together. "Please," he said, his tone beseeching. "I am truly sorry about what happened. I went back the next morning, to make things right, but your landlord said you'd moved out."

"Moved out?" she scoffed. Then her brow furrowed deeper. "I was thrown out thanks to you. He blamed me for the damage you and your friends caused. Now, do as I say and unhand me!"

"I mean ye no harm," he assured, releasing her arm straight away.

She wasted no time. Turning, she maneuvered through the dense crowd filling the nave. Glancing back, she saw a determined glint in the man's sky-blue eyes as he moved through the crowd after her, but his large frame slowed his progress while she easily darted through the gaps.

Stepping through the south door, she dashed across the courtyard where the Priory monks were walking, their heads bowed solemnly. She crossed to the covered walkway and slid down behind one of the large columns and laid her head against the cool stone and closed her eyes.

Keep breathing.

Keep fighting.

She fisted her hands against the deep pain in her chest, an ache that had gripped her heart from the moment her mother expelled her last breath. With every passing moment the pain grew, swelling inside her, threatening to choke the very life from her body.

Not that her life was worth very much. She shook her head, furious at her weakness.

Sure, she was penniless, homeless, and worst of all, so very alone, but she was a Fergusson and made of stronger stuff than most!

But without her loom, she had no way to improve her circumstances.

Damn that red-haired giant!

Fury, as swift as an arrow, pierced her despair, engulfing her sorrowful heart in bitter flames. Looking down, she stared at her empty hands. She had nothing, just like so many other women she had seen walking the streets of Durham, having to resort to selling the only thing they could—their bodies.

She took a deep breath. She had not come to Durham Cathedral to pray for herself. She had come to mourn her mother.

"Please, God," she prayed. "Take care of her. Tell her not to worry about me."

"My child."

She glanced up and saw an old man with a rim of white hair around his bald head. His robe was crisp white and about his neck draped an emerald-green stole. He was an important clergyman, whether a priest or a deacon, she did not know. Quickly, she dropped her gaze and stood up, then dipped in a low curtsy. "Forgive me," she said, keeping her gaze downcast.

"And what grievous act have you committed that you require my forgiveness?" he asked, his fatherly tone soothing her heart.

"Nothing," she said quickly, still maintaining her pious stance, but then she realized she'd just lied. "Well, truthfully, I did have wicked thoughts about someone a few moments ago."

He chuckled softly. "Such thoughts race through all men's heads, even my own, but you needn't seek forgiveness now. When next you go to confession, you can mention your thoughts again. Now, what did this person do to vex you?"

Clenching her fists, she resisted kicking at the stone on the ground as fury pulsed through her. Not meeting the holy man's gaze, she gritted out. "He and his companions destroyed my loom, my livelihood."

"Well, that is, indeed, a grievous offense. Did these men act maliciously?"

She lifted her shoulders. "I do not know what manner of men they are or what motivated their actions. What I do know is that I am hungry and no longer have a way to earn my keep."

Keeping her head bowed, she waited for his response. As more time passed, and he still had said naught, she assumed he was dismissing her. "Thank you, Father—"

"Bishop," he interjected.

She rounded her shoulders, sinking her head lower still. "Forgive me, Bishop. I did not know."

This time he laughed outright. "If only all God's children sought contrition as frequently as you." He gently laid his hand on her bowed head. "I am sorry for the loss of your loom and the insecurity you now face, but I can feel your sorrow. It runs deeper than the worries of the flesh. Something else troubles you."

My mother is dead, her heart screamed.

A knot formed in her throat.

"Breathe," she whispered, chasing away her tears. "Fight."

But what did she have left to fight for?

"I did not hear your words, my child. My ears are old."

She couldn't speak of her mother, not without breaking down, and she had vowed long ago to be strong. She took a deep breath and blurted. "I am lost."

He rested his hand on her bowed head. "Then mayhap, it is time to go home."

Her heart sank further still as images of Toonan flashed in her mind's eye. A bitter taste filled her mouth. "I don't have a home."

"Are you certain?"

She nodded, still not looking up.

"What is your name, child?"

She met his gaze for the first time. "Jo," she answered.

His eyes flashed wide for a moment.

Startled by the sudden surprise she glimpsed in his gaze, she stepped back.

"Do not be afraid," he soothed, reaching out his hand to her. "I didn't mean to frighten you. It is just...your eyes...they are most unusual."

The bishop's comment did not surprise her. She was used to people remarking on her eyes. "I have my father's eyes."

"Was your father a weaver?"

"My father was a great many things, but it was my mother who taught me the art of weaving."

"Jo, how old are you?"

"I am ten and seven."

"Remarkable," he muttered. "Tell me, Jo, where is your father now?"

She swallowed hard. "I have every reason to believe he's dead."

"And your mother?"

She pressed her hand to her mouth and turned away.

"What is it, my child? Is she ill? Is that why you've come to the cathedral, to pray for her health at Saint Cuthbert's tomb?"

She shook her head. "'Tis too late for that. I came to pray for her soul."

To her surprise, tears flooded the bishop's eyes. "I am so sorry for your loss, my child. Tell me, were you with her?"

"Yes." Jo closed her eyes. "She lost consciousness in the end and died peacefully".

"I am glad to know she did not suffer."

Jo nodded.

A sad smile curved his lips as he considered her. At length, he asked, "Who will you turn to now? Where will you go?"

She lifted her shoulders. "I do not know."

He drew closer, his faded blue eyes filled with concern. "Then, you are, in fact, truly alone."

"I...I have my dog Ruby."

His face brightened. "Your Ruby, is she brave?"

She nodded.

"Fierce?"

"Terrifying."

"Then she will protect you?"

"That I do not doubt."

He took her hand and led her to a stone bench. "Sit with me and tell me something."

"Yes, Bishop?"

"Do you trust me?"

She chewed the inside of her cheek. "Is it a sin to admit that I do not know?"

"No, it just means you're careful, which, in my mind, is one of the greatest virtues. God did not give you life to be reckless with it."

A slight smile curved her lips. "When I used to play chess with my father, he would always tell me to be bold but never reckless."

"Your father was a wise man."

"Indeed, he was," she agreed softly.

The bishop cleared his throat. "Now, what I have in mind requires courage and would, indeed, be a bold decision."

"I've learned courage," she said quietly, remembering the silly, carefree girl she'd once been.

He took her hand, looking fervently into her eyes. "Then go to the Highlands to Haddington Abbey."

Her eyes widened. "But that is so far."

"Yes, but you're a fighter, of this I'm certain. You'll manage, and when you arrive, ask for Abbot Matthew. Tell him that I sent you."

"I don't understand. What will the Abbot do for me?"

"The good abbot has found many orphans a home."

"At ten and seven, I hardly think anyone will open their home to me as they would a child."

"The abbot may not find you a family, but he will find you a home and a purpose."

"A purpose?"

He squeezed her hand. "As long as you have purpose, you can never be truly lost."

She sat straighter, his words filling her with hope.

"Now, a woman traveling on her own will draw attention—that is the one aspect of my plan which teeters on the bounds of recklessness. But you do have your Ruby. So, if you decide, in the end, that you do trust me and you boldly take a leap of faith and head north, keep off the roads and stick to the woods. Avoid all villages and towns."

"But what if the abbot doesn't believe me when I tell him you sent me?"

"All the abbot need do is look into your eyes to know you speak the truth." He cupped her cheek. "You've grit, my child, which is a gift from God that no man can take away. Be determined, and never give up."

The bishop's words, mirrored those of her mother, filling her heart with even greater hope. "Thank you, Bishop!" She dropped to her knees and kissed his ring. "Thank you with my whole heart."

She rose. "Forgive me, but if I'm to even consider traveling north, I must go. I have a lot of work to do."

He chuckled. "Still, you ask for my forgiveness when I can see the goodness in your heart reflected in your eyes. There is naught for me to forgive. Go with my blessings." He stood and placed his hand softly on her head. "May the Lord keep you and watch over you."

Dipping in a low curtsy, Jo spun on her heels and hastened across the courtyard. Determination imbued her stride. The bishop was right. She did have grit, and she was not going to give up without a fight. Her pride be damned. She needed coin, and if she hurried, she could make it to Lorna's tavern before it got too busy.

Chapter Nine

"I am going to beat that man to within an inch of life!"

"Ian, ye need to calm down," Ramsay said, keeping pace beside him. "Ye know what happens when ye get all riled up."

Ignoring his friend's warning, Ian turned onto Tivoli Street.

"We're already taking a great risk just by coming here again," Ramsay continued, "Edward's spies are likely keeping a closer watch on Drummond. For pity's sake, MacLemore may not even be there. Ye should have heeded my advice. We could have broken into his house and strung him up by his toes and..."

Fury coursed through Ian's veins, blazing red-hot at the mere mention of MacLemore's name. "We don't know where the devil lives!"

"A trivial point easily remedied had ye but given me a few hours to find out..."

"We haven't time," Ian snarled. "'Tis the lass I need to find, and he's our only tie to her." He thundered toward Jo's door, heedless of the consequences.

"Calmly," Ramsay called out, but Ian was in no mood to be calm. He kicked the door open. MacLemore looked up with wide eyes from where he sat at Jo's table adding coins to an already full purse. The man's gaze darted from Ian to Ramsay, then back to his task. "You two again. What do you want?" he said, his voice gruff.

"Where is the lass who used to rent this space?"

"I already told ye when ye came by here two days ago," the landlord answered without looking up. "She moved out."

Ian crossed his arms over his chest. "She told me that ye threw her out!"

MacLemore's eyes flashed with anger. He stood up. "That I did and good riddance. I don't rent to whores!"

In a flash, Ian seized the dirk from his boot, lunged forward, and pressed his weapon to the blackguard's neck. "Where is she?"

"I'm not her keeper," the man gritted out.

Ian shifted the tip of his knife from MacLemore's throat to his most prized appendage. "Tell me what ye know about her before I make yer long-suffering wife a very happy woman."

Sweat beaded up on the man's brow. "Her...her father was a weaver from London, taught her the trade. He's...he's dead. Her mother is ill. The old bitty's days are numbered by the sounds of it. That's where ye'll likely find her. She'll be at the Durham priory with her mother."

Ian released his hold on MacLemore and turned to Ramsay. "Yer hammer, please."

Ramsay reached behind his back and withdrew his hammer. "Are ye going to break his legs?"

"I'm still thinking about it," Ian replied.

MacLemore crumpled to the ground. "Don't hurt me. Please, I'm begging ye!"

Ian clasped the hammer, glowering down at the squirming coward from his great height. Of course, he wasn't going to break the legs of an unarmed man. Instead, Ian looked up. With a few swings of the hammer, he busted through the recent patch before handing the blacksmith back his tool.

"Feel better?" Ramsay asked.

"A wee bit," Ian replied. Then he looked down at the man still groveling at his feet. "Stand up!"

MacLemore scrambled upright. "Please, I need my legs and my prick."

Ian snaked out his hand, seized the coward's throat, and shoved him into the wall. "We'll be watching ye," he said, his voice deadly soft. "Treat yer tenants better. Next time, I'll not be so merciful."

Ian snatched the heavy purse off the table. "I'll see this returned to its rightful owner."

Ramsay followed him out the door. "I thought for sure ye were going to kill him."

Ian took a deep breath, his hands shaking with restrained fury. "So did I."

"What happened? What held ye back?"

"My honor." Ian motioned to the tavern across the way. "Come on. I need a drink."

JO RAN HER SLEEVE ACROSS her forehead, wiping at the beads of sweat before they could sting her eyes. Between the fire, keeping the pottage hot for those wanting a meal, and the dozens of hulky, sweaty male bodies, Lorna's tavern felt like the inside of a brazier.

Her forearm on the bar, she laid her head on the crook of her elbow and shut her eyes, trying to block out the surrounding din, for a moment, a breath, but then she felt a hand on her back. She jerked upright and locked eyes with her new boss.

"Oh, it's you, Lorna," Jo said, relieved that she had not been touched by one of the drunken revelers.

Lorna hoisted herself onto one of the stools and reached into her bountiful décolletage, withdrawing a handkerchief from the bosom of her tunic, and dabbed at the sweat glistening on her powdered face. Her brassy hair was piled on top of her head with loose tendrils framing her round face. Smiling, she patted Jo's hand. "Working upstairs with the other girls isn't nearly as hard as serving ale down here. The men are kind. They know I don't tolerate mistreatment of my girls. And you'll earn upstairs with one quick romp what will take ye a fortnight to earn down here."

"No thank you," Jo said simply.

Anger flashed in Lorna's eyes. "So, you think you're better than the lot upstairs, do you?"

Jo shook her head fervently. "No...I...I." She didn't know what to say. She certainly did not think ill of Lorna and the other women. They welcomed men into their beds to use their soft, pliant bodies, but what their customers did not realize was that the women were soldiers—fighting for their very lives. Without husbands or fathers to provide for them, their choices were few. Jo did not blame them. Still, she wanted no part of it.

Lorna shrugged, and once again patted Jo's hand. "Well, it's not for everyone, but as lovely as you are, you could fill your purse faster than you ever dreamed possible. Especially your first time. Virgins are highly prized." She leaned closer, her gaze probing. "Are you a virgin?"

Jo's mouth fell open in shock. Blushing, she tried to think of how she was to respond. Of course she was a virgin, but that was, in no way, Lorna's business? Still, she needed the job and didn't want to push Lorna too far.

Suddenly, Conrad, Lorna's muscular and perpetually angry barkeep, slammed four tankards down in front of her. "Get these over to those louts in the corner, compliments of me before they start punching each other out." Veins strained against the skin of his thick neck, which he bent first to one side, then the other. "Do it now, before I go over there and shut them up with my fists."

Relieved for the sudden distraction, Jo seized two tankards in each hand. "Sorry, Lorna," she said quickly and turned about, scanning the busy tavern.

Four men occupied one of the corner tables. They were all speaking at the same time and wildly gesticulating. She noted their empty drinking vessels had already been overturned on the table, waylaid no doubt by the action of their impassioned hands.

She glanced back at Conrad and dared ask, "Are ye certain they need more ale?"

"Better their hands be occupied gripping the handle of a tankard, than fisted and pummeling each other in the face," the barkeep explained. "Now, get on with ye!"

The air was thick with potential conflict as Jo rushed forward, careful not to slosh ale on the floor. She couldn't help but doubt Conrad's logic. More drink just meant drunker men, but what did she know? She was just a lady who had become a weaver and now a barmaid, trying desperately to survive with both feet on the ground.

Jo slammed the tankards on the table. Four sets of eyes looked at her.

"Compliments of Conrad."

The men glanced over at the mighty barkeep, whose brow furrowed deeply while he crossed his thick, muscular arms across his chest. Looking properly contrite, the men each took up a tankard and raised them in thanks to Conrad.

Jo chuckled as she turned.

Well played, Conrad.

She certainly had no experience dealing with hordes of intoxicated men, although the last two days she'd spent shuffling drinks across the room, she had learned a thing or two: How to spin away from groping hands before they found her arse. How to maneuver through the room without getting knocked into or run over. Luckily for her, she was trim and nimble and could find her way as a stream winds around clusters of rocks. Looking about the room at the dull gazes and hearing the cacophony of slurred speech, she decided rocks was an apt description for the tavern's patronage. They were all as dense as stone.

She cleared several plates off a table. One had a small piece of grizzle, which she claimed before setting the wooden vessels into the water bucket behind the bar to soak. "I have to take a quick break," she told Conrad, wanting to run out back to the outer kitchen where Lorna had let her roll out a pallet in the corner of the pantry. Ruby was waiting for her there and would, no doubt, enjoy the morsel she had hidden in her hand.

"Not now," he barked. "Two more customers just arrived."

She turned around. Familiar blue eyes locked with hers.

Chapter Ten

The tavern fell silent as heads turned to watch the newcomers, doubtless owing to the Scotsmen's great height and impressive builds.

"Do you know them?" Conrad asked quietly behind her.

She nodded. "In a manner of speaking."

"What do they want with you?"

The blond giant had claimed an empty table in the back of the room, but the red-haired one was walking straight toward her with a determined glint in his eyes.

She crossed her arms over her chest. "I'm not certain, but, doubtless, I'm about to find out." An instant later, she stood, craning her neck back to meet his gaze.

"I can't believe 'tis ye!" He smiled, and not for the first time, her stomach danced at the sight of his sensually handsome countenance.

Why did her tormentor have to be so bloody gorgeous?

She steeled her shoulders and placed her hands on her hips. "After you destroyed my loom, how else do you think I would make a living?"

He raked his hand through his hair. "I am so deeply sorry. We are completely to blame for everything, and we fully intend to right what has been made so very wrong." He scanned the room. "I will never forgive myself for having brought you so low—"

"I'm a barmaid," she snapped, interrupting him. "Not a grave robber. You've made your apologies. Now, why don't you turn right around and head back the way you came. You're bad luck, plain and simple."

Another damnable smile broke across his face, and once again, she was struck by the masculine cut to his jaw and his deep-set blue eyes. "Ye're luck is about to change. Can ye take a break and join my friend and I for an ale?"

She gestured behind her to where Conrad was eying them with suspicion. "I don't think I'll be allowed."

The red-haired giant stepped past her and put his plate-sized hands on the bar. "Jo needs a break."

Judging by the tightness of Conrad's expression, he wanted to tell the Scotsman to sod off, but even Conrad appeared small next to her handsome tormentor.

Conrad waved a dismissive hand. "I was going to tell her to take a rest anyway."

Jo hid her smile behind her hand. That, she knew, was a lie.

Having earned the attention of the rest of the bar, she felt dozens of gazes on her as she joined the men at a back table.

Before he sat down, her tormentor bowed to her. "My name is Ian MacVie, and this here is Ramsay MacTavish."

She nodded stiffly in greeting to the blond giant, who was also as handsome as he was large, but she refused the blush trying to warm her cheeks. Gorgeous or not, neither man could be trusted. "State your business. I've work to do. My loom isn't going to replace itself."

Ian's blue eyes brightened. She squirmed in her seat at the sight, then cast her gaze down, deciding it best if she just not look at him.

"We both regret the trouble we've obviously caused ye. Please allow us to set things right. We can buy ye a loom and set ye up in a new shop."

She straightened in her seat but kept her gaze downcast. Were they truly offering to compensate her? She cleared her throat. "I'll need coin to purchase supplies, yarn and such."

"Agreed."

She looked up in disbelief, but then her eyes narrowed. "Are you toying with me?"

He appeared taken aback by her comment. "Of course not. We wouldn't dream of making light of our actions. Ye have my word. I have a purse heavy with coin just for ye."

Her heart started to race. She reached out her hand. "All right then," she said. "Give it to me."

Ian shook his head. "Not here. I will get a room upstairs. When ye're through with work, ye can join me there—"

"I should have known," she snapped. Pressing her hands on the table, she stood up and stormed away without a backward glance.

"Men are all the same," she fumed to Ruby who padded alongside her as she paced the kitchen, fury coursing through her body.

"Is everything all right?"

Jo stopped in her tracks.

Lorna was leaning against the doorframe, wearing a curious expression. "I saw you talking to those men. You seemed to be acquainted."

Jo nodded. "I wish I could say that I didn't know them, but they are the reason I'm in this mess. I thought they were going to compensate me for the damages, but as it turns out..." Her voice trailed off. She had been about to say that they had only wanted to buy what was not for sale, but she didn't want to insult Lorna—she needed this job and her makeshift bed in the back kitchen now more than ever. "They're as rotten as I first suspected."

"I should warn you—they both just took rooms upstairs."

"No matter," Jo shrugged, trying to regain her calm. "I don't need them or their coin. I will work hard and before long, I'll have my loom and a fresh start."

Lorna smiled at her. "I admire your grit, Jo. You remind me of myself when I was your age. I was determined to own my own drinking house." She made a sweeping gesture. "See for yourself what a little grit can do."

Emboldened, Jo nodded fiercely. "Just like you, I'll never give up. And I'm not going to stop with a loom and a roof over my head. One day, I'm going to open my very own fabric shop."

"You know," Lorna began, but her tone was suddenly hesitant, which immediately made Jo tense. "New Castle has a bustling marketplace."

Jo gave Lorna a quizzical look. "Why do you suggest New Castle? Why wouldn't I set up shop right here in Durham?"

"Oh, no reason," Lorna chirped, fidgeting with her tunic. "You just mentioned a fresh start."

Jo put her hands on her hips. "What aren't you telling me, Lorna?"

Lorna glanced around uneasily as if checking to make certain they were alone. "MacLemore is talking about you to anyone who will listen."

A sick feeling invaded Jo's stomach. "What sort of things is he saying?"

Lorna sighed. "He's telling people that you're a whore and a liar."

Tears came on so suddenly that a sob escaped her lips before she pressed her hand to her mouth, choking down the emotion.

Lorna's brow pinched together. "Oh, pet," she crooned, opening her arms, but Jo resisted the woman's warmth, remembering her mother's words...

Be strong, Jo. Let no one see your weakness. Even the most well-intentioned will use it against you if they ever find themselves in trouble.

"I'm all right," Jo forced herself to say.

Lorna gently rubbed Jo's arm. Inwardly, she savored the contact, letting Lorna soothe her weary, broken heart.

"Your mother's death is still fresh. I can see the pain in your eyes." Lorna's own eyes brimmed with tears. "My mother passed away nearly five years ago, and I still miss her every day. May God rest her soul." She squeezed Jo's arm and then cleared her throat. "I know you don't want me to fuss over you, but take my advice, from one tough woman to another; you need to cry out your heartache. It will eat a hole inside you if you don't."

"Thank you, Lorna." She cleared her throat, then dusted her hands off on her apron. "I better get back to work. If I'm to leave town sooner than later, I'll need coin for supplies."

"Do you have a place to go?"

Jo dragged her fingers across her forehead, which had started pounding. She closed her eyes, thinking about Lorna's question.

A place to go...

She couldn't go home to Toonan, not after the numerous times over the last two years that she had promised her mother. Even on her death bed, her mother had, once again, made Jo swear she would never return to Toonan on her own.

Then she remembered the bishop's advice. *Go to Haddington Abbey. The abbot will welcome you. He will give you a purpose.*

If a fresh start was what she needed, God had given her one.

She looked at Lorna. "Don't worry about me. I have a place to go."

Jo stared hard at the door in front of her, which she had been doing for what felt like the better part of an hour.

"Just knock," she softly hissed at herself.

A purse awaited her on the other side of the door. All she had to do to get it was...

"Blast," she cursed aloud, feeling her cheeks flush just at the idea of giving herself to Ian. She shook the innocent thoughts from her head. "What does it matter? The world already thinks me a whore."

She raised her fist to knock, but let her hand fall back to her side. Pressing her forehead into the door, she squeezed her eyes shut against the pain twisting her heart. "Keep breathing, keep fighting."

Forgive me, Da.

She rapped her knuckles on the door.

After a moment, the door swung wide. Ian flashed her a sleepy smile. "I had given up on ye coming."

She swallowed hard, taking in the sleek, sinewy contours of his bare chest and muscular shoulders. She craned her neck back to meet his gaze. Dear God, did he have to be so big?

"I've come," she said lamely, not knowing what to say.

He stepped aside, a lazy smile curving his lips. "Welcome." Gesturing to the table near the brazier, he said, "I sent for some food. There's bread and cheese and pigeon pies that I bought at market earlier today."

Her legs felt flimsy as she stepped into the room.

Keep breathing. Keep fighting.

She glanced at the table. Despite her gnawing hunger, she couldn't think about food. "I'm not hungry."

He smiled. "No matter, join me for a drink then. I have warm mead and wine."

Why did he delay?

"Could we just get right to it?" she blurted, wishing her humiliation to be over.

He jerked his head up from where he stood, pouring the wine. She could see the surprise on his face. "Er...if that is yer wish." Then he pointed to the bed. "At least make yerself comfortable."

He turned away, crossing the room to a rough-hewn wooden chair in the corner where he seized a satchel and began digging around in it.

Make yerself comfortable—she knew what that meant.

Swallowing hard, she seized her tunic. Her hands trembling, she started to pull the wool over her head.

"What in blazes are ye doing, lass!"

She jumped, her heart racing. Was she doing it wrong? She tried to pull her tunic back on, but her nerves made her hands shake. She couldn't find the hole for her head. "Damn it," she cursed.

"Hold still, lass. Let me help ye." Ian tugged her tunic back in place. "Are ye hot or sick?"

"I...I thought," she swallowed hard.

He must have changed his mind, but she needed his coin to get north. "Don't you still want me?"

His eyes flashed wide. "Nay...I mean aye—ye're beautiful and fiery and exciting, but that's not why I asked ye to come up here."

"Do you mean to say that you're simply going to give me the money?"

"Och, lass," he crooned, lightly clasping her hand. "It looks like I owe ye another apology. I'm afraid that I didn't make myself clear earlier. Ye see, I asked ye up here because I didn't want anyone downstairs to see me give ye such a big bag of coin. I worried someone might try to relieve ye of it before ye had a chance to buy yer new loom."

She staggered back. "Oh, God, what you must think of me." Stumbling toward the door, she cried, "I have to get out of here!"

"Wait!"

She froze, her fingers a breath from the door handle.

"Please."

Hearing his gentle plea, she slowly turned around, although she could not bring herself to meet his gaze.

"Hold out yer hand," he said softly.

Cautiously, she reached out her hand.

Despite his massive size, his touch was feather soft as he cradled her palm in his. Gently, slowly, he smoothed his thumb across her palm.

"How long have ye been a weaver?"

She looked up, surprised by his question. "I first learned when I was very young."

"Do ye scrub and dye yer own wool?"

"When the job demands it, I do."

He seemed to consider her hand for another moment, but then he cleared his throat and said, "close yer eyes."

She cocked a wary brow at him.

"Don't ye trust me?"

"Is that supposed to be a jest?" she said dryly.

He chuckled. "All right. Don't close yer eyes. In fact, be sure ye don't blink at all." From behind his back, he produced a bag of coin, which he set in her hand. "Ye will find enough to pay for what Ramsay's great arse shattered, plus a wee extra, which I feel ye more than deserve to truly compensate ye for yer trouble."

The weight of the purse made her hand dip. Her heart pounded. "Thank you," she said breathlessly and turned on her heel, rushing to the door. Throwing it open, she stepped out into the hallway, but then she paused and looked back, once more, taking in the sight of his half-clad, sinewy physique. "I'm going to forget all about you," she lied. "Promise that you'll forget about me, too, especially...you know...our little misunderstanding."

Heat shone in his sky-blue eyes, making her heart race faster.

"Never," he vowed softly. "I'll never forget ye."

Chapter Eleven

Ian lay awake unable to rid his thoughts of Jo's mismatched eyes; her tall, sleek curves; and fiery courage. He could not remember in his twenty-six years ever being so profoundly impacted by a woman, especially one he knew so little about. What he did know, he was not sure he believed.

MacLemore had said that her father had been a weaver from London. Certainly, she could work a loom. He had seen the evidence. But her hands, although lightly calloused, were not the chapped, coarse hands of someone accustomed to the dregs of continuous labor. Of course, prior to her father's death and her mother's decline, she may have enjoyed a more leisurely life, especially if her father had been successful, which could explain her schooled bearing and soft skin. Members of the guilds, whether baker, weaver, tailor, or any of the organized trades, enjoyed prosperity beyond what the common laborer could ever earn.

He sat up and swung his legs over the side of the bed. Leaning forward, his forearms resting on his thighs, he gazed unseeing at the wall, his mind racing to solve the mystery that was Jo. She was a woman alone with no one to rely on but herself. This could certainly explain her guarded reserve and distrustful nature, but he knew there was more to her story. In fact, when it came to Jo, he had only one certitude—there was far more to her than met the eye. She was clearly hiding something—what? Well, he could only imagine. And imaging Jo was not only pleasing, but he also had no choice in the matter. Despite how he had tried to forget her and get some rest, he was living up to his promise—he would never forget her.

At dawn's first light, he left his room, determined to catch her before she started work for the day. Mayhap, she would consent to walk with him for a spell or at least break their fast together in the tavern. More than anything, he just wanted to sit with her, to look into her intriguing eyes, and listen to her speak from the heart. For a moment, he imagined what she would look like if she were to smile, or better yet, if she were to laugh out loud. The very idea of being the one to get Jo to let her guard down filled him with such excitement that he raced down the stairs.

The common was quiet. Two men sat in the corner. Judging by the ashen pallor of their skin and their slumped shoulders, he wondered if they had only just roused themselves from a drunken sleep on Lorna's table. The owner of the tavern was busy wiping down the bar. At Ian's approach, Lorna scowled.

"If you're looking for Jo, she's gone."

"When will she be back?"

"She's not coming back."

Ian's eyes flashed wide. "What do ye mean she's not coming back? Where else would she go? Isn't her mother ill? Surely, she's not leaving while her mother is sick."

"Her mother's dead."

Ian closed his eyes upon hearing such ill tidings. His heart ached for her. Now more than ever, he was determined to help her. "When did she leave?"

"She bid me farewell last night. Said she was going to make a fresh start."

Ian turned his back to Lorna to conceal his disappointment. He knew that Jo would not continue to work at the tavern for long, but he didn't think she would act so quickly.

"She's gone," he said softly.

"Aye, she up and quit." Lorna's words jarred him out of his state of shock. He took a deep breath and dismissed his selfish feelings. Instead, a slight smile curved his lips as he imagined a newly emboldened Jo, setting out at first light, purse in hand, to start a new life.

"I wish her every happiness. 'Tis as it should be," he said, more to himself than Lorna.

"What do you know about it?" Lorna snapped. "She was the best help I've ever had. Not too mention, fine to look upon."

Ian set the coin he owed Lorna on the table. "I'm certain that another comely lass, hard on her luck, will show up at yer door looking for a job," he said dryly.

"One can only hope."

Ian raised a disapproving brow at the tavern owner before turning on his heel and heading out the door.

Jo lingered in his thoughts as he made his way to the stables where he would meet Ramsay. They had to ride to Haddington Abbey to give their report to Abbot Matthew. Ian approached the town's livery and pushed open the swinging doors. Straightaway, he saw Ramsay, his head and shoulders visible above the stalls.

"Good morrow," the blacksmith called out. "My plan was to ready our horses, then get yer lazy arse out of bed, but I see ye're as anxious as I am to head north."

"Aye, that I am," Ian agreed, although in truth he had no wish to leave Durham, at least not without making sure Jo truly was all right. What if she encountered trouble while she was setting her affairs in order? He had given her such a large sum of money, large enough to draw the eye of a thief, if she were to take out the purse in front of the wrong men. Mayhap, he would remain in Durham for another day or two. He could track her down and stay with her until she was settled in a new home.

He walked purposefully down the walkway. "I want ye to go ahead without me."

Ramsay looked up from fitting the bridle onto his horse's muzzle. "But we've accomplished what we set out to do. This mission's over. Why in the name of all things decent would ye wish to stay in England another moment?"

"My reasons have naught to do with the cause," he began to explain as he passed a stall where a slim figure was bent over examining one of the back hooves of a large black stallion. He froze before taking two steps back and looking again at the figure. Long chestnut hair skimmed the ground.

It couldn't possible be her. "Jo?" he asked hesitantly.

The figure jerked straight. He met bright mismatched eyes. "Ian," she said simply.

A smile he couldn't contain stretched his lips wide. "Jo, I didn't think I would see ye again. I thought ye were likely out purchasing a new loo—" His words trailed off as his gaze settled on the satchel in the corner and the cloak draped over her shoulders. "Wait," he said. "What are ye doing here?"

"I'm leaving Durham," she stated while adjusting the length of her stirrups.

"I can see that, but where are ye going?"

She looked up at him and lifted her shoulders, not volunteering an answer.

He pressed his lips in a grim line as he took in the stubborn glint in her eyes. "Who are ye traveling with?"

Her eyes narrowed on him. "Ruby."

Ian jumped back startled as the door in the next stall rattled hard on its hinges and a fierce barking ensued.

"I can't saddle the horse safely with her in the same stall. Anyway, I don't think there would be room for the three of us in here."

Having recovered from his initial surprise, Ian peered over the stall at Ruby who snarled and lunged at the door, her eyes wild with bloodlust.

"Good, lass," Ian crooned, his words sending the dog into an even greater frenzy. "Sweet pup," he said, smiling. Then he cleared his throat. "All jesting aside, ye cannot travel alone with only Ruby as escort. 'Tis foolhardy."

She put her hands on her hips. "I dare ye to get in there and tell her that."

Ian shook his head. "Jo, I'm serious. Ye cannot travel the countryside alone. 'Tis madness."

Her eyes flashed with anger. "I don't care what you think."

A chuckle from the other side of the stables drew both their gazes.

"Or what you think, blacksmith," she snapped at Ramsay before turning back to face Ian. "Good day," she said curtly.

His gaze passed down her tall, slim form and her unbound chestnut waves. She lifted a small satchel, secured it to the saddle, and grasped the reins, turning to leave, but Ian stood in her path.

"Ye've hardly any supplies."

She shrugged. "I intend to get them in another town." A shadow crossed her face. "I want to put Durham behind me. Now, if you'll excuse me."

"Jo, ye need to take a deep breath—trust me, I know all about having to calm down."

"I don't need to calm down. I need you to get out of my way!"

"Listen, I know about yer mother. I'm so very sorry for yer loss, but I think yer heartache is making ye act rashly."

She looked away, shaking her head slightly. "Lorna talks too much."

"Ye can't mean to travel alone."

Jo looked him hard in the eye. "You just said that you know about my mother. So it stands to reason that you know why I am traveling alone—I'm not a simpleton, nor am I guided by my grief. I know what I do is dangerous, but I don't have anyone, just Ruby."

"Ye have me."

She dropped her gaze, but not before he glimpsed her suffering. When, once again, she looked up her eyes were clear, her face impassive. Without a word, she started to walk forward, the hooves of her massive stallion pounding the packed earth.

He moved to stand in front of the stall, his broad frame filling the doorway.

"You're big," she said. "But Star is bigger and Ruby's meaner."

Ian backed out of the stallion's way and further still as she released Ruby from the stall. The half-wolf lunged at him, but Jo gripped the short leash, straining to hold the animal back.

"Do you still doubt that Ruby will protect me?"

Ian raked his hand through his hair. "As fierce as yer dog is, she wouldn't have a chance against a broad sword."

Jo's gaze swept over the two massive warriors. She imagined them both with weapons raised at the ready, and their faces twisted in rage. In that moment, she knew Ian was right. Ruby was only a true threat to him if caught off guard and unarmed. But then, she remembered the bishop's warning.

Trust no one.

She straightened her spine resolutely. "We will manage." Then she started forward, leading Star and Ruby from the livery.

Ramsay came to stand at Ian's side while he watched Jo pass through the stable gates. "My guess is that I'll be reporting back to Abbot Matthew myself."

"Do not forget to tell the abbot about the bishop's plan to restore the Saints. And ye must track David, Paul, and Nick down on yer own. I will join ye as soon as I can." Ian stormed across the walkway to the stall housing his own mount. "I can't let her travel alone."

Ramsay chuckled. "But didn't ye hear what she said? She clearly does not want yer help. What are ye going to do? Follow her?"

Ian nodded. "That's exactly what I'm going to do."

Chuckling, Ramsay pulled his horse toward the gate. "When our paths cross again, my friend," he called out.

Ian saddled his own horse and quickly left the stables. Jo had refused his aid, but in this one matter, he could not honor her wishes. He would protect her, even from her own folly. As he stepped out into the sunshine, the cobbled thoroughfare stretching out ahead of him, Jo's less-than-inconspicuous black horse was easy to spot. Ian led his own chestnut stallion at a distance, careful not to be seen. She need not know that she traveled with an armed escort. What mattered was that he would keep her safe and close, although not as close as he would like.

Chapter Twelve

As the gates of Durham receded in the distance, fire burned red-hot in Jo's soul. She bent low over the saddle and kicked her mount hard in the flanks. Ruby raced at her side, her pink tongue flapping.

Her heart ached for her mother and for the answers only her mother had known. Why had they fled Toonan? Who was responsible for the loss of her parents and the contented life she'd once known? Pain twisted her shattered heart as still more questions plagued her mind.

Was she foolish to follow the advice of the old bishop?

Would this Abbot Matthew truly welcome her and give her life a new purpose?

The one thing she knew for certain was the workings of her own heart. She was tired of hiding, tired of being afraid. More than anything, she wanted security and belonging. But in a world torn apart by war and prejudice, did such a place even exist? Could Haddington Abbey be the haven she sought?

There was only one way to find out.

She breathed deep the fresh air and allowed the scent of the earth on the wind to mask her sadness. Pushing her mount faster, she upturned her face. The heat of the sun caressed her cheeks. Too long had she been confined within Durham's city walls, caged by cobblestone, fear of her landlord's roving hands, and the constant threats of poverty. Freedom now pulsed in her veins and imbued her body with strength. She knew the risks she faced traveling north with only Ruby to protect her, but life's hardships had taught her many lessons. She was not the same girl who had first set out with her mother two years ago. Anyway, what choice did she have? Despite the dangers of the roads, she would stay her course.

AFTER FOLLOWING JO at a distance for several hours, Ian could have drawn the sleek lines of her back, ramrod straight in the saddle, and the graceful waves of her rich brown hair, glistening in the sunshine. Her willful determination was visible in her carriage.

At first, it had been easy enough to follow her astride her massive stead. Travelers filled the roads beyond Durham, but now he had to keep back, moving carefully and slowly to ensure that his presence went undetected.

To his surprise, they were heading north. He had thought she might wish to return to London from which her father hailed. He could only assume she had no remaining family there to draw her south. Mayhap she wanted to make a fresh start in New Castle. The city did boast a flourishing marketplace. He kept his cloak over his head, despite the warmth of the late summer day, to ensure his red hair did not give him away were she to catch a glimpse of him from the distance as they crossed rolling moorland.

When the sun began to set, he saw the torch fire of a hamlet called Trang in the distance. It was a few miles south of New Castle proper. On several occasions, Ian had stayed in the small village at Gull Tavern. It was a clean, reputable establishment run by an elderly couple. The only other place for the weary traveler to rest was the Sheep's Head Tavern, a haven for unsavory locals bent on gambling and drinking themselves into stupors and raucous brawling.

After Jo gave her horse over to the young groomsman at the village livery, she and Ruby set out through the main road. Ian quickly gave his own horse over before hastening after her, still cautious to keep his distance.

She stopped at the first tavern she encountered, the Sheep's Head.

"Nay, lass. Keep walking. The Gull is just up ahead," Ian whispered under his breath as he continued to watch. "Blast!" he softly cursed as she turned and entered the disreputable drinking house.

Following, he peered through the window. The common room was still reasonably calm given the early hour, although he spied four dirty, rough-looking men sitting in the corner, raising their tankards. Ale sloshed on the table as they rammed their cups together. Ian scowled. He knew it was only a matter of time before the room would be crowded with similar men, ready to drink the night away.

He slipped through the door, claiming a small table in the darkest corner while Jo conversed with the barkeep, Ruby's leash gripped tight in her hand.

"Your beast has to stay outside," the bartender said, casting Ruby a look of contempt.

In response, Ruby growled, baring her teeth.

"She'll be no trouble, so long as no one gives me trouble," Jo said courageously.

The bartender's scowl deepened. "Did you not hear what I said, girl?"

But Jo would not be so easily deterred. "Then I will keep her in my room upstairs."

Ian smiled. She certainly had gumption.

The bartender considered her. "That will cost you another farthing."

Jo pressed what appeared to be a few coins into the barkeeps hand. Ian was relieved that she'd had the sense not to bring the large purse he had given her out in the open. "Can I have supper sent upstairs?"

"Where do you think you are? The King's palace. You'll eat in the common room like everyone else."

Jo disappeared upstairs with Ruby whose low throated growl could be heard even after she and Jo passed from view. A short while later, Jo returned and claimed the table nearest the bar and sat with her back to Ian...and the rest of the room.

His shoulders tensed as he watched every man in the room shift his gaze on her. It was clear by the sudden pointing and the leering smiles that numerous conversations in the room had turned salacious in nature—the object of desire none other than Jo, not that she could be aware of the trouble her presence had stirred.

Ian gripped the edge of the table, his knuckles whitening from the strain. "She should know better than to turn her back to a room," he whispered aloud.

At least, she was making it easy for him to remain unseen.

After several moments, a young woman passed through the door behind the bar, holding a tray. She headed straight for Jo's table and set a steaming trencher in front of her. An instant later the barkeep arrived. His leering smile revealed his own desire for Jo as he set a tankard in front of her. Thankfully, the barkeep did not linger. Ian sat back, willing himself to relax a little while she ate.

No sooner did he let his guard down than one of the four men in the corner stood up, downed his ale, and headed straight toward her. In a flash, Ian was on his feet and intercepted the man. "Turn around and sit back down," he hissed, scowling at the smaller man from beneath his drawn hood.

The man glowered back and gestured to Jo. "I saw her first—"

Ian's hand lashed out, catching the man by the throat. "If ye know what's good for ye, ye'll sit down and leave the lass alone."

Ian squeezed until the man's head started bobbing up and down to show he would heed Ian's warning. Releasing him, the man scurried away, and Ian glanced at Jo to ensure her back was still turned away from him. Then he whisked his hood off his head and scowled a warning to the room, turning to make certain he met the gaze of each and every man. His message was simple—*keep away from the girl or deal with me.*

JO WIPED UP THE LAST of the thick sauce from her wooden trencher with a hunk of bread before downing the rest of her ale. Then she stood and glanced quickly behind her at the room. The men at various tables glanced at her, but their gazes did not linger. Satisfied, she turned back around. She knew that by showing her back to the room, she had conveyed one simple message—*I'm not interested in being bothered. Don't talk to me.*

This was her first night traveling alone, which she knew was dangerous for anyone, especially a woman, but she also believed in herself. She had common sense and nerve. Head held high, she ascended the stairs to her room. Once inside, she locked the door, spread her cloak out over the moldy, straw mattress and called Ruby to her.

"Here you go, girl," she crooned, petting Ruby's long back, and feeding her some thick pieces of mutton she had saved from her stew. After Ruby gobbled down her dinner, Jo rose and crossed the room to a pitcher and basin on a stand in the corner.

"No surprise, but it's empty," she said dryly to Ruby who sat alert, waiting for Jo's next move.

"I'll be right back," she put her hand on the door handle. "I'll just pop down to the bar and fetch some—"

Ruby started growling, her teeth bared. "What's the matter girl," she muttered. "Is someone out there?" She put her ear against the door, listening for movement, but all she could hear were muffled voices rising up from the common room. Seizing Ruby's leash, she opened the door. Ruby lunged forward, growling and gnashing her teeth. Jo leaned out just in time to see a tall, cloaked figure hurrying down the hall before disappearing into another guest room.

"That was odd," she said to Ruby who continued staring in the direction of the stranger, a low growl in her throat. Jo turned around to put Ruby back inside, but then she changed her mind. "The barkeep be damned." Firmly grasping Ruby's leash, she decided to make the journey back downstairs with a sharp-fanged escort.

Chapter Thirteen

Ian sat upon a rock and gazed out over the surrounding birch trees to the clearing below. Jo stood at the edge of a small pool, dipping her toes in the water while her stallion drank. She let go of the reins and pulled her tunic up above her knees, stepping further into the pool. The hint of a smile curved her mouth. He licked his lips, so enticed was he by what he was witnessing. Certainly, the shape of her comely calves tempted his gaze, but it was her bearing that he found so bewitching.

There was a lightness to her face that he had never seen before. He chuckled softly when she suddenly kicked at the water playfully. He was so accustomed to her pinched brow and the grim set to her lips. Now, she seemed so young and carefree. She could not be more than ten and seven or eight, but so often she appeared older than that. He leaned forward on the rock when her gaze suddenly darted around her, scanning the surrounding trees. Then, she dipped under her horse's neck to scan the other side of the pool.

What was she up to?

In the next moment, he knew the answer. He swallowed hard, his mouth suddenly dry, as she inched her tunic up over her head, revealing her thin kirtle, which hugged her sleek curves. Despite how much he longed to see the womanly curves beneath her undergarment, he forced himself to turn away when she reached for the hem of her kirtle and started to pull that up, too. Then he heard a splash. He turned back just to see her toes dip beneath the water. Moments later, she broke the surface, her long hair slicked back, her face upturned. Her laughter reached his ears, warming his heart.

He could have watched her all day, for the rest of his life really, but he knew it was not right to intrude upon such an intimate scene. With a sigh, he turned away from the glory of water sluicing off her bare shoulders and decided to forage for mushrooms that he could leave in her path for her dinner.

Scanning the forest floor, he tried to focus on his chosen task, but his thoughts remained transfixed on her beautiful form, making it hard to concentrate. At last, spying a cluster of plump mushrooms, partially hidden beneath a scattering of ferns, he bent over, reaching out his hand, but then he jumped at the sound of a piercing scream. He whirled around and took off, head down, sprinting as fast as he could back to the pool.

JO DOVE BENEATH THE surface, the icy water rushing over her body, cooling her, and reviving her senses. She felt free, unencumbered by layers of clothing. Pushing off the bottom, she sprang toward the surface, but when her face emerged, Ruby's snarling seized her attention. She whirled around in the water in time to see a stout man in filthy rags rush at Ruby with a club. Air rushed into her lungs, powering the scream that fled her lips. Ruby sprang at her assailant. He cried out, dropped his club to shield his face and fell back, scurrying out from under Ruby who had left her mark on the man's cheek.

Backing up to the shoreline, Ruby snarled and growled, daring one of the men to attempt to get past her to where her mistress remained, shoulder deep in water. The stout man wiped at the marks on his face and growled when he saw the blood.

"I'll kill that stupid dog!"

"You stay away from her," Jo shouted. She felt helpless. If only she had her own dirk. She would charge out of the pool and slit the man's throat for even threatening Ruby.

But she was unarmed and naked.

Gripping a knife in his hand, another man, tall with broad shoulders and clad in a patched and greasy tunic, chuckled at his companion. "Tomlin, that's no dog. You just tried to best a wolf with naught but a stick. What you need is a dagger," he said, his voice thick and greedy, eying Ruby as if he was imagining what she would look like skinned and turning on a spit.

"Think you can do better with that," Tomlin snorted, gesturing to the other man's so-called dagger. "It's smaller than your prick."

Jo didn't care how small his knife or prick were. All she cared about was Ruby. "Come here, girl," Jo bellowed as the man slowly crept closer and closer to her beloved companion who was snarling, gnashing her jaws, her haunches ready to propel her toward the approaching menace.

But what if it was Ruby's blood that was spilled?

"No Ruby!" Jo screamed, pushing through the water to get to her, heedless of her lack of weapon or her state of undress. "Get away from her!"

Lewdly urging Jo on, the man with the knife sneered, "That's right. Come rescue your mutt. Let me see that beautiful body."

Jo reached the shore and rose out from beneath the surface, water sluicing off her shoulders. The men gawked at her wet, bare breasts. Just as Jo lunged for Ruby, a ferocious battle cry rang out and a flash of red whooshed down from the high rocks on one side of the pool. Before she knew what was happening, a familiar giant splashed down in the water between her and her assailants. He rose up, his stance strong, ready to fight.

IAN SNAPPED HIS WRIST, sending his dagger soaring through the air. It sunk deep into one the villain's shoulders. Crying out, the man dropped his club and fell back, his face twisted with pain. The other two men charged at him, their faces ugly with rage. Ian plunged his sword into his attacker's belly just as the other man raised his hand, dagger flashing in the sunlight, poised to sink into Ian's neck. Ian jerked back. The dagger stabbed naught but air. Then, in a flash of teeth and fur, Ruby clamped down on the man's wrist. He cried out, Ruby thrashing her head, mangling his flesh before releasing her grip. The man scurried backward, cradling his gushing wound, his face red and teeth clenched against the pain. Leaving the dead man behind, the others stumbled off into the wood.

But for Ian the fight wasn't over yet.

Ruby turned on him, snarling and snapping her jaws. He scurried back. Bending to seize a sturdy branch off the ground, he used it to fend her off.

Jo flashed past him, her long hair and arms concealing her nakedness, not that he could have taken more than a passing glance with the wolf-dog wanting to mangle his throat. "Call her off!"

Wrapped in her cloak, Jo appeared in front of him and grabbed Ruby's leash. "Come on, girl," she said, straining to pull her away. "She's hard to control when she feels I am threatened."

"I would never hurt ye."

"Unless you know a way to make her understand that, then you'll just have to go," she snapped. "I can only hold her off for so long."

"Ye're mad if ye think I'm leaving ye alone in the woods after ye were just set upon by three lusty, drunken woodsmen."

"I'm not alone."

"If those men had been more than common thieves armed with more than kitchen knives and sticks, ye and Ruby would be dead. She can only protect ye against unarmed or poorly armed men...like me, at the moment," he gritted, struggling to hold the stick that Ruby had lashed down on with her powerful jaws. "What ye need is an escort."

Still Ruby struggled with lethal intent.

"I appreciate your concern, but it's no use," Jo snapped impatiently. "She doesn't like anyone. Ruby," she commanded, her voice booming. "Stand down!"

Finally, Jo was able to pull the powerful animal back a few feet.

Ian rested his hands on his thighs, catching his breath as he looked the beast in the eyes. Yellow eyes stared back at his, untrusting, challenging, angry—not unlike her owner, except for the color.

But what if he could change all that?

He stood straight and crossed his arms over his chest. "If I can get her to like me, may I journey with ye."

Jo stared at him for a moment, her face a stony, unreadable mask. Then she looked away. "I don't need a guard."

He cleared his throat. "The dead man on the ground leads me to believe otherwise."

She looked back at him, her eyes flashing. "Let me say it like this, I don't want a guard."

"Then how about a friend?"

She faltered. He knew he must have said the unexpected by the way she paused. Her gaze dropped to Ruby who was still struggling to reach Ian's throat.

"It's impossible. Look at her. In case you don't realize it, she wants to kill you."

"Just give me a chance," Ian said. "I have a way with frightened creatures."

"She's not frightened. She's angry."

Ian stared at her for a moment before he said, "I just saved your life. She's not angry with me; she's scared. I just need to show her that I'm a good man, a man she can trust."

Keeping both herself and Ruby at a distance, Jo shrugged, imparting an air of indifference, which did not quite reach her eyes. Her gaze betrayed her nervousness, her worry, and something else Ian decided to believe was hope.

He shifted his gaze from the suspicious lass to her protective companion. Squatting down, he tried to make himself as small as he could. Dropping his gaze and lowering his head he said to the dog, "We just fought side by side—that makes us brothers."

"She's a girl," Jo interjected.

"All right, so not brothers, but definitely family."

Ian lowered his gaze further still and got down on his knees, bringing his head low to the ground. He swallowed.

"Let her go."

"Let her go? Are you mad?"

"Mayhap a wee bit but do it anyway."

"She's not just noise and bravado. She really will attack you."

"I believe anyone can learn trust when the person asking is worthy. I am a flawed man, make no mistake about that, but I'm a good one. She knows I am." He took a deep breath. "Let her go."

"All right, but don't say I didn't warn you."

Ruby lunged at him, barking and growling. Ian kept his gaze downcast but felt her hot breath on his face. She was so close and so very fierce, but then she danced back. He looked up, and an instant later she lunged forward again, snarling. Ian kept his breathing steady, his gaze averted, and didn't flinch. Again, Ruby stopped short of sinking her teeth into his flesh. Then, with a low-throated growl, her hackles raised, she bore down on Ian but did not snarl or snap her jaws. She nosed forward, all the while issuing the same low, warning growl. She sniffed at him, then retreated back to Jo's side, still issuing a muted growl in the back of her throat.

"Good girl," Jo exclaimed, scratching Ruby behind the ear while she gripped her cloak tightly around her naked body.

Ian rolled onto his back and expelled a long breath. "Well, that was a start."

"She didn't eat your face. I hope that's not how you measure the start of every good relationship."

He lifted his head to meet her gaze. "Ye can pretend to be unaffected by what just happened, but ye and I both know that was momentous."

"All right," she conceded. "That went much better than I expected."

He sat up, smiling. "Then we have an accord?"

"I suppose I did give you my word, but..." Her eyes narrowed on him suspiciously.

"But what?" he asked.

She straightened, clasping her cloak tightly around her. "Have you been following me this whole time?" she said accusingly.

He nodded. "Aye, in fact, I haven't taken my eyes off ye...except, of course, just now before ye were attacked."

She seemed to consider his words before saying, "Why did you take your eyes off me?"

"Ye were taking a bath. What kind of rogue do ye think I am?"

She shrugged. "Not all men are as honorable as you."

"I know plenty of men, all my brothers included, who wouldn't spy on a woman bathing. Yer body is just that, yers. Now, with a clear invitation, I would certainly be inclined to see more of ye, but not without yer permission. With that in mind—" Ian turned around to give her privacy. "Ye need to situate yerself. We shouldn't linger just in case that fool on the ground over there has more friends hiding in the woods."

After a few moments, she said, "I'm decent."

He turned back around. "Then let us head on our way."

She stood with her hands on her hips, giving him a hard look. "So, it's *our* way now, is it?"

"Ye did say that if I could get Ruby to like me, that I could travel with ye."

As if the dog understood, Ruby growled at him.

"Not biting you is not the same as liking you," Jo said defensively.

"I concede she's only being cordial and is not yet ready to have a warm cuddle with me by a roaring fire. If ye prefer, ye can pretend yer traveling alone, and I can just go back to following ye."

"Fine," she said, her voice clipped. "You can join me and Ruby but keep your questions to yourself. All right?"

Ian contained the smile that fought to spread wide across his face. God's blood, but he loved her gumption. "I learned long ago not to question a woman, especially one with secrets."

Her eyes flashed wide. "What makes you think I have secrets?"

He cocked a brow at her but said nothing. "Where are we heading?"

"You'll see," she said stiffly.

He chuckled. "I told ye, women always have secrets."

Chapter Fourteen

After riding in silence for more than an hour, they cleared the forest and crossed a wide field, which brought them to a road. "It forks up ahead. I ken ye won't tell me where we're going, but how about a general direction?"

"North."

He knew her answer was clipped intentionally. "Northeast or west?"

"Does it matter?"

He gestured to the two roads. "We must make a choice."

She clicked her tongue, nudging her horse across the road onto the adjacent field. "No roads," she said.

"Wait!"

She brought her mount to a halt.

Taking in the stubborn tilt to her chin, he ran his hand through his hair. "No roads? Are ye certain?"

She simply nodded in reply.

He considered her for a moment, her tall seat and intelligent gaze. He knew there was so much more to his English weaver than she would ever let on. He had so many questions, but he also knew, if pressed, that she would only grow more suspicious or withdraw from him altogether. As one of Scotland's rebel sons, he was no stranger to secrets, but ensuring her safety was made more difficult by not knowing where they were going or what they would face when they arrived.

"How far north?" he asked, thinking it was an innocent enough question.

"Far."

"All the way to the border?"

She nodded in reply.

"Beyond the border into Scotland?"

Again, she nodded.

He smiled. "What business does an English lass have in Scotland?"

"My father was English, but my mother was Scottish."

He was surprised by her forthright answer. "I did not realize that. Then, we must be journeying to yer mother's people."

"In a manner of speaking." The glint in her eye told him she was being deliberately vague.

"I believe ye enjoy keeping me in the dark," he said, ensuring the mood stayed light. The only way he was going to get a straight answer from her was if she let her guard down.

To his surprise, she smiled. "Are you too pampered to travel through the wilds. Must you seek the comforts of town?"

"I'm a sailor and a fisherman by trade. I've slept more nights under the stars than beneath a roof."

"I'm not surprised. For you, a roof is something to walk upon rather than to sleep beneath."

He threw his head back with laughter. "I'll have to be lighter on my toes next time I walk the ridge of a roof."

Her gaze slowly traveled the full length of him. "I think you'd best pray for a miracle if you ever wish to be accused of lightness on your feet."

He gave her an appraising look. "Ye're on the taller side for a woman."

She sat straighter in her seat, showing off her full height. "I'm glad you noticed." She nudged her horse with her heels. "Now, enough talk. Come on, Ruby. Let's ride!"

Over rolling moorland they rode. In the distance, he saw the small hamlet of Cridhe. The setting sun cast streaks of gold and pink hues across the horizon. Overhead, however, thick, dark clouds dotted the shadowy sky, shifting and spreading.

"We won't be sleeping under the stars tonight," he said as the evening sky was quickly devoured by the gathering storm clouds.

Jo turned her gaze heavenward and nodded grimly. "The sky was red this morning." Then she turned to face him, her expression determined. "I've no wish to sleep on the sodden earth. Do as you'd like, but I shall carry on."

Ian nodded. "Ye could certainly do that, although yer horse and Ruby might not be as eager to continue as ye."

She stroked Star's mane, her brow pinched with concern. Then she turned her attention to the large dog, sitting on the ground, panting.

"I know a place not far from here where we can find shelter," Ian offered.

"No villages," she warned.

He smiled softly. "I promise ye."

The tension fled her shoulders. "All right, then, lead on."

For the first time since they had set out, he led the way. To reach the shelter before the sky opened and unleashed the storm, they galloped over the open moors, Ruby racing to keep up. Normally, he would have cut through Cridhe to reach their destination, but instead he skirted around the village.

Before too long, they reached their camp for the night, an ancient long barrow. Two massive stones stood like sentries and formed a natural entrance to a wide, open circle, surrounded by tall stones, except where another passage opened, leading into a deep tunnel that dipped beneath the ground.

"We can leave the horses here," Ian said after they had passed into the open circle. "'Tis an ancient burial mound, but do not fash yerself. This will not be the first night I've slept here to escape a storm."

She dismounted and peered into the tunnel entrance, Ruby sniffing the ground behind her. "Do you mean to say there are bodies laid to rest in there."

"Only behind the walls. Ye can't see any of them. There is just one long tunnel with openings that branch off on both sides. Thieves have broken through to where the dead have been laid, but the walls have since been resealed. And remember, this was built by godless men who lived on this island long before the Gaels, Normans, or Vikings ever came to these shores. I assure ye 'tis perfectly safe."

Jo shook her head. "We might offend the spirits that rest here?"

Ian smiled patiently. "The souls that herein lie are ancient and wise. They ken when a heart is good. We've naught to fear."

She chewed her lip, betraying her uncertainty.

"If ye'd rather go back to the village, I know a lovely inn run by a plump older woman by the name of Mistress Bea. She keeps a thick pottage bubbling on the hearth day and night for travelers. And her feather ticks are free of fleas. Ye'll sleep like a babe at ol' Bea's."

She seemed to consider the inn, but only for a moment. With a deep breath, she took a resolute first step down into the cavernous tomb. "This will do," she said stiffly. Then she hesitated. "It's so dark."

"It won't be once we build a fire." He turned to his horse, removing his saddle bags. "It will be dry and warm. Ye'll see."

After they tended the horses and gathered their supplies, Jo once again hesitantly peered into the darkness.

"I will go first, if ye'd like," he offered.

She shook her head stubbornly. "'Tis no matter. Come on, girl."

Ruby sniffed at the entrance and whimpered.

"Don't you start," Jo scolded. "We have been in stickier situations than this."

Ian had to bend low to fit through the tunnel. "Keep straight. There's a branch up ahead into a chamber long enough to permit us to recline."

After a fair bit of stumbling on both their parts, and an unfortunate moment when he trailed too close to Ruby who snarled and nipped at his leg in warning, he followed them into a wide space with a low ceiling, requiring them both to remain hunched over. "These accommodations are not excellent for the tall."

Only silence met his jest.

Still, he smiled undeterred. "One of these days, I am going to make ye throw yer head back with laughter."

"If we had a small fire, you'd be able to see my brow arched in disbelief."

"Consider it done," he said, arranging the necessary supplies.

"What about the smoke?" she asked when he first struck the flint.

"'Tis drawn through the gaps and cracks in the walls and into the many chambers. 'Tis said that the barrow stretches far beyond this main tunnel."

Soon warm light filled the chamber, the flames casting dancing shadows on the walls. Bending low, he turned to retrieve some of the dried meat from his satchel, but Ruby was already there, sniffing and pawing at it.

"Let me get some for ye, lass," he said, but Ruby growled and bared her teeth, standing guard over the pack. He cleared his throat and looked at Jo. "Mayhap it would be best if ye sorted out supper."

Jo chuckled. "Good idea."

"Ye just laughed!"

"Only at your expense," she said dryly, but her lips curved in the barest hint of a smile that belied her somber tone.

"Thank ye," he said, taking her offering of a thick cut of the dried meat and an oatcake.

They ate in silence, her gaze scanning the ancient runes and pictures on the walls.

"I wonder what they were like," she said. "I mean the people who drew these pictures."

"I'm sure they were not much different than ye and I," he said keenly. "They had families, people they cared for."

"Do you have a family?" she asked.

He nodded. "I do. My parents are both dead and my wee sister, may God rest their souls, but I have four older brothers and an older sister."

Her eyes widened. "Such a large family."

He shrugged. "Not so large really, although it was a challenge to find a spot of ground in our one room cottage to lay out a pallet as we all grew taller." He smiled. "My parents did not count on us being so large, me especially, when they had settled in the midst of the busy market district of Berwick."

She leaned in, suddenly very attentive. "You grew up in Berwick?"

"Indeed," he answered. "What a fine city it once was."

"My father used to tell me stories of the great city. Were you there when it was sacked?"

"I was not in the city when Edward attacked, which is why I'm still alive. My parents and wee sister were not so lucky as the rest of us. They were slain by the English invaders. Rose—she's my eldest sister—her family was also slain, her three wee daughters and her husband."

Jo gasped. "That's awful."

"Those were dark years."

"How old were you?" she asked.

"Ten and five." He paused and then thought to ask, "How old were ye when yer da died?"

She didn't answer right away. Ian worried he had pushed too far, but then came her soft reply. "I was ten and five."

They locked eyes and for a moment a comfortable silence hung in the air. A connection had been made. He could feel her guard come down ever so slightly.

"Do ye have any other family to speak of?"

She looked away. "My family is dead."

He waited, hoping she would say more, but as the silence between them grew, he knew she had revealed all she would for the moment.

He handed her a costrel of ale.

She accepted and brought it to her lips, but then she hesitated. "This food and drink belong to you. I will pay you for them."

He shook his head slightly. "Do not fash yerself, lass. I'm happy to share."

Her brow wrinkled with suspicion. "Nothing is freely given in this world."

"'Tis a shameful day, indeed, when a fellow traveler is unwilling to share their supplies."

Still, he could tell she was not yet convinced.

"Listen to me, Jo. I wish to help ye, not for gain, or even to settle my debt, as I consider that to be paid in full. I want to help ye because I care what happens to ye. I don't want ye to be hungry or attacked by bandits. Is it so hard to imagine that I might just wish to help with no agenda of my own?"

"It is," she said simply. "I've known few men, and women for that matter, who consider others without first thinking of themselves."

"My parents were good people," he offered. "They taught us generosity and honor. I'm hardly perfect. I've made my mistakes, and I assure ye I will make many more before I join our bedfellows in the hereafter," he said, gesturing to the wall, behind which rested ancient souls long since dead.

Her lips upturned into an almost smile. At length, she released a long breath and flashed him a curious look. "You really are a decent man, aren't you?"

He nodded. "I promise ye, Jo. I mean ye no harm."

Without reply, she laid down and curled into Ruby, who sighed when she felt her mistress's warmth.

Ian sat back and rested his head against the stones and watched his newfound lassies for a while. Then he closed his eyes and drifted off to sleep.

He jerked awake. The fire was nothing more than glowing embers. He sat up, seizing the handle of his broad sword, intent on discovering what had awoken him. Then, Jo stirred beside him and cried out. In the dim light he could see her brows pinched. Then, she whimpered, her head thrashing from side to side.

"Jo," he whispered and gently shook her shoulder.

"No," she cried.

"Jo," he said more urgently.

Ruby's head lifted. She growled low in her throat.

Jo started to tremble, her face red, pain twisting her features.

"Jo," he said more forcefully, lifting her into his arms. Ruby whined, nudging her nose at her mistress's face.

Jo's eyes flew wide. "No," she cried again, pushing against him.

"'Tis me. 'Tis Ian. Ye're having a bad dream!"

Her eyes darted from side to side, her breaths coming quick and short.

"'Tis all right, lass," he crooned.

She gripped his tunic. "I...I..."

"'Tis all right, Jo. Just breathe."

She shook her head furiously. "It's not all right. It can never be all right." She swallowed hard. "I dreamt of my father." Her eyes glistened with unshed tears. "And my mother..." Her voice broke, but she pressed her hand to her mouth, containing the emotion.

He could see her struggle not to feel, not to break, to remain strong. The weight on her heart must have been unbearable. He wrapped his arm around her. "'Tis all right to cry, lass."

She shook her head furiously. "Mustn't cry...I have to be strong. I promised my mother I'd stay strong."

His heart ached for her. "Och, lass," he began gently. "Ye can't keep it all locked up inside. Yer mum would want ye to grieve for her. How else will ye move on? When my mum died, I didn't think I'd ever stop crying." He held her closer. "Let yer tears fall."

She looked up at him, her flooded eyes beseeching, silently pleading for release. "I...I...I just don't understand how all of this happened," she began. Her grip on his tunic tightened, her knuckles whitening from the strain.

"Jo," he said firmly. "Yer mother is dead. Cry for her."

She opened her mouth as if to speak, but no words came out nor did she breathe. And, suddenly, her face crumpled. "My mother's dead," she cried. Shuddering, her arms surrounded him, and she sobbed into the crook of his neck.

He waited for her to say more, but only her tears fell. And despite how he longed to know the workings of her heart, what was driving her quest, and what he was actually protecting her from, he did not press her. She clung to him, and he held her, rocking her, crooning soft words of comfort. After a while, her breathing evened. Cradling her close, he held her while she slept. He prayed his strong arms and the beating of his heart in her ear would keep her demons, whatever they were, at bay.

Chapter Fifteen

Jo slowly opened her eyes. A furry, twitching ear came into view. Ruby was close at hand, curled up like a vast, tawny ball. Jo yawned. Her lids felt heavy. She grazed them with her fingers, feeling their puffiness and, suddenly, remembered the damn that had, at last, broken within her and the rush of emotion that had surged from her soul straight into Ian's strong embrace. Behind her, he still slept, his body curved around hers, his hand splayed wide across her stomach. His even breaths warmed her neck. She closed her eyes, savoring the intimacy, but then images of her nightmare flashed across her mind's eye, and she remembered...

In her dream she had been sitting in the solar with her father, playing chess, when he suddenly stood upright, knocking the table over. Game pieces scattered the ground. "We're out of time," he cried, and then the walls around them began to crumble. Thane and her mother appeared and dragged her away while her father was crushed beneath the debris.

The dream, which had brought the agony of loss to the surface of her heart, pained her still to remember. But the rawness of feeling, its sharp edges, had been softened by Ian's tender care. Long had it been since she'd felt another's comfort. And now, as she continued to lay within Ian's warm, strong arms, she closed her eyes, savoring the security of his embrace. As if sensing the direction of her thoughts, he shifted behind her, pulling her flush against him. His scent surrounded her.

128

She felt cocooned, pressed close to his sinewy torso. Then suddenly, she was struck by new images, and she remembered what she had dreamt *after* Ian had soothed her back to sleep.

She had dreamed of him, his kind blue eyes, his large capable hands. She closed her eyes, remembering...

They were in a glade beneath a blanket of stars. His eyes bore into hers, intense with wanting. Scooping her into his arms, he crossed the glade and lay her down in the soft grass. He stretched beside her, his head propped on his hand, his warm breath softly caressing her cheek. "I love ye, Josselyn," he whispered.

Her heart swelled. She smiled without constraint, her heart free to feel, to love, to want. She opened her arms to him. "I love ye, too."

"Good morrow," the real Ian said behind her.

She jumped a little at the sound of his voice, embarrassed by the intimacy of her dream.

She jerked upright before glancing his way, but the moment she met the warmth of his gaze she felt her face burn.

"There's nothing to be embarrassed about," he said quickly, sitting up and gently stroking her back with one of his big, strong hands. "'Twas only a dream."

Her hand flew to her mouth. Had he guessed? Did he know the sweet, sultry images coursing through her mind's eye? She had dreamt of him. And in her dream, he had been hers, and she belonged to him. And he kissed her...and it was glorious!

"How did you know about my dream?" she said, defensively.

He looked confused. "Because ye cried out in yer sleep."

"Oh God, please tell me I didn't do that!" Had she said his name? Did he know about how his dream kiss had made her feel?

"Don't ye remember? Ye had a nightmare—"

"Oh, yes, of course," she blurted, interrupting him. "Yes, my nightmare, I do remember...er...thank you for your comfort."

He grinned lazily, and his eyes once more grew sleepy. "Any time."

Her gaze dropped to his full lips, lips that had felt both soft and strong all at the same time. She shook her head and stood up quickly, banging her head on the low ceiling. She winced, and Ruby also jumped to her feet, shook out her fur, and kissed her mistress's cheek. When the pain radiating through her skull dissipated, she gave Ruby a quick scratch behind the ear. Then, she took a deep breath to calm down before she dared meet Ian's gaze. "Thank you," she said stiffly. "For last night, I mean."

"Are ye sure ye don't want to sit down and talk about it."

Yes, she did.

In fact, she wanted to cry in his arms again. She wanted to sit with him and lose herself in his blue eyes and tell him everything, all her secrets, all her fears. She wanted to watch him laugh and to listen to his stories. And if she were completely honest with herself, not only did she not think him false in anyway, she truly believed he was all things good and big and strong.

Still, she reluctantly shook her head. Despite how she longed to, she would not sit with Ian and share of her soul.

After all, both her mother and Bishop Lamberton had told her to trust no one.

Ian stretched his long arm, reaching for his sack. "Let us break our fast, then head on our way." He glanced around at the cave paintings. "We have intruded upon the spirits long enough."

He handed her a thick piece of dried meat before offering some to Ruby.

"Here ye go, lass," Ian said, holding out a piece for her.

Ruby growled, her keen eyes locked with his.

"'Tis all right," he crooned softly. "I won't hurt ye."

Ruby took a tentative step toward him only to dance back, settling next to Jo.

"Here ye go." He tossed the meat. No sooner did it land at Ruby's feet, than she sniffed it and scooped it up in her strong jaws.

"One of these days, ye're going to let me pet ye," Ian said to Ruby.

Jo laughed when Ruby growled in response.

"Wishful thinking, I'm afraid," she said.

He smiled at her and this time she could not refuse the heat that warmed her cheeks.

"Ye laughed again."

The way he was looking at her, with admiration in his eyes, made her suddenly feel like there was no right place to set her own gaze. Nervously, she cleared her throat and picked at some dried mud on her tunic. "Once again, I believe I laughed at your expense." She'd tried to shrug away the moment, but her voice didn't have its usual coolness.

She dared look up at him and his gaze intensified as a slow smile curved one side of his sensual mouth. "I will just have to make myself the fool more often."

Her stomach flipped. She dropped her gaze. Blessed Mother, what had come over her? Could a simple dream truly unravel her stubborn defenses? But then she remembered his sensual touch as he lay with her in the glade—it had been no simple dream.

He tossed another piece of dried meat at Ruby. "Anyway, I'm a patient man. She'll come around when she is certain I'm trustworthy."

"How can you be so sure?" Jo asked.

Ian smiled gently. "I told ye before; dogs can sense a person's character. I have my flaws, to be sure—"

"For instance?"

"I will let ye discover them on yer own," he smiled. "Although, I will tell ye, I've a wicked temper when truly provoked."

She thought about the fire she had glimpsed in his eyes when he attacked her assailants in the wood. "Our encounter with those thieves taught me that much."

He nodded. "But as ye've already said, I am, all in all, a decent man—Ruby will soon learn as much for herself." He leaned closer, his gaze intent. "And I hope ye will, too."

She frowned. "I know you're decent. I said as much already."

"Aye, but ye can't just know something—ye have to believe it." He gave her a playful but appraising look. "There's a part of ye that's resisting what ye claim to know, the part that's forgotten how to trust." He took her hand. "Breathe out the last of yer wariness and let me in. Yer not alone any longer, Jo." He squeezed her hand, pressing it to his chest. "I'm not going anywhere."

A fresh well of emotion rose in her throat. More than anything, she wanted him to cradle her in his arms again and soothe her with endless words of comfort. "Do you promise," she whispered.

"I promise."

She drew a deep, shaky breath. "I cannot trust you, not fully, anyway. I made a promise, you see, to my mother. But I am grateful to you, Ian. Grateful to you and...and I'm grateful *for* you."

He smiled almost boyishly and rubbed his hand over his stubbly beard as if at a loss for words. "'Tis a dream to hear ye say that."

Her eyes flashed wide. *Not more talk of dreams*!

Hunched over, she started off for the cave entrance. "Let's not tarry any longer."

ANOTHER DAY OF RIDING passed, during which Jo kept her thoughts, her words, and her gaze to herself. Day turned to night and still she kept her silence. Ian remained as patient as ever. Every now and again, while he was brushing down his horse or preparing supper, he flashed her a curious expression. And more than once, she noticed him appraising her, his brow pinched with worry. But he stayed his tongue, never probing her with questions or pressuring her to speak her mind, which was a blessing as she wouldn't have had a clue what to say. She'd never been more confused. Her mind raced, consumed by the same questions that had been plaguing her for years, and now—she glanced over at Ian—now she had a new list of questions.

But as the moon rose high in the sky, and the time to lie down drew near, her mind began to quiet, and a singular notion came to dominate her thoughts—she wanted to lie, once more, in Ian's strong embrace, to feel the warmth of his body surrounding her and to know the touch of his hand on her cheek.

"Ian."

"Aye."

She jerked around when she heard him answer. "Did I just say that out loud?"

His lips curved in a sideways grin. "Ye said my name."

She cleared her throat. "Of course I did. Goodnight, Ian."

He drew closer, grazing the back of his fingers down her cheek as if he had read her mind. Her breath hitched.

"Goodnight, lass." Then his gaze shifted to Ruby. He reached to pet her, but she backed away, only this time she didn't growl, she whimpered.

Jo squatted down and buried her face in Ruby's neck. "I understand what you're going through," she whispered. "You want to like him, but you don't know how."

Ian laid a wide plaid on the ground before lying down on one side of the blanket. Jo stretched out on the other side and patted the spot between them. She needed Ruby to guard her, but not from danger of Ian or and unknown attack. She wanted Ruby to guard her from herself, for Jo did not doubt that once asleep, her body would roll toward Ian by sheer attraction, alone.

Chapter Sixteen

The next day as they rode, Ian glanced sidelong at Jo. There was an ease to her carriage and a lightness to her face. "I would not go so far as to say ye seemed relaxed this morrow, but ye do appear, shall we say, less guarded."

She raised a brow at him, a soft smile curving her lips, but she did not reply.

He looked overhead. The sun was beginning it's descent. "We've crossed into Scotland."

Her eyes brightened. "Really? How can you tell?"

He smiled. "I've made this journey a time or two. It just occurred to me that we did not stop for dinner. Are ye hungry?"

She shook her head. "Nay."

They rode on in silence for a while longer, then to his surprise she said, "Tell me something?"

His mouth fell open for a moment as he stared at her, speechless, but then he shook his head, remembering himself. "Forgive me. Ye've hardly spoken since yesterday. So, what would ye like to know?"

She shrugged. "Tell me anything. I like listening to you talk."

"All right then," he said searching his mind for something simple and joyful to tell. Straightaway, his mind returned to his family, and he remembered the last time he had seen his sister, Rose. "I'm going to be a merchant," he began.

She looked straight at him, raising a skeptical brow. "With a fleet of ships, I suppose."

He smiled, knowing she had assumed he was only jesting. "Mayhap one day, but I'll start with the Messenger."

"I see, so you have a ship in mind, then?"

"'Tis my sister's ship. She's a beauty."

"Your sister or the Messenger?"

He laughed. "Both."

She canted her head to the side, clearly trying to discern whether he was jesting. "Your sister really owns a merchant ship?"

"Indeed, she does. It was payment for a service she rendered a wealthy English Captain."

"What sort of service?"

A slight smile curved his lips. "That story is Rose's to tell. Anyway, she wants me to captain the Messenger when I'm ready."

Her eyes brightened. "You're truly in earnest?"

"I'm as serious as I've ever been."

Her eyes narrowed on him. "Then why are you not out there right now, sailing beneath the clouds?"

He couldn't tell her the truth—that he was a member of a secret alliance, advancing the cause of Scottish sovereignty. He, like all of Scotland's agents, guarded this secret well and would never speak casually of their cause, especially to an English lass with secrets of her own. His lips curved in a half smile. "How could I protect ye from the middle of the sea?"

She blushed, fueling his desire. And then her stomach growled, deepening the color of her cheeks.

He chuckled. "I thought ye said ye weren't hungry?"

"I didn't want to slow our progress. To be honest, I'm so hungry I could gnaw on my slippers."

"We haven't supplies for a proper feast, but I think I can put together a meal that might be tastier than yer slippers."

JO WAS RELIEVED WHEN they stopped a short while later.

"Behind those trees and down a slight hill is a stream. We can wash, tend to the horses and rest," he said.

"And eat," she chimed in.

He laughed. The sound was deep and masculine and sent a chill coursing up her spine. She squatted down and buried her face in Ruby's furry neck. "How are you, girl?"

Ruby wagged her tail in answer.

"Come on, lass," Ian said, drawing her gaze. "I'll race ye down to the stream for a swim."

Jo jerked up right. "I shouldn't...I mean, of course, I need to wash but..."

He chuckled. "I was talking to Ruby."

Jo's face burned. "Of course you were...I was just..." She stood straight and rushed off in the opposite direction, Ruby padding along behind her. "I'm going to gather some wood for a fire," she called without looking back. When she passed a tree, she quickly stepped to the side to conceal herself behind the wide trunk. Laying her head back against the bark, she released a long, slow breath.

"You have to get a hold of yourself, Jo."

Once upon a time, she had giggled with Ruby in her chamber about the man her father would have one day consented for her to marry. Romance, companionship, love—these were all things to which she had once aspired. The past years had almost blotted them from her mind, her memory, her heart...almost.

Trust no one.

But mama!

Trust no one.

But Bishop!

"Trust no one," she whispered to herself and hung her head. Then she straightened and pushed back her shoulders. "Keep breathing." She scanned the ground for wood. "Keep fighting."

With her arms full and her heart resolute, she retraced her steps back to camp just as Ian came up the slope. First, she spied his long hair, wet and slicked back away from his face. Next, his broad, muscular shoulders and chest came into view. She froze. He was singing as he continued up the gentle slope, his quiet voice deep and rich.

Dear God Above, was this meant to be some kind of test?

She chewed her bottom lip as she watched his stomach, ridged with hard muscle, shifting and tightening with his every step.

If it was a test, then she was failing horribly.

He crested the slope and smiled at her, his tunic gripped casually in his hand. Biting her lip, her gaze devoured the chiseled lines of muscles forming a V starting from the bottom of his sinewy torso and disappearing beneath his hose, which were slung low on his hips.

"Keep breathing," she whispered frantically under her breath.

"It felt good to wash away the dust of the road," he said smiling at her. Then he shook out his hair, the contours of his muscles rippling like the river from which he'd just emerged.

She swallowed hard. "Keep fighting."

"What did ye say?"

She met his gaze. Droplets of water clung to his long lashes, making his blue eyes shine brighter than ever. She dropped the firewood where she stood and stormed past him. "I'm going to bathe."

"I thought ye wanted to eat first?"

She didn't look back. She couldn't. If she did, she might charge at him and throw her arms around his neck and kiss him as she had in her dream.

"Ye said ye were nigh starving," he called after her. "Ye threatened to gnaw on yer shoes."

In truth, she was ready to gnaw on him.

She sped up, resisting the urge to sprint to the river. Ruby padded along beside her. When they reached the shore, Jo whisked her tunic over her head and waded into the briskly moving water. Crouching low, she cupped her hands and splashed her face. The icy water rushed down her neck and chest.

"Breathe," she whispered to herself.

She didn't understand what was happening. Never had a man had such an affect on her. Ian left her breathless and befuddled. She was even finding it difficult to meet his gaze without smiling like a halfwit. Her stomach flipped and danced when he drew near. The most innocent of touches—their hands grazing as they reached for the costrel or his hand on her waist while helping her into the saddle—sent her mind reeling.

"That's enough," she chided herself.

Nothing good could come of the feelings and flutterings plaguing her body.

For pity's sake, she had been sent on a journey by a bishop to meet an abbot, all the while her thoughts lingered on temptations of the flesh. It was sacrilegious! Wasn't it?

She turned to ask Ruby her opinion, but she was no where to be seen. Jo frowned. Ruby's watchful eye was always trained on her. Where could she have gone?

Panic set in. Heart pounding, she sloshed through the current to shore, seized her tunic, and yanked it over her head. Dashing up the hill, she tugged it in place over her wet kirtle, then burst through the thicket, drawing to a full stop almost straightaway.

There, in the clearing, was Ruby, laying belly up in Ian's arms, licking his face while he scratched her stomach.

Her chest tightened. Clearly, Ruby had succumbed to her own desire.

But I want to be curled up in his strong arms!

He glanced up and flashed his heart-stopping smile. "I told ye I would win her over. I've got a way with stubborn lassies." He looked back down at Ruby with adoring eyes, and Jo had to resist storming off again.

For pity's sake, now she was jealous of her dog!

Chapter Seventeen

After another night sleeping under the stars with Ruby between her and her giant Scotsman, they packed up camp and set out, riding side by side, the morning sun slanting though the trees. She looked sidelong at Ian. The shadow of leaves dappled his face and hair, and when he passed through a beam of uninterrupted light, his eyes shone so blue that it stole her breath.

Their pace was easy and his carriage, relaxed. She turned away to hide her smile when once again he started to hum. After a few moments, his soft singing reached her ears.

Smiling, she cut him another sidelong glance. "You do that often, you know?"

"And what is it that I do?" His attentive eyes sent a shiver up her spine. She stared, lost in two beautiful deep blue seas.

"Jo," he said, his lips curved in a sideways smile.

"Yes," she said absently.

"Ye were informing me of some habitual practice of mine."

She blushed and shook the dreamy haze from her thoughts. "Humming and singing softly under your breath. You do this often, very often, actually."

He raised his brows. "Is this a problem?"

She shook her head, her smile fixed in place. "I like it. It's just..."

"'Tis just...what?"

"It's just that you're so big. It strikes me as funny that a man who clears a pathway in a crowded marketplace—solely because people close at hand are intimidated by his sheer size—hums with such frequency."

He smiled. "I am a big man, but I'm also a decent man...remember?"

She blushed remembering their fireside conversation, a conversation they'd had on the same night that her dream had unleashed her already burgeoning desire.

He continued, "Like most people I am a great many things—brother, son, friend, fisherman, sailor."

"Lover?" she asked softly.

He met her gaze. "What are you asking exactly?"

The heat she glimpsed in his eyes emboldened her. So what if she acted upon her desire? It didn't mean that she had to surrender everything to him. She could still protect her true identity.

She glanced over at Ruby who was now running closer to Ian's mount than hers. Ruby had let her guard down, hadn't she?

Anyway, Jo had grown accustomed to fighting for what she wanted, and God above, forgive her, but she wanted Ian. "Do you have a girl waiting for you back at home?"

A soft smile played about his lips as he slowly shook his head.

She took a deep breath. She wanted to ask him to kiss her. "Ian—"

"Aye, lass."

What was she doing? She couldn't. But then how could she not? Better than most, she knew that life could change in the blink of an eye, and moments, lifetimes can be stolen away, lost forever.

"Will you kiss me?" she blurted. Her gaze dropped to the ground. "I've never been kissed before."

An instant later, she was flying off her horse and onto his lap. She glimpsed the heat of passion in his eyes before she closed her own, and his lips claimed hers. His arms and masculine scent surrounded her. His taste filled her senses. She quivered, sweet rapturous desire pulsing through her. She pressed herself closer. Her arms came around his neck. His lips were so tender, so warm. His touch was everything she had dreamt it would be and more...

She gasped when his tongue slid into her mouth, tasting and teasing soft moans from her lips.

When he gently pulled away, he looked down into her upturned face. "How was that?"

"Like lightning," she breathed.

HE PULLED AWAY, LOOKING deep into her limpid eyes. "I've never met anyone like ye before." He grazed his thumb across her full bottom lip. "Ye've courage, Jo—it lives in ye. It runs soul-deep."

Trembling in his arms, she shook her head. "It's an act, nothing more. I'm afraid all the time."

He cupped her cheeks. "Courage burns through fear. I'm a warrior—I have fought alongside men charging to meet their death but who may never have been brave enough to expose the workings of their heart. It takes greater courage to be willingly vulnerable, to cry for loss, to ask to be kissed, than it does to stand and fight one's enemy." He leaned closer. "The intensity behind yer eyes stirs my soul." He placed a feather soft kiss on one of her eyelids. It fluttered beneath his touch. "One brown eye." Then he kissed the other. "One blue."

His gaze dropped to her lips. Slowly, his own lips claimed hers once more. He savored the taste of her tremulous mouth. She moaned softly as her arms came around his neck. He deepened his kiss. His burgeoning desire blazed red-hot, coursing through his body, his heart pounding, his breaths quickening, but then he froze. Something had whizzed past his head.

He jerked away, his gaze scanning the ground. An arrow stabbed the earth not far from Star's hooves.

"Hold on to me," he growled as he dug his heel into his horse's flanks, holding tightly to Jo's reins. He cut through the trees. A volley of arrows shot past their heads, lodging in tree trunks as they passed.

"Ruby," she cried out. "Come on!"

He pulled her close against his chest.

"Stay low." They ducked under a branch. He cut hard to the right, then yanked on the reins. Up ahead, a line of riders blocked their way.

Ian glanced behind them. Archers surrounded them, their bows taut.

Jo slid to the ground and seized Ruby around the neck, holding her back from charging their attackers. "Stay low," Ian hissed, withdrawing his blade from the scabbard strapped to his back. He circled his horse around, scanning the surrounding forest that was coming alive as a ragged crew continued to pour forth from the trees. Both men and women boasted swords and arrows. They wore threadbare clothes but looked well-fed unlike the many tinkers and exiled, lawless tribes of men Ian had encountered living in the wood over the years.

"Good morrow," one of the riders said before clicking his tongue. His horse stepped forward. "My name is Godfrey. I welcome ye to our domain."

"Ye've a thing or two to learn about hospitality," Ian replied, not lowering his sword.

"We're a welcoming lot to those who know how to bring out our amiable side."

Ian narrowed his gaze. "Are ye the leader of this band of forest dwellers?"

"I am that."

"Then tell yer mates to lower their arrows and I'll consider sheathing my blade."

"Ye're outnumbered."

"I will bring down more men than ye count with yer boots on before ye've managed to steal my last breath. Are ye willing to lose that many of yer followers? If ye are, some might question yer position."

A smile spread across Godfrey's face. "I like ye, and I don't doubt ye would slaughter us plenty before we could kill a warrior-beast such as yerself. But..." His gaze dropped to Jo on the ground. "But what about the lass? Are you willing to let her die before ye've even heard our terms for safe passage through these woods?"

Fury fought to claim Ian as he scanned the surrounding archers. "Put them down," he snarled.

Godfrey reached out a placating hand. "Steady there. We're just talking."

"Ye're threatening my woman. Stand down!"

Godfrey calmly continued, "We ask not for coin or the fine weapon ye hold or yer woman, who is, indeed, treasure. All of this can be over, if ye give us the dog."

Jo gasped. Ian glanced down. She squeezed Ruby, despite how the dog struggled to break free from her grip to charge at their assailants.

"Ye're wasting yer time. The dog heeds no one but her," Ian said.

Godfrey smiled. "For a pack of her pups, I'll sacrifice a finger or two."

"You can't have her. You'll have to kill me first," Jo shouted.

"Yer woman is English," Godfrey observed. He eyed her for a moment. "Another reason to avoid bloodshed all together."

"Walk away now and no one has to die," Ian snarled.

Godfrey raised his hand and the archers pulled tighter on their strings. "Make peace with us or with our maker. The choice is yers."

Ian glanced down at Jo and Ruby, then back at Godfrey. "I offer ye my horse," he growled.

Godfrey's eyes widened in surprise. "Ye'd part with yer fine steed over a mutt?"

"The dog has no price," Ian said firmly. "I will die to protect them both."

Godfrey's gaze settled once more on Jo and Ruby and his expression softened. "I accept," he said, bowing with a flourish.

Ian dismounted, taking his saddlebags and blanket before offering Godfrey the reins. "Take the stallion, then let us on our way."

Godfrey nudged his horse forward, accepting the reins. Ian turned away and reached down, securing the leash around Ruby's neck before helping Jo mount Star.

"Take care of him," Ian told Godfrey.

"I always care for what is mine," the woodsman replied.

Ian started to lead Star forward, but neither Godfrey nor his followers moved to let them pass.

"We had an accord," Ian growled.

"I'm afraid we can't let ye pass," Godfrey replied cheerfully.

"But you gave us your word," Jo snapped.

Godfrey clapped his hands, and the archers lowered their arrows. "Ye cannot leave without first celebrating with us."

"What is there to celebrate?" Ian replied stonily.

Godfrey's smile widened. "Our possession of this fine stallion, of course." He held out his hand. "Not to mention 'tis July ninth—the feast day of Saint Godfrey, my saint's day."

Ian wanted nothing more than to charge at the man, rip him down from his horse, and beat him bloody.

"I can see yer still vexed with us, but we're not bad men," Godfrey offered.

A woman among the archers cleared her throat.

"Or women," he said, winking in the woman's direction. "But we are wanted, lawless souls, guilty of crimes ranging from theft of bread to defiance against our lords. We choose not to kneel and call anyone other than ourselves master." Godfrey climbed down from his horse and moved to stand in front of Ian, his hand outstretched. "Do not let the wee theft of yer horse stand between ye and a night of feasting, music and dancing."

Ian held the man's gaze and saw only truth in the woodsman's eyes. Some outlaws were not bad or dangerous men, but like he and his brothers, they were rebels who refused to live out their lives beneath the yoke of other men.

Godfrey continued, "I offer ye true hospitality."

Ian looked up at Jo. "I believe we've paid for a share of food and wine. What say ye?"

He could see her hesitancy but was not surprised when she slowly nodded.

Holding tightly to Ruby's leash with one hand and the reins to their only horse in the other, Ian looked at Godfrey, his expression purposely holding a warning. "Lead on, then."

Godfrey whooped, his cheery smile unwavering. "This will be a night to remember!"

TENSION STIFFENED JO'S shoulders as they wove through the trees. But after a short while their attackers turned hosts began to greet her. The women who had taken aim at her with bow and arrow were now smiling warmly. Jo felt confused and apprehensive, but increasingly her caution was turning into excitement. As they carried on through the forest, children appeared, darting alongside them, pointing at the newcomers and calling out greetings to their parents. Further ahead, she spied the flicker of distant torch fire, and soon, she heard lilting notes of music.

Ian's deep voice rasped in her ear. "If ye're uncertain, we can make a break for it."

"Why would you think that?"

"Ye're trembling."

She looked up at him, biting her cheek to suppress her own smile. "I admit that I'm excited."

A glint of pleasure lit his blue eyes. "Ye're excited for the feast?"

Her mismatched eyes shone with intensity. "No...our first dance."

He kissed her hard on the mouth. "This *will* be a night to remember!"

Chapter Eighteen

The forest was alive with music and laughter. Her heart thundered with excitement, but she could still only see the bonfires belonging to the revelers flashing through the trees.

"I want ye to have the freedom to enjoy yerself. All I ask is that ye don't go where I can't see ye," Ian said quietly, his arm encircling her waist from behind.

Rocking in the saddle while they wended their way through the wood, she strained to see through the shadowy leaves. Ahead of them, Godfrey reined in his horse and brought a horn to his lips. A mournful wail rent the night, contrasting with the lively pipes and whistles. Moments later, another horn sounded in reply, and then like a curtain being drawn, the thick barrier of leafy branches lifted away, revealing a bustling hamlet. In the center of the glade blazed a massive bonfire, around which men, women, and children skipped, holding hands in a reel. Off to one side, musicians had gathered, pipers and lute players, and surrounding the festivities were several small huts of peat and thatch.

"Come, my new friends," Godfrey said as he leapt to the ground. Extending his arms wide, he continued, "help yerselves to food and drink."

Grasping Ruby's leash in one hand, Ian placed an arm around Jo's slim waist and set her feet on the ground.

"Dance with me," said a voice behind her.

She whirled around, meeting Godfrey's gaze.

"To show there's no hard feelings," he said to Ian.

"'Tis not for me to decide," Ian replied. "She speaks for herself."

Jo's heart swelled at Ian's words. His confidence in her fueled her own to greater heights. She accepted Godfrey's hand. "Just once or twice around the fire then."

Her host was trim and light on his feet. His beaming smile matched those of everyone around them, the smile of free men and women who did not live under the yoke of another. The fire raged. Her heart raced. She skipped along to the music, circling the fire again and again. Breathless, she released Godfrey's hand and thanked him before crossing the glade to where several rustic trestle tables were set up, their surfaces laden with wooden platters of game, breads, and cakes. Ian stood, Ruby at his side, speaking with an older man whose face was mostly hidden behind a grizzly beard.

When she approached, Ian poured her a tankard of mead.

"Thank you," she said and downed the lot.

"Ye've danced up quite a thirst," he laughed, refilling her cup. Then he offered her a pheasant leg, which she heartily sank her teeth into, ripping off the succulent meat.

"Ye're wife has a good appetite. Ye know what that could mean," the old man said, nudging Ian.

"Oh, we're not—" Jo started to say, but Ian interrupted her.

"Expecting," he blurted, wrapping his arm around her waist. "But my wife and I are hoping to be blessed with a wee bairn in the coming year."

Her brows drew together. "But we're not—"

"Picky about what we have. Just as long as the good Lord blesses us with a wee bairn to love, we are happy with a son or a daughter."

"To many sons and daughters," the old man toasted, raising his cups.

Ian dipped his head. "Thank ye, Clyde. Now, if ye'll excuse us, I suddenly crave a dance with my wife."

Holding tightly to Ruby's leash, Ian swung Jo around and led her in a reel, circling the fire. Her mismatched eyes burned through him, her smile making his body crave her touch, her kiss.

At length, when they stopped to eat and drink some more, she asked him. "Why did you tell that old man that we were married?"

"I claimed ye for myself before someone else tried."

"Claimed me? You speak as if I am a horse or a sword which someone might barter or trade."

"I do not doubt that there are many decent souls gathered here this eventide. Still, these people govern themselves and my guess is that what Godfrey says goes. And he's had his eye on ye since he first came upon us in the woods."

Scanning the revelers, she spied Godfrey looking her way. He raised his cup to her. Instinctively, she planted her feet apart and put her hands on her hips as he walked toward them. "Clyde just told me that ye're man and wife." His gaze shifted to Jo. "It would be a lie if I claimed not to be disappointed." Then he turned and directed their gazes to a hut across the way. "That one is empty. If ye're married, then 'tis yers for the night."

"Ye're gracious, indeed," Ian said, stepping slightly in front of Jo.

Godfrey smiled. "And ye're lucky ye're so big or else I might challenge ye for her hand, married or not."

There was tension in the men's gazes, but then Godfrey smiled again. "More ale," he said, raising his cup high. "After all, 'tis my saint's day," he called out, and everyone cheered in response.

Ian pulled her into his arms. "I would like to kiss my wife."

Jo's heart leapt. She was breathless and hazy from the ale and the pleasure of being enclosed in Ian's strong embrace.

She laughed. "Your *wife* would like nothing more."

He kissed her long and hard. Then scooping her up, he carried her to one of the fallen logs that had been rolled near the fire. He sat down, cradling her in his arms, their kiss only breaking when Ruby nudged her head between them.

"Feeling left out, girl?" Jo laughed, nuzzling Ruby's neck.

A loud guffaw drew Jo's gaze. Clyde was staring at them with a big grin on his face.

"Ye must be newly weds," he observed.

Ian winked at her before he called, "Aye, we are that."

The old man's smile faltered, a concerned expression pinching his brow. "Be sure to enjoy the passion, lad." Then he gestured to an older woman with gray streaked curls and plump pink cheeks at his side and rolled his eyes. "It doesn't last."

The woman narrowed her eyes on him, but then to Jo's surprise, she stood up, seized her husband by the tunic and pulled him to his feet before planting a kiss on his lips. Jo laughed as the older man overcame his shock and wrapped his arm around his wife, bending her back as he deepened their kiss. Then he pulled away and strained to lift her into his arms, walking toward a small hut. "It will be a night to remember," he called out, teetering beneath her weight on his bowed, aged legs.

Jo turned and locked eyes with Ian. "Shall we also retire?"

Ian crooked his thumb beneath her chin and softly kissed her lips. Then he stood, cradling her in his arms. Tugging Ruby behind them, he carried her to their hut.

Once inside, he set her feet on the ground and released Ruby, who padded over to a corner and plopped on the ground, curling into a circle.

Jo gazed with unabashed longing at Ian. "Husband," she purred and stood on her tiptoes, circling her arms around his neck. A sensual smile curved her lips. "This *will* be a night to remember," she said softly.

Groaning, his intense eyes bore into hers. He crushed her against his chest. "I want ye, wife."

"I can barely draw breath," she blurted, gripping his tunic in her hands. "That is how much I want ye."

Slowly, he eased the fabric of her tunic over her head. She arched her back into his hand as he cupped her breast, teasing her nipple through the sheer fabric of her kirtle. Then he slid his thumbs beneath the straps of her undergarment and eased it off her shoulders and over her slim hips. She stepped free and stood in front of him, naked and vulnerable. A smile curved her lips—she had never felt stronger.

She seized his tunic, pushing the fabric high up his chest before he yanked it over his head. Then he eased his hose down so that he, too, was free to be loved by her hands—and how she had craved to touch him.

She swept her hands across his broad, muscular chest and down the hard ridges of his stomach. Gasping, she took in the sight of his thick, hard length and reached out, daring to touch his manhood.

"Ye're amazing," he groaned and pulled her close. Their lips and tongues clashed in a frenzy of passion. Kneeling together, she lay back on the pallet and reached for him.

He grabbed her hands and pinned them over her head with one hand while he swept his other hand over her breast. With his palm he gently caressed her nipple. Then he lowered his mouth, his hot breath, teasing her hard peak. He stroked her sensitive nub with his tongue, forcing a gasp from her lips. Then he seized it gently between his teeth. She cried out and writhed beneath him, soft moans escaping her lips. Sensation, wicked and carnal danced slowly, languidly throughout her whole body. Slowly, his lips and tongue trailed lower while his hand caressed her hip and smoothed over the dip of her stomach. She gasped as his fingers brushed the soft curls between her thighs.

"Open for me," he rasped.

She spread her thighs apart. An ache, agonizing and sweet all at once, filled her. He trailed his fingers slowly from her knee, up the inside of her thigh, his touch soft as a whisper.

"Oh, Ian," she groaned when he stroked the very heat of her.

IAN WATCHED HER DESIRE heighten as his touch softly grazed her flesh.

She bucked her hips against his hand, her body demanding more.

"Please, Ian!"

Groaning, he shifted his weight and slowly, he entered her. Her tight sheath constricted around him. He held his breath as he stretched her wider until he filled her. She wound her arms firmly around him, her face buried against his neck, and slowly he started to thrust. Her hips met his, her body slick with sweat. She clung to him as he thrust harder and faster. Her breath filled his ears. She wrapped her legs around his waist, meeting his hard passion with a furious demand all her own. And then she seized up in his arms and cried out. Shuddering and quaking, she clung to him. He drove deeper, her rapture tearing through him. Higher he climbed and higher. Then he cried out as wave after wave of pleasure shot through him.

Chapter Nineteen

Just before first light, they slipped away from the woodsmen's hamlet to avoid any further demands from Godfrey. Ruby thundered ahead of them, clearly eager to be on the road again without the restraint of her leash.

Jo looked up through the trees, gaging the direction of the sun. "We have to go east?"

Ian pulled on the reins, bringing Star to a halt. She twisted in front of him and looked up, meeting his gaze.

"Why have we stopped?" she asked.

"Given everything that has transpired between us, do ye think ye might trust me enough to tell me where we're going?"

Her face went pink. He pressed his lips to hers, unable to resist her innocent beauty. She reached out and cupped his cheek, deepening their kiss. Although it pained him, he pulled away, struggling to not lose his thoughts in the sultry haze of desire. "Where are we going, Jo?"

She cleared her throat and straightened in the saddle, looking forward. "Haddington Abbey."

He stiffened in his saddle. "Are ye certain?"

"Why?" she asked in a rush. "Is that bad? Should I not want to go there?"

"Nay, Haddington Abbey is safe. The Abbot is a good and kind man. I'm just surprised that yer going to a place that is so familiar to me. 'Tis a second home really."

She smiled. "I'm glad to hear it. The bishop said that I would find a purpose at the abbey."

"Bishop? Which bishop?"

"Bishop Lamberton. I met him when I was at the cathedral, incidentally, just after I ran into ye. In fact, I was greatly distressed at the time that he approached me. After learning I was alone and with no place to go, he told me about Haddington Abbey. He said that I should journey north and present myself to the Abbot, assuring me that I would be welcome."

"Abbot Matthew will certainly welcome ye—this I do not doubt, but forgive me, Jo, I know the bishop well. I find it hard to believe that he would advise ye to make the long journey to Haddington alone."

"Even so, 'tis true. I told him about Ruby, and he seemed to think I could be all right with just her at my side, although he did ask that we keep to the wood and avoid roads and villages." She raised a brow at him. "He also told me not to trust anyone." Then a smile curved her lips. "That is one promise I did break."

When they arrived at the abbey, Jo couldn't help but feel utterly ridiculous. "Mayhap, we should move onto the next village. I'm certain to be an asset to a small hamlet. I can set up my shop and—"

He shook his head. "Ye're in the Highlands now, Jo. Everyone weaves their own fabric." His expression became serious. "Listen, I can tell ye're nervous, but ye must see this through to the finish. The bishop sent ye here for a reason, and it must have been an important one to have encouraged ye to risk traveling alone." He cupped her cheeks. "The Abbot is like a father to me. In fact, had I not followed ye when ye first set out from Durham, this would have been my destination. I mean, 'tis all too much to just be a coincidence. Somehow, we've been brought together for a reason, Jo. And I do not doubt 'tis yer destiny to walk through those doors."

She swallowed hard. Her chest tightened. With every passing moment, her emotions unraveled more and more. She could not have said why, but her initial feelings of foolishness upon seeing the Abbey had given way to full-blown fear, which worsened with every breath she took. But she remembered Ian's words...

Courage burns through fear.

"All right," she said with a resoluteness she did not truly feel. "I'll do it."

She kept her hands clasped together to try to stop them from shaking, while Ian tied Star and Ruby to a nearby hitching post. Then, gently, he took her arm and led her along the cobbled walkway to the abbey's imposing double doors. Jo closed her eyes, allowing Ian to be her guide.

Keep breathing.

Keep fighting.

She did not need to open her eyes to know when they had crossed the threshold into the abbey. The air felt cool. Their footsteps echoed. The smell of incense surrounded her.

"Good morrow, Brother Mark," she heard Ian say.

Still, she kept her eyes closed and her head down.

"The Abbot has just finished the prayer service for Prime. He's in his chamber."

"Thank ye," she heard Ian say, and then, once again, her feet were walking as if of their own accord, her every thought focused solely on breathing and not turning and fleeing as fast as her feet could take her. And then, before she knew what was happening, she heard Ian present her to the Abbot.

Still, she kept her eyes closed and her gaze downcast.

Keep breathing.

Keep fighting.

"Why have ye come to see me, my child?"

She took a deep breath. "Bishop Lamberton of Durham Cathedral sent me to you," she burst out, louder than intended, her voice unsteady. Raw emotion twisted her heart, and to her own bewilderment, she suddenly was near to bursting into tears.

The abbot took her hand and gently led her to a chair by the hearth. "Sit with me."

Still not meeting the abbot's gaze, she sat, perched on the edge.

"Now, tell me, my child, why have ye come?"

She gripped the arms of her chair. "The bishop said you might have a purpose for me. He...he..." She pressed her hands to her cheeks, her skin hot. "I'm sorry...I don't know what's wrong with me."

The abbot knelt in front of her. Still, she did not meet his gaze. "Go on," he urged her.

"There's a weight on my chest." She shook her head. "I can't explain it. I'm..." A mirthless laugh fled her lips. "I'm afraid."

"Do ye fear me?"

"Nay, I fear that all has been for naught, that ye will cast me away. That Ian will reject me. That I will be alone again, and I will not know why? I just want to know why!" A sob tore from her throat.

"Look at me," the abbot said gently.

Taking a deep breath, she lifted her chin and met his gaze.

His eyes narrowed slightly. He cupped her cheeks, scrutizing her face. Then a smile crinkled his eyes.

"Bless my heart. Why, hello Lady Joselyn."

Chapter Twenty

Her eyes flashed wide. "But...how...how did you know," she stammered.

"The likeness ye bear to yer father is uncanny." Still keeping her face upturned, he gently tapped under her eye. "One blue." Then he tapped under the other. "One brown, plus yer hair, yer features. Ye're Laird Malcom Fergusson's daughter. If I were allowed to, I would bet my life on it." He cupped her cheek, his gaze intent. "I believe I may have some of the answers yer heart seeks. And my guess, my hope, is that ye might have some answers for me."

"Wait a moment," Ian burst out, coming to stand in front of them. "Before either of ye continue, I believe *I* am the one most in need of answers."

An uncertain smile curved Jo's lips. She stood up and pressed her hands to his chest. "Just remember to keep breathing. All right?" she said softly.

Ian nodded and she took a deep breath. "I may not have been entirely honest with ye about who I am," she began, speaking for the first time in nearly two years using her Scottish brogue. "My name is Lady Josselyn Fergusson. 'Tis nice to meet ye, Ian MacVie."

Ian blew out a long breath and closed his eyes.

She gripped his tunic. "Are ye all right? Are ye mad? Please, look at me!"

Ian opened his eyes. "I'm not mad. I'm...well, I don't ken what I am." He turned her hand over and grazed his thumb across her palm. "That explains yer smooth skin and noble carriage. I was beginning to blame the latter on sheer stubbornness."

The abbot drew closer and motioned to the chairs. "I think 'tis probably best if ye sit down, Ian. In fact, let us all sit together, for there is much to discuss."

After they had each taken a seat, Jo began by recounting the day she'd fled Toonan with her mother, leaving her father behind.

"And yer mother never told ye why ye left?" the abbot asked.

"Nay, she only said that we weren't safe at Toonan. Later, she told me that father was dead, and that his murderers were hunting for us. There's little more to tell. We made a life in Durham. Mum's illness worsened. She died. In my grief, I went to the Cathedral to pray where I met the bishop. And here I am."

"Now, I understand," Ian said to her surprise.

"Good," Jo said dryly. "Because I understand nothing."

"The bishop recognized ye as Laird Fergusson's daughter. He sent ye here counting on the abbot drawing the same conclusion."

The abbot nodded. "Their likeness in undeniable. In fact, I wonder, Ian, why ye did not see it?"

"Of course I knew Laird Fergusson by reputation, but I never actually met him."

Jo took a deep breath before she asked Ian, "Are ye angry at me for lying to ye?"

He reached out and brought her hand to his lips. "Nay, of course not, ye were only protecting yerself, but there's still something that I'm confused about."

"Go on," the abbot urged.

"I ken why the bishop wanted Jo to come here, knowing that ye'd recognize her and provide her with a safe haven. But why would he encourage her to travel here on her own, taking such a risk, if only to secure her safety. It doesn't make any sense."

"The bishop had another motive. He carried a hope in his heart, one that I share. Ye see, my lady, yer father was entrusted with the task of concealing a vast treasure, some of which was stolen by Ian's brothers." The abbot smiled. "Yer lives are more connected than either of ye may realize, and judging by yer familiarity with each other," he said, looking pointedly at Ian's hand resting on Jo's thigh. "Ye're more connected than *I*, at first, realized."

Jo blushed.

"But no matter," the abbot said quickly. "We will come back to that. Now, as I was saying, a few years ago, Ian's brothers broke into Westminster Abbey and stole the King's very own treasure, which had been stored in the Chapter House, jewels, foreign coin, solid gold platters—items of immeasurable wealth but also distinctly royal. This meant that the items could not be easily traded or sold at market. Only the bishop had the necessary connections to turn the wealth into usable coin, with which we funded Scotland's army. Only, he had to be careful not to move too much at once.

"And so, he divided the wealth in half and mixed each portion with other riches stolen by Scotland's agents like yerself, Ian, and Ramsay, Nick, David and all the others. One half, he slowly worked through; meanwhile the other half he gave to yer father, my lady, to conceal until the bishop was ready for it. Now, 'tis important to note that only the bishop and I knew that Laird Fergusson had been given the treasure, but neither of us knew where he'd hidden it...and we still don't. But, somehow, word had spread that he was the treasure's keeper, and an army led by Baron Wharncliffe and Clan Fergusson's neighbor, Laird Stewart, marched on Toonan to take it back."

Jo's eyes flashed wide. "Then, that is why Father sent us away, because they were going to lay siege to Toonan."

"I do not doubt that yer father sent ye and yer mother away, in part, to ensure yer safety."

"What other reason might he have had," Ian asked.

"When we questioned Toonan's steward, he told us that yer father had already decided to surrender himself to avoid any bloodshed, but still insisted his wife and daughter be safeguarded away, despite Lady Clara's questionable health."

"Wait," Jo exclaimed, hope swelling within her heart. "Thane is alive!"

The abbot smiled. "He is, indeed, although he suffered injury at the hands of the Stewart's warriors, he survived and was eventually released by the baron when it was clear he did not have the information the English lord sought."

"What about Captain William and Ruby and Cook and—"

The abbot reached over and patted Jo's hand. "No one was hurt. Yer father ordered the gates to be opened and surrendered himself straightaway."

Her chest tightened. "Then my father is dead."

The abbot nodded softly.

Ian's fist came down hard on the arm of his chair. "Was Clan Stewart brought to task?"

"When we questioned Laird Stewart, he said he had been coerced by the baron, who had threatened to march on Stewart Castle with the full might of King Edward's army, if they did not back the baron's men."

Ian snorted. "So he claims."

"Indeed," the abbot answered dryly. "His loyalties change with the wind."

"Did...did my father...did he..." She couldn't bring herself to ask the question plaguing her heart.

"Ye want to know if yer father revealed the treasure's location," the abbot said knowingly.

She swallowed hard and nodded.

"Nay, lass. Our sources tell us that bands of English soldiers are still out there, searching Scotland for both the treasure and for ye."

She pressed her hand to her chest. "Me? But why?"

"Because there are some who believe yer father told ye and Lady Clara where it was hidden before ye fled so, that the secret did not die with him."

"And this hope is one ye and the bishop share," Ian said knowingly.

The abbot nodded, looking expectantly at Jo.

"I'm sorry to disappoint ye," Jo began, "I never knew about the treasure, and if my father had confided the secret to my mother, it died with her."

"Did ye and Lady Clara ever try to return to Toonan?" the abbot asked.

"Never, my mother told me it wasn't safe. In fact, even on her death bed, she made me promise again never to return on my own."

The abbot gave Jo a curious look.

"What is it?" she asked.

"Knowing Malcom as well as I did, he may have told ye without being explicit. What I mean to say is that he may have told ye without ye even realizing what he was saying."

"Like a clue?" she asked.

The abbot nodded. "Mayhap, when he said goodbye, he revealed something."

She shook her head. "I don't think so. That day is a blur in my mind, but I remember his last words as though etched on my heart. They were words of love."

A sad smile curved the abbot's lips. "As well they should have been, for yer father loved ye and yer mother so very deeply." He sat straighter, his voice brightening. "And ye're alive and now ye're safe, which is of the greatest importance."

"Then the treasure is lost?" she asked.

The abbot lifted his shoulders. "It very well may be. Only God truly knows that answer. Now, tell me how yer paths crossed."

Ian winked at her. "Shall I tell him, wife, or would ye prefer the honor?"

"Wife?" Abbot Matthew said, his eyes flashing wide.

"'Tis not what you think, Abbot," Jo said, laughing. "Ian, tell him the truth."

"Well, if ye remember, abbot, ye sent Ramsay and I to Durham to meet with Drummond. Well, he turned out to be Jo's neighbor."

"I see," the abbot chimed in. "So then, Drummond introduced ye two?"

"Not exactly," Ian began with a grimace. "When we were at Drummond's, Ramsay and I had to make a break for it out Drummond's second story window—"

"On to my roof," Jo interjected. "There I was, abbot, working at my loom. I stood up and crossed the room for a drink, and an instant later, a giant blacksmith crashed through my roof and—"

"Flattened her loom with his arse," Ian finished before turning to Jo. "I don't mean to make light of it."

She chuckled. "'Tis distant enough now that I can see the humor in it all."

The abbot cleared his throat. "This is all very interesting, but when did ye get married?"

"We didn't," Jo replied. "Not really."

Ian reached out and took her hand in his. "We encountered a band of exiles in the woods on our journey here. After robbing us, we were invited to a celebration of sorts. I naturally told them Jo was my wife to protect her virtue."

The abbot raised his brow sternly. "And is her virtue still intact?"

Ian rubbed the back of his neck, his face turning as crimson as his hair. "We may have gotten a wee bit carried away."

"What is that supposed to mean?"

Jo looked down, unable to meet the abbot's gaze.

"I'll tell ye what it means." Ian turned and knelt in front of Jo, taking her hands in his. "I love ye," he vowed fervently. "In fact, I've been in love with ye since the first moment I laid eyes on ye and yer snarling dog."

Jo's stomach leapt. Smiling, she said, "I can't say I loved ye quite that long. In fact, after ye fell on my loom, I wanted to sic Ruby on ye."

"And now?" the abbot chimed in.

She locked eyes with Ian, and when she spoke, her voice trembled with feeling. "I made my heart hard so that I wouldn't feel or cry or surrender. For two years, I've done naught but breathe and fight...until I lost all reason for doing both." She gripped his tunic. "And then this giant, red-haired, stubborn Scotsman dropped into my life and vowed to protect me...even from myself." Tears filled her eyes. "And he became my friend. He showed me it took strength to cry and to feel...and to love." Her tears blurred the ardent expression on his face. "Ian MacVie, I love ye. And I will keep breathing, and I will keep loving ye all the rest of my days."

He crushed his lips to hers, long and hard. Then he jerked away, his blue eyes meeting hers. "Will ye marry me then, Jo?"

She threw her arms around his neck. "I will!"

Ian scooped her into his arms and spun her around. Then he turned to the abbot. "What say ye, Abbot? Will ye marry us?"

The abbot chuckled, shaking his head slightly. "As yer brother, Rory, knows, I cannot solemnize yer union, however, I can speak with Father John. Mayhap he can hear yer vows after Sext."

They locked eyes. Her heart raced wildly.

"My wife," he breathed, his voice reverent. He cupped her cheeks, and slowly lowered his head, his lips claiming hers. She groaned softly and stood on her tiptoes, her arms twining around his neck, and she kissed him with all her love, all her passion.

The abbot cleared his throat.

They broke apart, both breathless and wanting more.

"I think it best not to wait," Abbot Matthew said in a rush, then stood and darted across the room toward the door. "I will just go and speak with Father John now."

JO USED HER FINGERS to work the tangles free from her hair, which she left unbound, her brown waves falling loose down her back. She looked down at her shabby tunic and chipped away at some dried mud. A memory of the beautiful tunic her mother had made for her fifteenth birthday flashed in her mind's eye and a sad smile curved her lips. "I love ye, Mama."

"There are beautiful flowers this time of year in the garden."

She whirled around. The abbot walked toward her, holding a circle of blossoms in one hand. "I took the liberty of weaving ye a crown, Lady Josselyn."

Jo curtsied. "It has been a long time since I've been called that."

Smiling tenderly, the abbot placed the crown on her head. "Yer father was a valiant man and a true servant to Scotland. I was honored to call him friend." Then he bowed to her. "It would be my honor to walk ye down the aisle."

Tears stung her eyes. "I miss them."

Brows drawn, the abbot straightened and clasped both her hands in his. "They are smiling down at ye from heaven. This match would have made them happy. Ye could not have entrusted yer heart to a finer man, but I need not recommend Ian's good character to ye. Doubtless, he has proven his worth already."

Jo smiled through her tears. "He is all things good and kind."

The abbot offered her his arm. "Are ye ready to marry Scotland's gentle giant, then?"

"I can hardly believe this is all real, but aye, Abbot, I am."

She walked into the nearly empty chapel on the abbot's arm. Straightaway, she locked eyes with Ian who awaited her at the altar. He, too, wore his travel-stained tunic, belted at the waist over fitted hose that showed the strength of his muscular thighs. His long, unruly, red hair was secured at the nape of his neck. She had to stop herself from sprinting ahead and throwing her arms around his neck.

Their walk up the aisle felt like an eternity, and when she finally stood in front of him everything else fell away. The walls of the chapel, the stained-glass windows, Father John's gentle features, everything but Ian faded into a haze of color and sound. Their words, the priest's, Ian's, even her own responses, seemed otherworldly. Her only certitude, in that moment, she placed in the man standing opposite her. She was marrying Ian, which meant all was right in the world, for she did not doubt that angels had sent him to her.

Her loom had been broken so that her heart could heal and be filled with love, once again.

After the ceremony, the abbot led them out to the garden where a table had been laid with simple fare. Together, they ate and laughed. Jo felt a lightness in her heart that she hadn't known since before fleeing Toonan. Not only had she found her soul's true mate, but her heart was no longer plagued with unanswered questions. Her understanding of why they'd had to flee her home did nothing to lessen her sadness or grief; if anything, she felt it more acutely than ever. But now it was not clouded by the unknown, and so she could face it plainly.

And as always, she would keep breathing and keep fighting, only now, she could also keep loving.

When the hour to retire arrived, the abbot led them to an empty chamber. He blessed the narrow platform bed before he bade them goodnight. When Ian shut the door behind him, her heart leapt. Her stomach danced. "I'm nervous," she said breathlessly.

A slow smile curved Ian's lips. "Don't be." He clasped her waist. "'Tis just me, Ian, and ye're just ye, Jo."

His words soothed her nerves, releasing her hunger. She pressed her hands to his chest, walking him backward until he had no choice but to sit on the bed. Then she stood in front of him and boldly slid off her clothing, slowly, sensually.

"Ye're infinitely beautiful," he breathed, his gaze journeying over her nakedness, his eyes burning with hunger.

She climbed onto him, straggling his lap and flung her head back. His lips claimed her throat, his lips tender, his teeth biting.

With a growl, he suddenly stood and thrust her from him. In a flash, his clothing was heaped on the floor, and he seized her, kissing her with wild abandon. She closed her eyes and wrapped her arms around his neck. He lifted her into his arms and laid her on the narrow bed. His hard body moved over hers. An ache burned deep within her, hot and wild. She arched her back, her body wanting to be closer. Her hands rushed over his shoulders, savoring his hard strength. Then she gasped as his warm breath teased her nipple. She shivered just as his tongue flicked out, sending currents of pleasure rushing between her thighs. She groaned, spreading her legs wide. He moved his lips lower, across her quaking stomach to the very heat of her. Throwing her head back, she cried out. It was more than she could bear.

Ian shifted over her, settling himself between her thighs and swiftly entered her. Heat blazed through her. She wrapped her legs around his waist. With every thrust, he sank deeper and faster. She clung to him, squeezing her eyes shut against the mounting agony sweetly building, spiraling, climbing higher and higher. Then she cried out, the sound mingling with his. Together, they reached fulfillment, as wave after wave of pleasure racked their bodies.

Chapter Twenty One

After Prime, Ian led Jo out into the garden. To his surprise, her gaze passed over the flowers and well-tended vegetable patches. Instead, she hurried over to the small table beneath a flowering tree and surveyed the chess set he'd laid out for later in the day, when the abbot would be free to play. "Abbot Matthew and I always enjoy a game when I visit," he explained.

Her uncanny eyes shone brightly as she continued to consider the pieces. "Who usually wins?"

Ian rubbed the back of his neck, a mock, sheepish grin on his face. "As a matter of fact, the abbot *always* wins."

Laughing, she picked up the white queen and tossed it absently in her hand. "I love to play."

"Really?" He sat down in front of the black pieces and raised his brow at her. "Should I be worried?"

She took the stool opposite him, a mischievous glint in her eye. "Ye may wish to say a prayer or two."

Shaking his head in amazement as she whisked his knight off its square and settled it next to the ever growing cluster of black pieces on her side of the board, he leaned across the table and pressed a quick kiss to her lips. "I love my incredible wife!"

She smiled and lifted her shoulders, modestly. "I wasn't always as accomplished, but my father forced me to practice everyday."

"Ye used to play together?"

She nodded, and a sad smile curved her lips. "We played nearly every afternoon, as often as he could get away from his duties, but it took years for me to become a proficient player. In fact, I remember asking him, when I was just a wee lass, why he wasted his time teaching me. At the time, I never thought that I would improve." She leaned closer. "And do ye ken what he told me?"

Resting his chin in his hand, Ian gazed at his wife. "Nay," he said unhurriedly, enamored as he watched the last of her guard fall away.

A wistful smile curved her lips. "He said, 'time spent with ye is never a waste, for time is the greatest gift anyone can give'." She laughed. "After that, if he wanted to play chess, he would always say to me...'Do ye feel like wasting time?'"

Just as Ian was thinking that he could never tire of listening to Jo's laughter, the lyrical sound faded, and her smiled disappeared.

He sat straight.

She stiffened tensely in her seat.

"What is it, Jo?" He reached across the table, covering her hand with his. Her mouth had gone slack. Unshed tears glimmered in her eyes beneath her pinched brow. Her sudden grief made his own heart ache. "Talk to me, Jo!"

"Those were his last words to me," she said in a rush. "He cupped my cheek and said 'remember, time is the greatest gift anyone can give'."

Tears slid past the confines of her lids. Ian stood and circled around the table to take her into his arms. But she pressed her hand against his chest to stop him. "Wait," she said, her voice suddenly hard.

Ian froze. "What is it?"

But she didn't reply. Her tears stopped, and she gripped the table, her knuckles whitening from the strain.

His heart started to race. "What's happening, Jo?"

She stood, still not heeding his words, and began to pace the garden, muttering, her brow heavy with concentration. Then she whirled around, hardness replacing the light in her eyes. "Ian, take me home."

He frowned. "I thought ye never wanted to go back to Durham."

"Not Durham. Take me to my true home. Take me to Toonan."

His eyes widened. "I can't do that. I already promised the abbot that I wouldn't. In his words, I'm not to go traipsing through the Scottish countryside with ye. 'Tis too risky. Whomever wishes to find ye, could still be out there."

"I don't care!"

"I do! Both the abbot and the bishop knew ye at a glance. The abbot believes yer resemblance to yer father is the very reason yer mother took ye as far south as Durham, in the first place."

She stubbornly jutted out her chin. "I promised my mother I would never return to Toonan alone. Are ye going to take me or will ye force me to break my word."

Ian raked his hand through his hair. "I'm sorry, Jo, but Toonan is likely still being watched. We can't just walk through the front gate."

She put her hand on her hips. "Husband, do ye think me a simpleton? I don't plan to walk through the front gate."

It was two days hard ride to Toonan. When the castle came into view, Jo's heart soared and ached all at once.

She was home.

Memories came flooding back. It had been nearly three years since she glimpsed Toonan, but it felt as if a lifetime had passed. She'd fled, clinging to her mother, sobbing for the loss of her father, her heart riddled by fear and grief.

There was so much about that girl—the one she saw in her mind's eye, racing through Toonan in her beautiful new tunic—that left Jo feeling unsettled. That girl had been kindhearted but also pampered and naïve.

That had been Lady Josselyn.

Now, she was just Jo—a commoner, a weaver, a woman grown. But she, suddenly, shook her head. That wasn't right either. She wasn't an English peasant.

If she wasn't a Scottish lady or an English peasant, then who was she?

In that moment, she looked sidelong at Ian, who sat tall in his saddle, humming.

A slight smile upturned her lips. She knew exactly who she was. She was Jo MacVie, Ian MacVie's wife. And like her husband and her parents before her, she was a Scottish rebel.

And now, she was on a mission to fulfill her father's legacy and to advance the cause of Scottish independence... For, in her heart, she knew her father had given her the very clues needed to solve the mystery of the missing treasure.

Pulling on the reins, she brought her horse to a halt. In the distance, loomed the gates of Toonan's outer wall. Her kin resided behind those gates, people she loved with her whole heart. Instantly, she started to fret over how they'd managed without her father or mother to care for them, but she took a deep breath. The abbot had said that Thane and Captain William were both alive and well. Together, Jo was confident they had the skills to run Toonan.

She closed her eyes against the memory of Thane's anguished face as he was dragged away by the Stewart warriors. She shook her head, fighting against the flood of heartbreak rushing to the fore of her mind. But she couldn't escape it. Memories hurtled toward her—the anguish etched on her father's face as he watched them rush from his sight; Ruby sobbing uncontrollably; Lady Clara, who had always been so gentle with her, becoming hard and unyielding as the iron wrought for the very swords from which they hid.

Jo gasped, suddenly, understanding why her mother had been so hard on her. She turned, seeking Ian's gaze. "She knew she was going to die and leave me all alone." Tears stung her eyes. She looked to Toonan. "She knew then, before we'd even left the gates that her health was failing. She was hard on me so that I would become tough enough to face any challenge head on."

Ian nodded. "That I do not doubt. 'Tis believed that men are stronger than women." Ian shook his head. "There's no greater force on earth and I wager in heaven, than a mother's love. She did what she thought she had to, to ensure ye kept on going."

"Keep breathing. Keep fighting," Jo muttered. Then she looked Ian hard in the eye. "That is what she told me. 'If ye can breathe, ye can fight.'"

A light shone in Ian's eyes. "'Tis odd that ye should say that, because I met a pilgrim outside Durham Cathedral, an older woman about half yer size, who gave me the same advice." He took a deep breath. "I'm still breathing." Then he winked at her. "So why don't we go find that treasure?"

She gasped. "How did ye know that is why I wanted to come here?"

He chuckled. "Because I ken my wife is no simpleton."

She laughed, remembering her cheeky remark back at the abbey. "Does the abbot know why we've really come?"

Ian nodded. "He needed a worthy reason for why the monks were being tasked with the responsibility of caring for Ruby, who, as ye know, was less than gracious to her hosts."

"With any luck, we shall return to Haddington with a prize to make up for the...er...inconvenience. With that in mind..." Sitting straighter in her saddle, she took a deep breath. "Let's keep fighting!"

"I have just one question—how do we get in?" Ian asked.

"Follow me," she said, turning her horse down a grassy slope that would lead them to the forest.

Chapter Twenty Two

S he wove through the trees, Ian wending behind her, and stopped in front of an old well.

Sliding from her mount, she tied the reins to a tree. "Here we are," she said, moving to the edge of the well and peering down into the black hole. Moss clung to the stone sides, the tufted greenery visible in the dim forest light, creeping downward until it disappeared from view, consumed by shadow.

"How far does it go before it levels off into the tunnel?" Ian asked, peering down beside her.

"The depth of the well doesn't matter. The tunnel isn't at its bottom." She pointed down one side. "It shoots off there. We must scale down to it, then crawl through for a spell. If I remember correctly, it isn't long before the tunnel heightens, and we'll be able to stand." She turned, her gaze taking in his great height. "Well, ye might have to duck yer head."

He shot her a skeptical look. "Will I fit through the initial hole?"

Jo lifted her shoulders. "There's only one way to find out."

She grabbed the length of rope from her saddlebag and handed it to Ian. "When I was eight or nine, my father brought me here and showed me what to do. First, we must tie one end of the rope here." She draped the rope over the piece of the well house that was suspended above the opening.

Ian's brow furrowed. "At the time, I'm certain that was advisable, but the years have weathered this wood." He crossed to a young but sturdy-looking pine and secured the rope around it. Then he turned and tied the other end around her waist.

"Are ye ready?"

She nodded, gripping the rope. "Lower me down."

Slowly, he dangled her down into the well. It took several tries for her to get a hold of the tunnel lip, but she found her grip and pulled herself inside. The air was thick and damp. She considered the space over her head and the width of the cave.

"Ye'll fit," she called out. "Barely," she added under her breath.

"All right. I'm coming but move away from the entrance. I'm going to ready a torch."

After a few moments, Ian's head and shoulders appeared in the tunnel entrance. He passed her the torch before he pulled himself behind her. His shoulders brushed the sides of the tunnel as they crawled over stones that were wet and slick. Eventually, the narrow tunnel broadened and heightened. It was carved into the earth and framed in wood. Tree roots dangled above their heads, many stretching thirstily into the ground, digging deeper into the earth at their feet, creating a tangled web through which they had to weave. In places, the frame had weakened, releasing piles of loose dirt to the ground.

Finally, their path began to ascend, and soon the wood supports ended, and once more, stone reinforced their way. When they reached a stairwell, Ian stopped her. "Where does this lead?"

"To my parent's chamber."

Jo's heart hammered in her chest, not only from the exertion of climbing the stairs but from the myriad emotions building within her: Soon, she would be standing outside her parent's chamber...but they would not be inside. Likewise, she would be within Toonan...but no one could know she was there. One moment, excitement shot through her, then the next, she was crestfallen and wanted nothing more than to turn back.

But she would not surrender now.

Not after coming so far.

Once upon a time, she had been a girl, so very afraid with no sense of the strength she'd had inside her. And all that while, it was there...the will to survive. Her mother and father had known that she was made of tougher stuff, and she had proven just that to herself again and again.

They reached the door. She took a deep breath. Ian stood behind her, holding the torch high. Steeling her shoulders, she lifted the latch, leaning back to allow room for the door to pull open, revealing the back of a heavy tapestry. Stepping inside, she carefully inched along the chamber wall, concealed by the densely woven fabric. Reaching the tapestry's edge, she started to peer around it, but suddenly Ian grabbed her arm and shook his head. Furrowing her brow, she listened and heard what had made him pause. Footfalls sounded across the floor, and for a moment, her heart gave way to hope.

What if it was her father? What if he'd managed to escape the baron, and the abbot's spies had yet to hear of the good tidings? Or mayhap Laird Stewart's loyalties had truly shifted back to their rightful place, supporting his own countrymen, and he negotiated her father's release?

Her heart pounding in her chest, her breathing shallow, she shook off Ian's grip and peeked out. Someone crouched near the hearth, striking flint. Slim and narrowly built, she knew instantly that it was not her father. Curious, she continued to watch. The person was bent low and in shadow, but when he straightened, Jo's heart leapt.

"Thane!" she cried, bursting out from behind the tapestry.

"Jo, come back," she heard Ian hiss.

"It's all right," she said quickly, glancing back.

Thane whirled around, his eyes wide, his hand pressed to his chest. "Lady Josselyn," he gasped and fell to his knees. "It cannot be." Then he smiled, tears flooding his eyes as he jumped to his feet and charged toward her. "Lady Josselyn," he cried, his voice cracking.

Chapter Twenty Three

Jo raced forward and threw her arms around Thane's neck, a sob tearing from her throat.

"Yer home!" Toonan's steward squeezed her so tightly, she could hardly draw breath, but she didn't care. Her heart swelled with joy and relief. He pulled away just enough to cup her cheeks. "Let me see ye," he said, tears streaming down his cheeks. "Are ye real?"

She nodded, her lips pressed tight against the fresh wave of emotion barreling up her throat. Again, he crushed her close. "I never thought I would see ye again." Then he pulled away slightly, his gaze darting around the room. "Where is Lady Clara?"

The knot tightened in her throat.

Thane's brows drew together. He gripped her upper arms. "Where is yer mother?"

Josselyn shook her head, her tears flowing freely. "She's..."

Thane closed his eyes. "Nay," he whispered and hung his head. Stepping backward, he sat on the edge of her parent's bed, resting his head in his hands. After several moments, he looked up, his face was slack and his eyes heavy. "How?" he croaked.

Jo sat beside him, taking his hand in hers. "She wasted away."

Thane clenched his fists. "Damnation," he cursed, his nostrils flaring. Then he released a heavy sigh, scrubbing his hand over his face. At length, he turned to her. In his eyes, Jo glimpsed his anger and sorrow, both clearly vying for domination. "I'm so very sorry, my lady." He held out his empty hands, his shoulders slumping. "For so long, I've waited for yer mother's return." He gestured to the dancing flames. "Every night, I've lit yer parent's hearth, praying that she would…" He shook his head. "I had hoped…" His voice trailed off. But then he took a deep breath and sat straighter, shifting to angle his body toward Jo. Taking her hands in his, his eyes brightened. "But all hope is not lost." A smile suddenly curved his lips. "Ye're here. Toonan's lady has returned!"

Toonan's lady? Her?

In her heart, she'd become Jo, never believing she would ever enter Toonan's keep again. Since her mother's passing, not once had it occurred to her that she was now Lady of Clan Fergusson.

Ian came forward then, drawing both their gazes.

Thane's eyes narrowed on her husband. He stood up. "Who is this man?"

Ian stepped closer, but Thane cut to his left, shielding Jo.

"Ye needn't worry, Thane," she said, easing out from behind him and moving to stand at Ian's side. "This is Ian." She met her husband's gaze and drank in the sight of him. Never could she have chosen a better man to be laird to her people. She did not doubt that they would welcome Ian into their hearts when the time was right.

She smiled up into his sky-blue gaze before turning to Thane. "He's my husband," she said, proudly.

"Yer husband?" Thane exclaimed. His gaze scanned Ian's large frame with purpose. "Ye're a warrior, that much I can see, but who are ye?"

"My father's family hail from Clan MacVie in the Hebrides, but I grew up in the city of Berwick before it was seized by King Edward."

"Have ye a title, wealth, position of any kind?"

"As ye've said, I'm a warrior, and a fisherman by trade."

Thane stood silently for a moment, his gaze darting between Jo and Ian. He raked his hand through his hair. "I will not lie, Lady Josselyn—I had hoped yer marriage would bring wealth and opportunity to our clan, but I'm trying to imagine what yer father would have said. His first concern would not have been title or riches, or else he never would have refused the Stewart's proposal for ye to marry his son, despite how advantageous that alliance might have been for Clan Fergusson." Thane stopped pacing in front of Ian. "I suppose if Laird Malcom were here right now, he would want to know...are ye a good man?"

"Put yer mind at ease," Ian said warmly. "I love Lady Josselyn with my whole heart."

Jo blushed, hearing Ian use her title for the first time. He pulled her close as he continued, "I vow always to protect her, to cherish her, to raise her high." He shifted his gaze, locking eyes with her. "She's my wife." Then he turned back to Thane and outstretched his hand. "I offer my loyalty and my sword to Clan Fergusson."

With a nod of approval, Thane shook Ian's hand. "Clan Fergusson is grateful to ye. I am grateful to ye." Then he turned back to Jo. "I am happy for ye, my lady, but..." A bewildered expression settled on his face. "Where have ye been? Yer warriors have scoured the Highlands looking for ye?"

A sad smile curved her lips. "I've been no where near the Highlands."

"But..." Thane sputtered. "Where else could ye have gone?"

"After ye were defeated and taken by the Stewart, Mother realized that ye had our only coin. Without the resources to travel safely north, she took us south."

His eyes widened. "Ye've been in England?" His nostrils flared, and he puffed out his chest. "Lady Clara took ye where no one would think to look for ye, even me." His eyes shone with pride.

"Indeed," Jo said. "She thought of everything. We sold her wedding ring and our clothing and journeyed to Durham. We found a room for rent, bought a loom, and earned our keep."

"Ye've been living as a commoner?"

She nodded.

Thane's lips settled in a grim line. He shook his head. "Had I been stronger, faster with a sword, I might have spared ye and Lady Clara these hardships."

"Ye did yer best to protect us, Thane." She took his hand. "I am just so grateful that ye're alive. I thought I lost ye, too." Jo took a deep breath. "What happened to ye? After they took ye."

Thane expelled a long breath and raked his hand through his thinning hair. "The Stewart released me when yer father surrendered. It was part of his terms." He lifted his shoulders. "And I've done what I could to keep the clan going while we watched for yer return." Thane's face broke into a smile. "And here ye are, but why did ye take the hidden passage? Why did ye not come through the gate? Yer people will celebrate yer return!"

"I've not returned," she said softly. "Not yet anyway."

Thane cocked his brow at her. "What do ye mean? Ye're here before my very eyes."

"I made a promise to my mother."

Thane shook his head furiously. "But yer people need ye!"

Jo reached out and gently took Thane's hand. "My parents have been taken from me. The only thing I can do now to honor their memory, is to keep my promises."

Thane's shoulders slumped. "Then why have ye come?"

"I've a promise to keep."

"But ye just said yer mother told ye to keep away."

"Not to my mother. The promise I keep is to my father. I promised him that I would remember."

Thane's brow furrowed the instant before his eyes flashed wide. "The treasure," he said knowingly.

She nodded.

"Did yer father tell ye where it was hidden before we left?"

"Nay," she answered.

"Then it had to be yer mother. Lady Clara told ye," he said, his words coming out in a rush.

"Nay," Jo answered. "I never knew why we fled. Mama only told me that we had to hide, that we had to conceal ourselves. She instructed me to keep my head down, to never look anyone in the eye, but she never told me who might be after us. I learned about the treasure only days ago from a great friend to my father, the Abbot Matthew of Haddington Abbey. He told me that men have hunted for us, believing that we knew where to find it."

Thane nodded grimly. "Yer mother was right to hide away. I'm certain that bands of men have scoured Scotland, searching for ye both, although I knew the futility of their hunt. Yer father spoke of the treasure to only a few trusted confidants, but he told me, in no uncertain terms, on the very day he was arrested that no man knew where the treasure was hidden."

A slight smile curved Jo's lips. "I am no man."

Thane's eyes flashed wide. "Then ye do know, but...but how—if yer father did not say or yer mother, how could ye possible know?"

Jo was about to say that her father had, indeed, told her, but then she faltered. She did not truly know. "I'm not certain, but I do believe my father tried to tell me. It was something he said to me when he bid me goodbye. I think he was giving me a clue."

"Where do we begin?" Thane asked eagerly.

"We need to get to my chambers without being seen."

"All right. 'Tis near supper; everyone should be in the Great Hall, even Samuel."

"Ruby's brother?"

"Aye, he aspires to be a clerk for the keep, and so I agreed to train him. Now, he's always at my heels, but no matter. Follow me. I will ensure no one sees ye."

Jo followed Thane, but then paused. She took hold of Ian's hand for strength, dreading what she was about to ask. "Did ye see my father when he was taken?"

Thane expelled a slow breath, then shook his head. "When I was released, yer father was already gone, but Captain William stood witness." Thane reached out and squeezed her other hand. "They arrested yer father hours after ye, and yer mother and I left. He was shown the respect due his station. They did not hurt him, nor were his hands bound. He was not permitted his sword, but he was given his own horse to ride and was allowed to carry his shield bearing the Fergusson crest through Toonan's gate." Thane expelled a long breath and closed his eyes. In a weak voice, he continued. "A missive came reporting that he was executed. I'm sorry, my lady."

Ian's arms came around her as she crumpled. There had been a part of her that clung to hope—the part of her that would always remain a wee lass who saw her father as an unbreakable mountain, always strong, always there, always protective. The certainty of his passing cut so deeply.

"Yer father and yer mother's legacies live on in ye," Thane soothed. "Now, that ye've returned—"

She lifted her face from Ian's shoulder and swiped at her tears. "Remember, Thane, I've not returned, but I hope to one day. I want nothing more than to care for my people."

Thane's eyes shone. "Yer words give my heart great joy. I will be patient for that day."

Ian cupped her cheek, drawing her gaze. "We don't need to do this. We can return to Haddington."

She shook her head, clearing away her tears. "While we still draw breath," she reminded him.

Ian nodded and turned to Thane. "Will ye take us to her chamber?"

"Of course," Thane said and crossed the room. He cracked open her parent's door and peered out before signaling the corridor was empty and for Jo and Ian to follow.

Chapter Twenty Four

Ian eased his broad sword from the scabbard strapped to his back before he took Jo's hand, leading her behind him. He was overjoyed by Jo's happiness in knowing Thane was alive, and the affection Thane bore for her was evident in his eyes—Ian did not doubt how well he loved her. Still, Jo's mother would never have cautioned her so strongly against returning to Toonan if she hadn't believed the danger to be very real. No one could guess what ill might await them, and he was not going to let his guard down until they were safely back at Haddington Abbey.

"My room is the final door on the left," she whispered behind him.

When they filed into Jo's chamber, he heard her gasp.

He turned to her, pulling her close. "What is it?"

Her gaze, glistening with unshed tears, darted around the room.

"I..." She clamped her hand over her mouth, fighting for calm. At length she spoke, her voice barely above a whisper. "This is where I last saw my father. It feels like a lifetime ago." She crossed to her dressing table and picked up her silver comb. "The lass that I was. I...I knew so little of the world." A mirthless laugh fled her lips. "When I think of what used to concern me, needlework, feast days, the excitement of a new tunic." She scanned her chambers. "I never knew hunger. I never understood the hardships faced by children left to fend for themselves or what few choices women had without a man to stand behind."

Thane's face was twisted with grief. "I blame myself for the hardships ye've endured. Had I been stronger, a warrior—"

Jo reached out and squeezed Thane's hand. "Do not blame yerself. Ye fought valiantly." She straightened, standing tall. "Anyway, the hardships I've endured have made me stronger. They've broadened my mind and have given me a greater capacity for compassion." Then her gaze shifted, and she locked eyes with Ian. "Not to mention, love."

A soft smile curved Ian's lips. He kissed her tenderly before seeking Thane's gaze. "Don't forget," Ian reminded Toonan's steward. "Because of ye, Jo and her mother were able to escape the baron. If it were not for ye, they may also have seen the inside of a prison."

Thane humbly bowed his head. "That will forever remain my one consolation." When he looked up his eyes shone with pride. "Yer parents are smiling down at the woman ye've become."

Jo took a deep breath. "I promise ye, Thane, when all this is, at last, put to rest, we will return and raise our people high."

Thane's eyes crinkled at the edges. "My heart has always known the strength of Clan Fergusson resides with its women—its mothers."

Ian's heart swelled at the sight of Jo's joy. He did not want to rush their reunion, but he was also keenly aware that they were trying to avoid alerting anyone to their presence. "Jo, we mustn't delay."

Jo nodded. Determination furrowed her brow as she crossed to the chess set on a table by the hearth and scanned the pieces, taking in their arrangement on the board.

Her chest tightened when she saw that the pieces were in play, and she remembered that she and her father had started a fresh game the day before she'd been forced to flee his side. Leaning over, she studied the pieces and their placement, but there was nothing out of the ordinary. Then she bent at the waist and looked beneath the table, expecting to find something secured to the underside or tucked into the intricate carvings of the table's legs. But there was nothing.

She looked up and met Thane's gaze. "Have ye moved this table or any of the pieces?"

"Nay, my lady. The family's chambers have been cleaned but not altered in anyway. Upon yer return, I wanted everything to be just as it was...well...as much as it could be, anyway," Thane continued, his voice somber.

She knew what he'd meant. Nothing could ever be the same as it was at Toonan, not without its laird and lady.

She squeezed his hand. "Thank ye for yer care." Then she turned and faced Ian, her heart starting to race. "I thought for sure..." She gripped her head in her hands. "I truly believed there would be something, some clue." She offered up her empty hands. "Why would those words be the last my father would ever say to me, if he wasn't trying to tell me something?"

Ian gently clasped her arms. "Take a deep breath. Try to calm yerself."

She closed her eyes and did as he'd bade.

"Now," he said, his voice soothing. "Think back. Can ye remember anything else?"

Keeping her eyes closed. "He took me in his arms. I was crying. He...he told me he loved me and to remember that time was the greatest gift anyone could give."

"Keep going," Ian urged. "What did he say to yer mother?"

Her brow furrowed with concentration. "He said that my mother...unlocked his heart. No." She shook her head. "He said she unlocked his passion and..." Her eyes flew open. "She is his queen!"

Turning back to the table, she seized the white queen and examined the piece, spying a small notch on the bottom." Driving her thumb nail into the groove, it popped off and a tiny scroll slid onto her palm.

Both Ian and Thane drew closer.

"I can't believe my eyes," Thane whispered, his voice reverent.

Her hands shaking, she unrolled the parchment.

"What does it say," Thane whispered.

"*An Ferbasach*," Jo read. Then she turned and looked at Ian. "The Conqueror."

Ian's brows drew together. "Kenneth MacAlpin, the first Scottish king, was known as the conqueror, but why does yer father write of him?"

Jo puzzled over the scrawled letters for only a moment longer before she turned to Thane and blurted, "The tapestry in the solar." Shifting her gaze to Ian, she explained, "It depicts the final battle when the Gaels defeated the Picts during their last uprising."

"We must hurry," Thane urged them. "Supper will be finishing soon!"

Jo led the way to the solar, taking long strides, driven by the profound realization that she was carrying out her father's work. Unknowingly, she'd long been the keeper of her father's legacy, and she was not going to let him down. Even from Heaven, he was relying on her. She glanced back at Ian, his hand still clutching his broad sword, and she was struck by how important that moment was, not just to her father, but to the cause. She took a deep breath, her heart hammering with excitement—if they found the treasure, then Ian, Abbot Matthew, and Bishop Lamberton could rebuild Scotland's army. Her breath caught—Her king was counting on her!

Thoughts tumbled around in her mind as they hastened toward the solar door.

Once inside, her gaze scanned the tapestries, each one a celebration of one of Scotland's great Kings. "There," she said, moving toward a massive tapestry that stretched nearly from ceiling to floor. A bloody battle was portrayed between the Gaels and Picts, and at its center was a crowned figure, standing on a wide flat rock—the Stone of Destiny.

She lifted the tapestry away from the wall, peering behind it.

"Ye won't find anything there," Thane said. "The castle was thoroughly searched by the baron. All the tapestries were taken down, including the one in yer parent's chamber, which of course means that passage is no longer truly secret. I almost had it filled in. I'm now relieved I decided against it."

Ian raised his brows. "Not as relieved as we are."

Jo fervently nodded her agreement before disappearing behind the hanging tribute to Scotland's first king, despite

Thane's discouragement. "There must be something," Ian heard her mutter.

Turning about, Ian considered the room. "What is on the other side of that wall?"

Thane looked to where he pointed. "A small prayer room."

Ian nodded and dropped his gaze, examining the rush-strewn floor. "What is below?"

"The kitchens, I believe."

Ian crouched down and rolled back one of the thin woven rugs and ran his hand over the stones, brushing away the dirt. Something caught his eye. He wet the back of his thumb and wiped at one of the stone tiles, revealing minute lettering. Struck by a thrill of sensation, he called to Jo.

She stepped out from behind the tapestry. "What have ye found?" she asked, crouching beside him. Ian didn't have to answer.

"*Alba*," she cried, having spotted the carving, and dug her fingers into the groves between the stones. "I can't quite fit my fingers under it," she said, her voice strained as she pulled on the flat stone. Her arms went lax after several moments. "It won't budge."

"Step back," Ian cautioned her. Fitting the tip of his sword into the groove between the slabs, he pulled down on the handle. Slowly the stone loosened, then gave way altogether, flipping over with a clatter.

"What do ye see?" Thane asked behind him as Ian peered into the hole.

"Only wood."

"Look," Jo said, lifting another tile with ease. "These have not been sealed."

Together, she and Ian removed the surrounding slabs, exposing more wood.

She eyed the planks. "Do ye suppose we have to break through?"

Ian smoothed his hand over the wood. Where the tile with the carving had been was a hole. Inserting two fingers, he felt around and grazed cool metal. "I've found a latch. 'Tis a door," he said in a rush, catching Jo's gaze, which glinted with excitement. He undid the latch and the door dropped away, swinging down.

"A stairwell," Thane exclaimed, standing above them, his hands resting on his knees.

Jo stood up, dusting her hands on her tunic. "Thane, lock the door. We do not want anyone entering the solar."

After Thane slid the bolt in place, Ian stood and sheathed his sword before squeezing Jo's hand. "Are ye ready?"

"This is my father's work," she beamed, nodding eagerly. "'Tis my duty."

Ian seized a torch from the wall, then turned, climbing backward down the steep stairs as if a ladder. After his head dipped well below the floor, the stairs started to circle around and around.

"We have to be below the kitchens by now," Thane said, behind them. "This passage must have been built in between the pantries."

Ian reached the last stair. In front of him was a doorway. He handed Jo the torch and unsheathed his sword, once more, before sliding back the lock and opening the door, his sword held at the ready. Shadows cast by the torch light danced upon the stone walls. The room was large and circular and empty but for a single chest in the center.

"Can it be?" Thane exclaimed crossing straightaway to a chest. He flipped back the lid and gasped. It was brimming with gold plates inlaid with gemstones the size of ripe black berries. There were bejeweled amulets on gold chains and bags of coin.

JO PLACED THE TORCH in a sconce, then hastened to join Thane at the chest. "I've never seen coins like these before," Jo said after Thane opened one of the teeming purses and shook a few into his hand.

Ian peered quickly over Thane's shoulder. "They're Flemish made," he said before he moved away and began to scan the surrounding walls, his brow drawn in concentration.

She stood straight. "Are ye all right?"

Ian nodded absently. "Check the other bags."

She uncinched the ties. "Two contain Flemish coin and a third holds...French marks," she said, recognizing the seal. She set the coin aside and continued her perusal of the treasure. "Look at this," she exclaimed to Thane as he knelt next to her. She held up a small crown, gleaming with emeralds. "I've never beheld such wealth before!"

"Nor have I," Thane chimed in, easing a string of round, glossy pearls from beneath a gilded chalice. He beamed at her. "Just consider the many ways we can help our people!"

Jo threw her arms around Thane's neck. "My father may be gone, but not his memory or his purpose." A short laugh burst from her lips and she sought Ian's gaze. He was still examining the wall. "The bishop did promise that if I journeyed to Haddington Abbey, I would find a purpose."

Ian smiled. "I've no doubt this is the very purpose the bishop had in mind."

Once again, her husband's gaze returned to the wall.

She raised a brow at him. "I ken yer a man who values life's simple pleasures, but we've discovered a fortune and ye've hardly looked at it."

He started to circle the room, his gaze lifting to scan the ceiling, then dropping to the floor. "Give me just a moment, and I will join ye."

"Look, my lady," Thane said, drawing her gaze. He had a gold coin pinched between his fingers. "With just this, we can buy enough seed to plant every Fergusson field from the Eastern Slope to the western shore."

"Oh, nay, Thane," she said, correcting the steward. "This treasure was not given to my father. He was only made its guardian. 'Tis not for our use. 'Tis for the cause." She scooped a handful of French marks. "This will make certain our lads, Scotland's lads, have food in their bellies, armor on their backs, and horses upon which to charge into battle. With this treasure, Scotland will once again be free and proud."

Thane smiled at her. "Ye're just like yer father."

Her heart swelled. "Thank ye, Thane."

His smile vanished. "I didn't mean it as a compliment."

Chapter Twenty Five

Jo screamed as Thane dragged her away from the chest toward the door, the tip of a dagger biting into her neck.

"Let her go," Ian snarled, thundering toward them, his sword raised high.

"Stay back," Thane growled. The dagger sank deeper into her flesh. She cried out, her neck throbbing.

Ian stopped in his tracks. The color drained from his face. "Jo!"

She felt blood trickle down her throat. "Ian!" Her heart thundered. What was happening? She tried to twist free. "Thane, let me go!"

"Nay," he hissed in her ear, his hold on her tightening. "Ye've brought this on yerself!"

The whites of Ian's eyes showed at he glared at Thane, his nostrils flaring, the cords in his neck throbbing. "Let her go, or I swear to God I'll kill ye!"

"Ye'll have to step over her dead body," Thane sneered.

"How could ye," she cried. Tears steamed down her cheeks. "I loved ye!"

"Ye love her, too," Ian roared. "Don't deny it!"

"So what if I do," Thane spat. "This isn't about love. This is about doing what is right by our clan!"

"Please, Thane, I don't understand. 'Tis me, Josselyn. Ye served my father—"

"I did serve him. Clan Fergusson served him. And what did he do when a king's fortune came into his possession? Did he feed his people? Did he strengthen our defenses? Did he build alliances? Nay! He hid it in a hole while our crops failed!"

"It was ye," Ian snarled, his face twisted with rage. "Ye betrayed Malcom!"

"Aye," Thane snapped. "It was me!"

Growling, Ian stepped forward.

Burning pain seared her throat. She cried out.

"Stay back! I'm warning ye. I will kill her."

Ian shook with rage but drew no closer.

Jo gasped for breath. Emotion choked her voice. "The...Stewart attacked ye...I saw men strike ye!"

"Aye," Thane spat in her ear. "Yer father nearly ruined everything when he sent ye away. I spent two days in their filthy, stinking prison before the guards would believe that I forged the alliance between the Stewart and Baron Wharncliffe."

Her heart raced, anger burning through her. "How could ye?"

"I did what I had to!"

Ian turned and seized a fistful of coin and ropes of pearls from the chest. "Ye betrayed yer laird and now threaten his daughter's life for naught but unusable riches!"

"What does a fisherman know of wealth," Thane scoffed.

"Yer a fool," Ian snarled. "This is no ordinary treasure. Laird Fergusson protected his people by hiding it away. There isn't a merchant out there who'd risk buying or bartering for what is clearly royal treasure. If yer laird had been as foolish as ye, he would have brought Longshank's hammer down upon yer people. Only the Church has the power and connections to use it."

"I don't need a corrupt abbot to turn this gold into seed," Thane hissed.

Jo screeched with fury. "Enough! I am Toonan's lady. Unhand me and surrender yer weapon!"

Thane's vice-like grip on her tightened. "Aye, Josselyn. Ye're, indeed, lady of Toonan...but not for long."

He thrust her from him. She stumbled into Ian's arms while Thane stepped through the doorway. "I'll come back in four days. Ye should both be dead by then." He locked eyes with Jo. "I take no pleasure in this." Then he slammed the door and slid the bolt in place.

"NAY," JO SCREAMED AND rushed forward, pounding her fists on the door. "Thane, Come back! Ye can't do this! My parents trusted ye! I trusted ye!"

"Jo, stop!" Ian trapped her wrists and turned her about, crushing her against his chest.

"Nay," she cried, struggling against his hold. "He cannot get away with this!"

"And he won't," Ian assured her.

"But we're trapped down here. No one will hear our screams. We're going to die!"

He cupped her cheeks in his hands. "Breathe, Jo. I promise ye, we're not going to die. Thane will not have his victory. Just breathe."

Her breaths continued quick and shallow, but then her nostrils flared as she inhaled deeply, filling her lungs.

"Good," he crooned. Then he ripped the hem of his tunic and pressed it to the slice on her neck. Releasing a long, slow breath, he, too fought for calm.

"How can ye be so certain?" she said blearily while he tore off another strip of fabric to wrap her wound.

Ian pointed to the single chest on the floor. "As certain as I am that yer father did not sacrifice his life for that—even more certain am I that the bishop did not send ye on a dangerous quest north for one chest full of treasure."

"I...I don't understand," she stammered, seizing the emerald crown. "How can ye think this meager, when I was nearly rendered speechless?"

He tied the bandage off, then gently clasped her hand and, once again, began to scan the walls. "Ye haven't seen what I've seen. Ramsay and I, my brothers, the other rebels, we've stolen a lot of gold over the years. There must be more," he muttered absently. "By reputation, yer father was a cunning and cautious man." He grazed his fingertips over the stones, looking for some kind of oddity. "He certainly didn't cart this treasure through yer front gates, nor did he carry it across the Great Hall, into the solar."

Her eyes widened as she understood his meaning. "Then, there must be another way in."

He nodded, a gentle smile curving his lips. "Which also means there's another way out." Turning in a circle, he scanned the walls, but nothing caught his eye. Still, he did not doubt his instincts for a moment. Kneeling, he removed bags of coin and heavy platters of gold from the chest before he pushed against the side, straining to move it, to ensure it did not conceal another trap door.

Jo knelt beside him, running her hand over the newly exposed stone floor. "Nothing," she said. Standing, she thrust her shoulders back. "No matter." She planted her feet solidly on the ground, hands on her hips, and joined him in surveying the room. "We must have missed something, that's all."

Walking forward, she pushed against the wall in front of her. He joined her, skimming his hands over the stones, pushing as he went to see if any were loose.

"I found something," she exclaimed, pulling at his tunic.

"Where?"

"Right here." She dusted off one of the stones. "See, there's an opening."

He leaned close, and sure enough, there was a coin-sized hole with irregular edges. Leaning close, he blew into the opening, clearing away the remaining dust. Then, he tried to push his finger inside, but only the tip could fit. "I can't tell what it is."

Jo nudged him aside. "Let me try." Her smallest finger slid into the hole with ease. "I can't quite...reach...the end." She sat back, her face slack, and shrugged her shoulders. "It just feels like jagged rock."

He raked his hand through his hair. "Damn it!" His frustration was mounting. "Start again. What did yer father say to ye?"

"Ye ken what he said. He told me that time is the greatest gift ye can give someone."

He shook his head. "Nay, not that, before that."

She lifted her shoulders. "He told my mother that she was his queen..."

Again, he shook his head, his mind racing. "Nay," he gritted, clenching his fists, angry with himself for beginning to doubt his own logic. "Keep going. There was more..."

"She...she unlocked his passion!" The words rushed from her lips, and she gasped. Her mismatched eyes flashed wide. "Ye don't think..."

A jolt of excitement shot through him. "Do ye still have it?"

Nodding her head furiously, she reached into her satchel and pulled out the white queen, which she thrust at him. "Ye do it!"

He took hold of the chess piece and turned to face the wall. Holding his breath, he inserted the queen, crown-end first, into the hole. It slid inside without resistance.

"It fits!" Jo clapped her hands together. "Now what?" she asked, her eyes dancing with excitement.

He took a deep breath. "We turn it."

"Can I do it?"

Nodding, his pulse racing, he stepped back.

She came forward, and hand trembling, she grasped the piece and made to turn it, but it didn't budge. Furrowing her brow, she clasped the queen with both hands and tried again. A vein in her neck stood out as she strained. Then, suddenly, it turned over, and a clicking noise echoed around them.

They locked eyes.

She swallowed hard.

"'Tis a moment for prayer, if ever there was one," he said, his voice barely above a whisper. Then, holding his breath, he pushed against the wall with all his might. Slowly, it inched forward. Chips of mortar and stone broke away, creating a cloud of dust. Beside him Jo coughed and waved her hands to disperse the cloud.

"There's an opening," she exclaimed.

Sure enough, there was a space wide enough even for him to slide through. Unsheathing his sword and seizing the torch from the sconce, he sidled sideways through the newly exposed passageway, into another room, and was so struck by what he saw that he nearly dropped the torch.

"Dear God above," Jo gasped, behind him.

Ian's mouth ran dry as he circled around, taking in the fullness of their discovery. The room teemed with treasure. Chests lined the floor in tall stacks. Bags of coin were heaped in piles. Many had opened, spilling out their shiny contents like frozen streams of silver and gold. Ian smiled. "This is more like what I expected."

"Aye," Jo laughed, her cheeks flushed. "And look over there!"

A grin he could not contain spread across his face as he followed her gaze to the door partly hidden by a towering pile of silk skeins. He started toward the new door but thought better of leaving the secret passage open into the real hidden treasure room. Straining, he slid the wall back into place. Then he rushed to help Jo move the fabric out of the way.

"Please do not be locked," she murmured and tried the latch. It opened without resistance. A rush of fresh air hit her face.

Ian peered down the long tunnel, certain to bring them to freedom. "Now, that's truly a beautiful sight to behold!"

Chapter Twenty Six

"Welcome home, Lady Josselyn," Ian said softly.

Jo let his words penetrate her mind as they approached the gates of Toonan. Her heart raced. "I wish the passageway from the treasure room had led to another place within the castle itself." Once more, her gaze scanned the looming battlements. She swallowed hard. "But now everyone will know that I've returned."

"The passage had to leave away from the castle for yer father to have smuggled in the treasure unseen." He squeezed her hand. "If ye're not ready to return to yer people, we can go back to the forest and use the tunnel in the well again."

She shook her head. "That will take too long." Reaching for his hand, she stopped in her tracks and looked up at him. "They will all believe I've returned for good. I cannot abandon them again. I know that when ye married me, ye may not have fully understood that I come with the responsibility of caring for an entire clan, but they are my people."

A gentle smile upturned Ian's lips. He cupped her cheek. "If 'tis me yer worried about, don't be. Jo MacVie, I don't care where we go, all I ask is that ye take me with ye." He gestured toward the keep, it's turrets beckoning to her. "If Toonan is yer home, then 'tis mine as well."

"But what about the Messenger and being a merchant?"

Ian raised a brow at her. "Let's solve one problem at a time."

She nodded in agreement and blew out a puff of air. "All right." Squaring her shoulders, she narrowed her eyes on

Toonan. "Then, let us go quickly. Everyone must be made aware of the traitor in their midst."

Ian took her hand, keeping pace alongside her. "I'm warning ye now. I'm likely to kill him."

Jo plowed ahead, her brow furrowed with determination. "Not if I do first!"

When they reached the gate, Jo approached it without hesitation. She'd promised her mother never to walk through the gates alone, and she'd kept that promise. She glanced up at Ian, whose long, wild red hair shone in the sun. His sky-blue eyes were alight with determined strength. Feeling the full force of his support, she looked up at the battlements expectantly.

"Make yerselves known," shouted one of the guards, peering down from above.

Jo took a deep breath. "I am yer lady!"

The man's eyes narrowed on her the instant before they flashed wide. "Lady Josselyn!"

The warriors along the wall gathered close, gaping down at her.

"Is it truly our lady?"

"Can it be?"

"Open the gates!"

As the portcullis started to rise, Ian squeezed her hand. "Thane is unlikely to surrender to yer authority but know that I will protect ye and yer people from his treachery."

She thrust her shoulders back, her head held high. "I'm not afraid."

She'd been tested time and again, and she'd survived. Her struggles had only made her stronger. And beside her stood a good man with limitless courage. Her father would have respected her choice in a mate, despite the humbleness of his birth, because of the merits of his heart and mind. And she did not doubt that her people would embrace Ian's goodness. And together, they would heal her clan and bring Thane to task.

A tremor of excitement shot through her, and her breath hitched. "I love ye, Ian."

A sensual smile curved his lips. "And I ye." He leaned down and kissed her, his lips soft and tender.

A moment later, the outer guard, a band of half a dozen men, passed through the gate. Motioning for the others to stay back, one man broke away from the group and approached her. The moment she saw his rugged features and creased brown eyes, a surge of emotion rushed up her throat.

"Captain William!"

Brows drawn, he hurried to her and dropped to his knees. "Lady Josselyn." He looked up at her, the struggle and uncertainty of the last two years painfully etched on his face. "We've searched everywhere for ye...We thought ye were lost or...dead."

She leaned over and wrapped her arms around the captain's neck. "I'm all right."

He stood, hugging her close. "All is not lost!" Her feet lifted off the ground. He spun her once around before setting her feet back down. "What of yer mother?" he said, his voice low.

Her chest tightened. She shook her head in answer.

He inhaled sharply, his nostrils flaring, as he closed his eyes against the ill tidings. "May she rest in peace," he murmured.

She squeezed his hand.

"I had hoped..." The captain's words trailed off, but he cleared his throat. "Now is not the time for sorrow." His face brightened. "Before we grieve, we must rejoice!"

Smiling, Jo stepped back and took Ian's hand. "Captain William, this man is my husband, Ian MacVie."

William's eyes widened. "Husband?" Then he dropped to one knee. "'Tis an honor."

Ian rubbed the back of his neck, his ears turning red. "Ye needn't kneel." He clasped William's arm and pulled him to his feet. "I am a man of action, no different than ye or any other warrior."

The captain smiled. "Welcome to Toonan, my laird."

"Laird?" Ian blurted, flashing Jo a questioning look.

"Ye're my husband." She winked at him. "Ye'll get used to the title."

"With yer permission, my lady," the captain began, "I would like to give ye an entrance into the courtyard worthy of the moment."

"Of course," Jo said calmly, although her stomach fluttered as she looked at the men over the captain's shoulder, smiling at her and speaking together in low voices.

The captain put his hands on her waist before he looked to Ian. "Do ye object?"

Ian held up his hands. "She is her own mistress. Ye already have all the permission ye need."

The captain smiled and met her gaze. "Are ye ready?"

She nodded, then squealed as he lifted her high in the air and settled her on his shoulder.

The men nearby cheered and led the way through the gate into the baily, where a crowd of her kinfolk had already begun to gather.

"Our lady has returned," the captain shouted.

The crowd erupted into a frenzy of cheers. Her gaze darted in every direction, spying familiar faces beaming up at her, and the moment her feet hit the ground she was surrounded by her people. Tears streaming, she embraced those whom she'd not seen for so very long.

"Ruby!" Jo's heart soared as she spied her dear friend pushing through the throng to reach her.

"My lady!" Ruby sobbed and threw her arms around Jo's neck.

Jo clung to her. She tried to speak but her voice was choked by tears. Finally, she blurted, "Ye've no idea how much I missed ye!"

"I thought I would never see you again," Ruby cried. "I thought ye were dead, we all did!" She jerked away, her face flushed with emotion. "Oh, my lady, wait until Thane finds out ye've returned!"

Jo's heart sank. She stumbled back, pressing her hand to her chest. For the briefest of moments, surrounded by her beloved kinfolk...she'd forgotten the steward's treachery. It came back in a rush that stole her breath and made her legs quake. "Ian!" Faces swam in front of her eyes. She clutched Ruby, scanning the crowd.

Never had she been so happy for her husband's great height. Pulling Ruby behind her, she made her way through the sea of well-wishers, greeting and hugging her way to Ian, who was in deep conversation with William. Noting the serious expressions on both their faces, she knew they were already discussing Thane.

At her approach, Ian took her hand and pulled her close. "Thane has left with a band of men."

Her eyes flashed wide. "Where has he gone?"

Captain William drew closer. "He claimed to know who betrayed yer father."

A sick feeling twisted her stomach. "Who has he accused?"

"Abbot Matthew of Haddington Abbey."

She sucked in a sharp breath and turned, meeting Ian's gaze. "But...how..."

Ian expelled a long breath. "I have spoken to William at length, and I believe Thane hopes to regain favor with Baron Wharncliffe by handing over the leader of the Scottish rebellion."

William nodded. "I knew something was the matter when Thane told me to gather my men. He barely looked me in the eye. And one moment he was muttering something about striking another deal, and then the next, he was shouting about the corruption of the Church and bringing the traitor to heel."

Heart pounding, she seized Ian's hand and started to pull him toward the gate. "This is all my fault. I'm the one who mentioned the abbot's name to him. We must ride!" She looked to the captain. "Assemble our warriors!"

"Wait," Ian said, calmly. "We mustn't be rash. Thane left here with at least ten men."

"We've other warriors," she urged him. "We must ride before he gets too far ahead."

"Ye don't want to pit yer people against each other, Fergusson fighting Fergusson."

"But surely, they will heed me, and take my word over Thane's. The fighting will be over before it starts."

"He has been their leader for more than two years now, my lady," William warned. "'Tis too risky to attack without jeopardizing innocent lives."

"Also, ye need yer warriors here to defend the keep, just in case I'm wrong and Thane tries to return," Ian added.

Captain William dropped to one knee in front of her. "My lady, he will never pass through the gates of Toonan again, this I vow!"

Jo took a deep breath and met Ian's gaze. "What are we going to do?"

"We ride north and find Ramsay and the other rebels."

"But what about the Abbot?"

"The abbey has no defenses. He's as good as taken, but Thane will not hurt him. He's too valuable." A hard glint entered Ian's eyes, the gentle giant, once more, yielding to the fierce warrior. "To save the abbot, we must call upon the Saints."

A shiver shot up her spine. "Who are the Saints?"

A sideways smile curved his lips. "I'll explain as we ride."

Chapter Twenty Seven

A crescent moon climbed the blackening sky, casting beams of cool light upon the sloping moors. Stars, myriad and wondrous, dotted the sky and pointed their way north while Jo listened with rapture to Ian's tales about the Saints and Scotland's secret network of Scottish rebels.

"My brothers and I were first asked to join the cause by Bishop Lamberton. After the Berwick massacre, we were exiles, living in the woods. Like ye, we needed a purpose, and so he gave us swords and horses and called us the Saints. At his command, we robbed English nobles on the road north into Scotland."

"Why did he call ye the Saints?"

"He wanted to protect our identities. During a heist we couldn't use our Christian names. And so, the bishop gave us saints' names. Mine was a simple choice for the bishop. Ian is the Gaelic form of John, and so he called me Saint John. As the eldest brother, Jack was the leader of our gang, and so rightfully called Saint Peter. Quinn, being the educated MacVie, was named for the philosopher, Saint Augustine. Now, before I tell ye about Alec, do ye know the story of Saint Paul?"

Jo nodded. "His birth name was Saul, and he was a Pharisee."

"Do ye remember how he came to believe in Christ?"

She thought back to her studies with Father Daniel in the loft above the chapel. "He experienced a powerful vision on the road to Damascus."

"Indeed, and that is why the bishop called Alec, Saint Paul. He has visions."

Jo's eyes flashed wide. "Alec's been gifted with the Sight?"

"Aye, although he may consider it more of a curse."

"This is fascinating. I never had any siblings."

Ian laughed. "Ye do now, and there is still one more, Rory."

"What did the bishop call him?"

"Saint Thomas."

Jo gasped. "As in Doubting Thomas? But why?"

Ian smiled. "Rory's loyalty and his character have never been questioned by the bishop, but in those days, Rory was, shall we say, a wee bit reckless. The bishop was just giving him a gentle reminder to heed Jack and to think before he acted."

She glanced sidelong at her husband. "What name would he have given me?"

A slow, sensual smile upturned his lips. "I could think of many names for ye, none of which should be repeated in church...lover, goddess, vixen—"

She swatted his shoulder playfully. "I see that look in yer eye, husband, but we cannot be waylaid." She cleared her throat. "Back to the subject at hand. Answer me this—even if yer names were protected, what about yer faces. Couldn't those ye robbed have told the magistrate what ye looked like?"

"They never saw our faces. The bishop gave us each black masks and shirts of gleaming black mail and around our necks hung large wooden crosses."

Jo shivered. "Ye must have been a wicked sight!"

Ian smiled. "That we were. We sent terror into the hearts of those English nobles, who were unlucky enough to meet the Saints on the road. Not that their terror was reasonably grounded."

"What do ye mean? Ye attacked, did ye not?"

"Aye, but we always adhered to a simple code; we were thieves not murderers." He lifted his shoulders. "Not that we were even truly thieves. Every coin, jewel, or trinket we stole fed the cause. English nobles have bled our countrymen dry. We were only taking back what was rightfully ours."

"Will yer brothers be at Ramsay's tavern?"

"Nay, they've all been unmasked, their identities revealed, and so they've gone into hiding to protect the other agents and the leaders of our cause."

Frowning, she asked, "Will I ever meet them?"

Ian reached across the space between their horses and squeezed her hand. "That I do not doubt, but for now we're riding to meet Ramsay, and with any luck, he's already assembled the other agents."

Jo chewed her lip. "There's just one thing I don't understand. I thought Ramsay was a blacksmith by trade, not a tavern owner."

"The Iron Shoe isn't an ordinary tavern. 'Tis underground, beneath Ramsay's shop and is only known to Scotland's agents. 'Tis a place to meet in secret. Many plans have been made over a tankard of Ramsay's finest brew."

"And ye're certain he'll be there?"

"Nay, but 'tis the first place we'll look."

She shot him a look of mock disapproval. "And here I thought I was the one keeping secrets. Ye've led me to believe ye're this decent man, a simple fisherman, a heroic warrior, a good Samaritan, rescuing women and dogs in distress, and all the while yer a thief, a spy, an outlaw—"

"Not quite," he chimed in. "My brothers are all wanted men; whereas, my identity has never been revealed. Ye won't see my likeness on the wall of a drinking house. So, yer only partly correct. I'm not actually an outlaw."

"Let us try to keep it that way—I would rather ye not have to go into hiding like yer brothers. But know this, if ye must run—I go where ye go."

He seized her off her horse and kissed her with all his love, all his passion. "The hour grows late, and our horses must rest."

She scanned the woods, spying a towering oak with a massive canopy that kept the underbrush at bay. "We could rest there."

But he shook his head. "I've another place in mind. I'm taking ye to the Harborage. 'Tis not far from here."

Jo scanned either side of the narrow path through which they rode. "Ian, I don't think we're going to find an inn out here."

He laughed. "The Harborage is our haven, a place for Scotland's rebels to rest without fear. There's a clear pool, amidst a wide, open glade, surrounded by tall dense trees. We built platforms to sleep upon high up in the branches."

"How do we get there?"

"Ye have to know where to go. There's no road except that which we make ourselves."

As they carried on, Jo asked, "What are the other agents like?"

"There are more agents than any of us know about. But Ramsay and I had a few agents in mind when the bishop charged us with canonizing new saints, David, Nick, and Paul. David is good man, quick to react, and given over to worrying. He's also as cocky as they come but has an incredible mind for tactics. Nick..." Ian blew out a long breath. "Nick is hard to describe. He's a fierce swordsman and a passionate rebel, but...he has anger in his heart."

"Why?"

A shadow passed over Ian's face, replacing his usual bright countenance with a sorrowful frown. "He has suffered greatly. Nick also hailed from Berwick. When the great city was attacked, he was at sea. His wife and three children were burned alive in their home."

Jo gasped, clasping her hand to her heart.

"He joined the cause, not because he sought justice. He wanted revenge. In recent years, however, my brother, Alec, helped him find some peace. He's no longer guided by vengeance alone, which has made him a wee bit softer." Ian took a deep breath before he continued, "Lastly, there's Paul. He's everything Nick is not. Despite the hardships he's faced, he remains quick to laugh. He is earnest and kind." Ian pulled on his reins. "Here we are," he said, gesturing to a particularly thick wall of bramble.

Jo looked around her at the inhospitable tangle of branch and bracken. "Where exactly are we other than the middle of the forest?"

He chuckled. "What? Is this not everything ye imagined a haven to be?"

Jo trudged through the dark woods, pulling her horse behind her. Dense underbrush obscured the ground, snagging at her tunic. Silvery beams of moonlight slanted through the trees, alighting upon Ian's broad shoulders as he led her deeper into the thicket. Towering pines reached for the stars, and scattered in all directions were fat oaks, adding to the lush canopy overhead.

River song reached her ears. She listened to the briskly flowing waters and imagined what her eyes could not see: a wending current, impeded only by slick, jutting rocks and stubborn saplings at the water's edge. Soon, the towering pines and gnarled oaks gave way to slender birch trees, which beckoned the moonlight with their sparsely adorned branches. Then, the river came out of hiding as the underbrush thinned and faded, leading them to the middle of an open glade, beautiful and strangely luminous beneath the summer moon.

"'Tis beautiful," she said, her voice reverent.

They fed and watered their horses and brushed away the burs clinging to their soft coats. Then, it was their turn to wash away the dirt and dust from the road.

Jo slipped off her leather shoes and eased her feet and calves into the icy pool. "This is glorious." She leaned back and gazed up at the velvety sky, broody and studded with diamonds.

"I never want to leave this place," she drawled, but then jerked upright. "We cannot linger."

Ian stiffened at her side, his hand moving to the hilt of his sword strapped to his back. "What's wrong. I heard nothing."

"Nothing's the matter," she said quickly. She expelled a slow breath and eased her shoulders down. "For a moment, I had forgotten our urgency." She gazed at the sleepy mist hovering above the water, lulling and otherworldly. "'Tis as though a spell has been cast over this place to make the weary traveler forget their worries."

"That's the idea, but ye needn't worry. As soon as our horses have rested enough, we will set out. I promise there are no sirens hiding among the trees, casting spells to make us slumber."

She grabbed his arm. "Are ye certain, because I just saw shadows moving through the trees over there."

Ian leapt to his feet, drawing his sword. "Get behind me," he growled.

Jo sidestepped behind his broad back and peered around his arm at the suddenly menacing forest, alive with the sound of snapping branches. She swallowed hard, gripping Ian's tunic in clenched fists. Then, a chilly silence claimed the night. All movement had stopped. Even the river seemed mute, drowned-out by the sound of her pounding heart.

Suddenly, a man sprang from the impenetrable forest, his sword at the ready. She gasped as she met his hard eyes, but to her surprise, the tension fled from Ian's back.

"*Alba gu bràth.*"

Still eying her with suspicion, the man sheathed his blade and walked toward them. He shook hands with Ian. "*Alba gu bràth.*"

"This is my wife, Jo," Ian said.

"*Alba gu bràth,*" she said, trying out the secret password of their cause for the first time while she dipped into a low curtsey.

The man shook his head disapprovingly but managed what she guessed might have been an attempt at a smile.

Chuckling, Ian turned to her. "Ye may have guessed that this is Nick."

"How could she have done that?" Nick scoffed.

Ian slapped Nick on the back. "I told her all about yer warm and friendly ways."

Nick looked back at her, his hard eyes impassive. "If warm and friendly is what ye want, Paul will be here at any moment." Then he turned to Ian. "The others are bringing along the horses. I came ahead to ensure the Harborage was secure."

No sooner had Nick made his announcement, than the forest came alive around them. Three men stepped into the glade, towing horses, the largest of which, she knew straightaway. The other two she guessed were David and Paul. David, she decided, was one with shoulder-length blond hair and intelligent green eyes. And the other man, with a boyish mop of brown curls, warm eyes, and a smile so broad she feared it would crack his face, had to be Paul.

"*Alba gu bràth*, Ian," Ramsay boomed.

"*Alba gu bràth*!"

The mighty blacksmith shook Ian's hand, then turned to her and smiled. "Hello again. So, ye let him join ye on yer travels after all."

She shrugged. "I couldn't very well let him travel on his own. Look at him." She shook her head and sighed. "He's defenseless against the dangers of the open road."

Ramsay threw his head back with laughter. "Ye're funny..." His eyes flashed wide. "And Scottish?" He whirled around, his numerous, long, blond braids, lifting off his back. "Is my memory faulty, or is she just pretending."

"She *was* pretending," Ian began. He turned to Jo and smiled encouragingly. Then he put his arm around her waist and stepped back to address the men. "Scotland's agents, it is my great honor and privilege to present to ye, Lady Josselyn Fergusson."

Ramsay's eyes flashed wide. "Lady! How is that even—"

But David reached out his hand, silencing the blacksmith. He stepped forward, his green eyes narrowing on her. "Are ye the daughter of Laird Malcom Fergusson?"

At the mention of her father's name, Ramsay's eyes widened still, and Paul's seemingly limitless smile faltered, his gaze becoming intent and eager. Even Nick was looking at her with undisguised interest.

She made her stance strong. "I am she."

David drew closer, looking at her intently. Then he gasped. "Of course, ye are. Look at ye. One brown eye and one blue." He dropped to one knee. "I had the honor of serving with yer father. He was a great man."

Ramsay, too, came forward and knelt. "I only knew him by reputation, but I ken what he has done for the cause. 'Tis an honor." He looked up and winked. "A surprise but an honor."

"What is going on," Nick snarled, his attention now on Ian.

Jo stiffened. "There's no need for anger."

"I'm not angry," Nick snapped at her before his gaze settled once more on Ian. "I'm curious to know why Ian is here in the Harborage with the daughter of Malcom Fergusson. Something's happened and I want to know what."

Ian nodded "Yer right, Nick. Something has happened."

Ramsay stood up. "Whatever it is, the Saints are ready to ride. We have our masks, black armor, wooden crosses, and we've a set for the new Saint Peter," he said looking pointedly at Ian.

"Good. Because we have our first mission."

"The abbot has given us orders?"

Ian shook his head grimly. "Nay, the abbot is our first mission. He's been taken."

An uproar ensued. Jo gripped Ian's hand tightly, her gaze darting from man to man as they all spoke at once, their faces twisted with fury.

"Whoever is responsible will pay," Nick snarled. "I will cut him from stem to stern!"

"I thought ye said yer brother softened him a wee bit?" she whispered in Ian's ear while the other agents continued to vent their surprise and anger.

"This is softer, if ye can imagine."

"Silence," Ramsay thundered, drawing everyone's attention. "Explain," the blacksmith said, the one word spoken with such vehemence, a shiver shot up Jo's spine.

Ian quickly told the agents about the treasure and Thane's treachery. "He left Toonan before we could escape and marched on Haddington with nearly a dozen men. As soon as we learned of his plan, Jo and I set out. We stopped here to rest our horses on our way to the Iron Shoe." He turned to Ramsay. "Ye can imagine my relief to find ye here."

Ramsay planted his feet wide and cracked his knuckles. "We can make it to Haddington before dawn."

"We don't ride for Haddington. Thane would have already succeeded in taking the abbot."

"How can ye be so certain," Paul asked.

"Haddington has little by way of defenses, and even if some of the monks had taken up arms to defend their leader, ye ken as well as I, that Abbot Matthew would have refused their championing. He would've surrendered himself before any blood could be spilled."

David nodded. "Ian's right."

"Thane hasn't the courage to act alone. He needs a nobleman to stand behind. I believe he rides south to make a new deal with Baron Wharncliffe."

Nick licked his lips, his eyes alight with bloodlust. "Then, we'll take them on the road south into England."

Jolts of excitement shot threw Jo as she watched the men prepare for action. After they'd dressed and readied their horses, Ramsay, David, Nick, and Paul stood side by side. They wore black tunics covered in black mail that glinted in the moonlight, black hose, tall black boots, and in their hands, they grasped black, hooded masks.

Ian, who also wore the Saint's garb, stood in front of them, holding five wooden crosses, strung on simple rope. "Ramsay, ye will be Saint James the Greater, given yer the tallest man, excluding me, I'd wager this world has known for a century."

Ian placed one of the crosses around Ramsay's neck. Then he moved to stand in front of David. "Ye led us into battle at Methven. And so ye shall be Saint Michael." After placing the cross around David's neck, Ian shifted his gaze to Nick. "Legend has it that Saint George slayed a dragon. Dragon fire blazes inside ye, but ye also have a valiant heart." He slid the rope over Nick's head. The newly dubbed Saint George gripped the wooden cross. "I will breathe fire tonight!" he vowed. Ian clamped his hand on Nick's shoulder. Then he turned to Paul. "Ye became one of Scotland's agents because ye wanted to see our people fed and clothed. Ye do not seek vengeance nor glory. Ye're Saint Martin."

After Ian honored Paul with his cross, Jo moved to stand at her husband's side. "May I?" She outstretched her hand, looking pointedly at the last cross he was holding. Ian placed it in her open palm.

"Bow yer head, Saint John." She passed the rope over his head. Then he straightened, his ardent gaze meeting hers. "Daughter of Scotland, are ye ready to ride?"

Her heart thumped in her chest. "Let us go save the Abbot! *Alba gu bràth*!"

Chapter Twenty Eight

Hooves pounded the earth in the distance. One side of Ian's lips upturned in a lazy smile. "I missed being a Saint." Lowering his black hooded mask over his face, he glanced back at the others.

"Jo, keep back until we've subdued the warriors under Thane's command."

She nodded her assent. "Remember, those are my clansmen." Brows drawn, her gaze darted to Nick.

"Jo, look at me."

She did as Ian had bidden her.

"Ye needn't fash yerself. We *all* understand what is at risk."

She nodded and turned her horse around, heading higher up the ridge to safety.

Ian turned back around, his gaze scanning his fellow agents. Their horses snorted and stomped at the ground. "Saints, masks on," he hissed. "Stick to the code. Ye're called by yer saint's name. The warriors we charge at are not our true enemy. Our aim is to steal away the abbot," he said looking pointedly at Nick. "Disarm, maim if ye must, but remember yerselves, lads...we're thieves, not murderers."

Narrowing his eyes to see through the slits in his mask, he scanned the ribbon of road beyond the trees. The coach they'd been tracking, which bore the seal of Haddington Abbey, careened into view along with nine Fergusson warriors, plus the driver.

Ramsay nosed his horse forward, stopping beside Ian. "Which one is Thane?"

"I don't see him. He must be in the coach." Ian stretched his neck to one side and then the other. He took up his reins. "Saints, let's ride!"

He kicked his horse in the flanks and reached the roadside at a gallop and met the Fergusson warriors head on. One thought raced through his mind—these were his kinsmen now. Steel rang in a harsh clash. Fury swept through him, but he kept it in check. One warrior charged at him. He parried, then swung. The flat side of his sword slammed his attacker's forearm. The warrior's blade dropped to the ground.

One warrior disarmed.

Ian swung around, parrying another blow. He sliced his sword down, knocking his attacker's blade to the ground.

Another warrior disarmed.

Sword raised high, he readied for the next assault, but only a cloud of dust stirred. He scanned the saints—none injured, all had kept their seats. Then he eyed the warriors on the ground. Some were clutching minor wounds, but none were dead. With a grunt of approval, Ian swung down from his horse. The other Saints followed. The defeated men's eyes flashed wide, and they scurried back to the carriage, which had been driven into a ditch.

In the early light of day, Ian knew they were a terrific sight with their great height and black hooded masks.

Ian turned to Ramsay and David, "St. James and St. Michael, secure the carriage. Get the abbot."

With a nod, Ramsay stormed over to the carriage with David following just behind.

Next, Ian motioned to Nick. "St. George, gather the weapons."

Then Ian turned to Paul. "St. Martin..." Ian took a deep breath and locked eyes with Thane, whom David had just pulled from the carriage. "Hold him and keep him away from me!"

"Ye're d...d...demons," Thane stammered,

"Nay," Nick growled, storming at Thane.

"St. George," Ian warned. "Stick to the code!"

Nick seized Thane's tunic in his fist, snatching him away from Paul. "We're not demons. We're Saints!" he snarled through his mask, then shot his fist up, slamming Thane under his chin. His head snapped back, and he crumpled to the ground.

An instant later, Jo rode down the slope.

Ian smiled at her, although he knew she couldn't see. "I told ye Saint George has grown soft."

THERE WAS A PART OF Jo, the part that seethed with fury at Thane's betrayal, that wished Nick was still as vicious as ever and had done as he'd threatened at the Harborage, slicing Thane from stem to stern. But when she dismounted from her horse, she drew a deep breath and remembered the Saint's code. She passed by Thane's crumpled form without a second glance. The person truly weighing on her mind was the abbot.

She hurried to the carriage, peered inside and, to her surprise, spied three men with burlap sacks on their heads, crammed together on the same seat, their bodies twisted awkwardly. None spoke, but each emitted strangled noises that were further muffled by the sacks.

"What's the delay?" Ian called.

She glanced at him over her shoulder. "He tied their wrists to the counterbalance." Turning back, she bit her lip while she watched Ramsay and David attempt to slice through their bindings.

"Is Thane dead yet?" David gritted. "Because if he's not, I claim the honor. These ropes are carving into their wrists." Then he leaned back. "Blast this damn mask! I can hardly see!"

"Keep it on, St. Michael," Ramsay warned him. "Stick to the code."

Jo scanned the prisoners; two wore hose while the other wore the robes of a monk. Reaching out, she whisked the rough fabric off the abbot's head. He squinted against the light and struggled to speak.

"He's gagged!"

"Jo," Ian called to her.

She backed out of the carriage and met his gaze. "Allow me to help," he said, brandishing a small dirk.

She nodded and stepped aside. Ian leaned into the carriage, and after a few short moments, the abbot emerged. Angry gashes marred his wrists, and the edges of his mouth looked cracked and sore, but otherwise, he seemed in good health.

"Abbot Matthew!"

"I'm all right, Lady Josselyn."

"Lady Josselyn!"

Jo whirled around. Ten Fergusson warriors were laying on their stomachs, face down with their hands on the backs of their heads while Nick paced in front of them.

"Who said that?"

"I did," the one nearest to her blurted.

"I don't remember giving ye permission to speak," Nick snarled.

"Stand down, St. George. Remember, these are my men. They were not aware of Thane's treachery." She rushed to the man's side. "Ye may rise."

He lifted his head and looked at her, his eyes widened and filled with unmistakable reverence. "It is ye!"

She nodded and swallowed hard against the sudden knot in her throat. "Forgive me, but I do not remember yer name."

"I am Hamish, the captain's youngest brother."

Jo smiled. "Of course."

Tears flooded his eyes, and he squeezed her hand. "Are ye truly here, my lady?"

She nodded and gently tugged on his arm. "Please rise."

Hamish stared cautiously at Nick. "Who are these...men?"

She glanced at Nick, who was glaring down at Hamish through the slits in his nightmarish mask. "Ye've naught to fear, Hamish. They're Scotland's heroes. If ye're loyal to me and loyal to Scotland, they will not harm ye."

"I am," Hamish said fervently. "We all are, everyone of us. In fact, we just marched on the house of a corrupt abbot who betrayed yer father. Thane can tell ye himself." His gaze scanned the roadside and carriage, then settled on Abbot Matthew. His eyes flashed wide. "'Tis him, there. He betrayed yer father. Thane can tell ye..." His words trailed off when he spied Thane unconscious on the ground.

Jo sought Hamish's gaze. "Thane lied to ye. He was the one who betrayed my father." She looked at the rest of the men still lying on ground. "Rise warriors of Clan Fergusson!"

Slowly, her kinsmen stood, their expressions fluctuating between awe and terror, depending upon whom they set their gazes. "The abbot is innocent."

Hamish made the sign of the cross. "Then we kidnapped a man of the cloth?" He dropped to his knees. "Dear Heavenly Father, forgive us!"

"Ye needn't be afraid," Jo soothed, helping Hamish, once again, to his feet. "Thane is to blame, and he, alone, will be held responsible. If my father were here—"

"He *is* here!"

Sucking in a sharp breath, Jo whirled around. Ian lumbered out of the carriage, supporting one of the other men to the ground. She could see now that his hose were badly tattered, and a tangled mess of straggly brown hair further obscured his downturned face. Suddenly dizzy, she stumbled back.

Nick grabbed her. "I've got ye."

She straightened, her heart pounding. Could it be?

"Da?" The word came out hoarse, choked from her throat.

The man slowly raised his head, his hair stiffly falling away from his face. "Josselyn," he croaked.

A sob tore from her throat. She rushed forward and threw her arms around him. "Da!" she cried again and again.

"Be careful," she heard Ian warn her. "He's badly hurt."

She pulled away, searching her father's face.

The slightest smile curved his lips. "I'll be all right now. I've got my wee lass." Tears leaked from the slits of his eyes, which squinted against the light. He wrapped her in one tremulous arm. He was painfully thin. She could feel his spine and ribs jutting through the skin of his back.

"Oh, Da!" She hugged him again, only gentler this time, and she cried unabashedly, tears of joy and of sorrow. Her father was battered and broken, but he was alive!

"Lady Josselyn!"

She pulled away slightly from her father's embrace to see who spoke. A young man with wheat colored hair and a spattering of freckles, stood next to Ramsay, who looked even larger than usual, standing next to the lad. She knew the young man instantly. He was Ruby's younger brother. "Samuel!" Brows drawn, she reached out to take his hand. "How came ye to be here?"

Squinting against the bright sunshine, he rubbed his head. "Thane took a club to me."

Her eyes flashed wide. "But why?"

"I saw him leave the keep. It was getting late. The sun was beginning to set. I...I followed him into the woods." Samuel gripped his head in his hands. "He was on his knees gazing down into what looked like a pit of some kind. I came up behind him and asked him if he needed my help, and he turned on me." He shook his hand. "That's all I remember." Then he took her hand. "But, my lady, ye're here, standing before my very eyes." Then Samuel's gaze shifted to her father, and his eyes shot wide. "My laird," he exclaimed and dropped to one knee, but he groaned again, gripping his head between his hands.

"I appreciate the gesture, lad," Malcom rasped. "But give yer head a rest."

"Listen, we all have a lot to talk about," Ian chimed in.

Jo turned and met his sky-blue gaze, visible through the slits of his mask. "But let us save our catching up for the carriage ride home." He turned to Ramsay. "St. James, help Samuel and Laird Fergusson back into the carriage." Then he turned to Paul. "St. Martin, give the Fergusson warriors back their swords and help them round up their horses. St. Michael, bind Thane's hands."

"Gladly," David said with relish.

"Then secure him to one of the horses," Ian continued. "Ye have the pleasure of escorting him to Toonan." Then Ian's gaze shifted to Nick. "Saint George, ride for Durham. Someone there needs a full accounting of all that has transpired."

Nick gave a curt nod before turning on his heel and walking toward his horse.

"Wait, St. George," Jo cried and hastened to his side. "There is a young baker named Joseph. He keeps a stand in the very heart of the market square. Will ye tell him that Jo said thank ye for his many kindnesses."

Nick dipped his head in acknowledgment of her request.

"Thank ye," she said. Turning on her heel, she started to walk away, but then she jerked around. "Wait, there is one more thing I wish ye to say to him." A smile curved her lips. "Tell him that my name is Josselyn."

Chapter Twenty Nine

With Ramsay in the box seat, driving the horses forward, the coach lumbered toward Toonan. Inside, Ian sat next to the abbot, and on the opposite bench, Jo sat, flanked by her father on one side and Samuel on the other. The latter had surrendered to his headache and had fallen asleep on his lady's shoulder.

As Malcom recounted his story, Jo's distress became increasingly apparent. But as much as Ian longed to spare her any further suffering, he knew she needed to know the truth.

"How could they have kept ye in a pit all this while!" Tears rushed down her cheeks.

"Thane couldn't very well lock me in Toonan's dungeon and expect my presence to go unnoticed. And the baron didn't want anyone else to know about the treasure. Had he brought me to Wharncliffe, he would have faced questions from his men." He released a long breath. "They kept me alive, hoping to track ye and yer mother down..." His voice broke. "They wanted to use ye, to threaten ye, to make me confess where I hid the treasure."

"Oh, Da! How ye have suffered."

"My suffering is nothing. 'Tis what happened to ye and yer mother..." He swallowed hard. "That is my only regret."

Jo rested her head on her father's shoulder, and they drove for some time in silence. Then at length Jo sat straight and looked at the abbot. "But why did Thane go after ye when he'd already found the treasure?"

"Ambition," her father said simply.

The abbot nodded. "My guess is that he hoped to gain recognition from King Edward by handing over the keeper of his stolen treasure and one of the leaders of Scotland's secret rebellion."

She nodded, but Ian could tell she still felt unsettled. "What is it, Jo?"

"'Tis just that he was already in possession of a fortune. What more could he have asked for?"

Malcom lifted his shoulders. "Titles, lands, a noble wife—who can truly know the workings of his heart? I will say that as misguided as he was, I do not doubt that he believed he was acting for the good of our people."

Jo stiffened. "Father, ye cannot mean to forgive Thane?"

Malcom patted her hand gently. "I do hope to one day. I don't care to be burdened by this hatred for the rest of my life. But if ye're worried about him being held responsible, ye needn't be. Thane will be exiled with only the clothes on his back, no horse, no coin."

She nodded. "'Tis fitting that he'll be made to struggle like Mama and me."

"Although, I dare say, he won't survive half so well as ye did," her father said, a sad smile curving his lips. "I'm proud of ye." He cleared his throat. "Now, Josselyn, I do have one question. Ye and this young man," Malcom said, gesturing to Ian who was sitting across from him, "Ye've both said that Thane discovered the treasure. Did he truly find it...all of it?"

Ian shook his head. "Nay, he did not." Leaning forward in his seat, Ian said, "Laird Fergusson, everything I've been told about ye over the years, about yer cunning and the fineness of yer character, I now know to be true without the inkling of doubt in my mind."

Malcom flashed him a curious look. "And who are ye?"

Ian's hand shot out for the laird to shake. "Ian MacVie. I'm yer...er...daughter's husband."

To Ian's surprise, a weak smile curved Laird Fergusson's lips. "So, my daughter married a MacVie. She couldn't have made a better match had I arranged one myself." He shifted his gaze and smiled warmly at his daughter. "Ye've always been a smart lass."

She laughed and her father chuckled, although his mirth soon deteriorated into a dreadful cough that racked his thin shoulders. "Rest now, Father. We will soon arrive at Toonan. I'll make ye well again. I promise." Despite the comfort of her words and the confidence of her tone, she flashed Ian a worried look.

He reached over and squeezed her hand encouragingly. "Keep breathing, Jo."

She took a deep breath. "Keep fighting."

"I like this new nickname...Jo," her father said, trying it out, his voice sleepy. "It suits ye, lass."

Two months later, Toonan's second harvest was underway, and her laird was on the mend, which meant that Jo and Ian could, at last, make the journey to Colonsay.

Ruby rushed into Jo and Ian's chamber. "Are ye certain ye do not wish me to pack yer trunks?" she asked, her words coming out in a rush.

Jo smiled calmly. "One satchel will suffice."

"But surely ye need more than that!"

"And who will carry the trunks on board?"

Ruby put her hands on her hips. "Yer husband and Ramsay are as mighty as the Argyle mountains."

"That doesn't mean I want them lugging trunks on and off the ship just so I can change for every meal."

Ruby sat down with a huff in one of the chairs. "Then what am I to do? Cook already packed yer provisions. Laird Malcom's bedlinen's have been changed. Ye're as self-sufficient as a nun." Just then, Ruby, the furry one with yellow eyes, leapt off Jo's new bed, fashioned to fit her husband's large frame, and padded over to her maid, nuzzling her furry head into Ruby's lap.

"I still can't get over how quickly she took to ye," Jo said, smiling at both her Rubys.

"She knows her namesake," Ruby crooned while she scratched the dog's soft, fluffy neck. Ruby barked her approval, then lapped at the maid's cheek.

"Remember to mind her while I'm away, and keep her out of the kitchens and away from the fields where the men train. And, of course, do not let her loose in the stables. And—"

"I ken she doesn't like anyone else accept ye, me, and yer husband."

"She doesn't like anyone else, yet" Jo corrected. She crossed to the hearth and reached down, smoothing her hand across Ruby's furry back. "Give her time, and she'll come around."

"To quote something ye once said to me," Ian said, appearing in the doorway. "Wishful thinking, wife."

Jo drank in the sight of Ian's broad shoulders and trim waist. His blue eyes shone with love. She rushed to his side and threw her arms around his neck and kissed him long and hard. "If ye remember, husband," she began when their lips parted, "in the end, I was wrong. Ruby succumbed to yer warmth and charm even before I did."

Wagging her tail, Ruby padded across the floor and jumped up, her front paws splayed across Ian's chest. "Don't fash yerself, lass," Ian crooned affectionately, burying his fingers in her fur and scratching behind her ears. "I love ye, too."

After Ruby lumbered down, standing, once more, on all fours, Ian turned to Jo. "The boat is ready. Ramsay is manning the steering rudder. Abbot Matthew is on board. 'Tis time to say goodbye to yer father."

"And to me," Ruby blurted, rushing to Jo's side.

Jo's chest hitched as she pulled Ruby close. They embraced each other as if for the last time.

"Remember, lassies, we're not going to Colonsay forever. 'Tis only a visit. We'll return in a month or two."

Jo took a deep breath, swallowing the knot in her throat. "I ken. 'Tis just that my heart isn't as smart as my head. The last time we said goodbye, we thought it was truly the last time." She stood straight and thrust her shoulders back. "But, of course, ye're right." Jo shifted her gaze from Ian back to her maid. "This is not goodbye."

Tears flooded Ruby's emerald eyes, but she smiled bravely. "Until we meet again."

Saying goodbye to her father was no easier. She climbed into bed beside him and snuggled up to his chest. Her hand rested on his heart. She savored the steady rhythm. "Ye look stronger everyday, Da."

"I feel stronger."

She sat up on her elbow and looked at him. His freshly shaven face boasted a healthy glow. The hollows of his cheeks had begun to fill out. She tapped her finger gently under his eye. "One brown eye." Then she tapped under the other. "And one blue."

His eyes crinkled around the edges as a smile spread across his face. "I love my wee lass. Be safe."

She nodded. "We shall return soon." She kissed his cheek and scooted off the bed. "I love ye, Da," she said, then set out across the room.

"Jo!"

She stopped in the doorway and turned back, looking at her father expectantly.

"When ye return, I'll be even stronger. Mayhap, we can waste some time."

Tears stung her eyes. "There is nothing I would love more."

Chapter Thirty

Epilogue

"**S**he's here!" Ian slowly shook his head in amazement as he gazed at the sleek merchant vessel off the coast of Colonsay.

Jo smiled. "She is a beauty!"

Ian seized her and crushed her to his chest. "The Messenger certainly is, but I meant Rose. I can't wait for ye two to meet."

He turned his gaze toward the crescent shore. "What do ye think, Abbot? Is it everything ye imagined Colonsay to be?"

The abbot smiled. "After sending off so many of my agents here, glad I am to see it with mine own eyes, although I won't mind telling ye, I'm most excited for the prospect of dry land."

"What about ye, blacksmith?"

Ramsay had barely stopped smiling from the moment they had stepped down into the skiff and set off from the mainland. He gripped the steering rudder in his massive fist and closed his eyes, deeply inhaling the tangy sea air. "'Tis grand, indeed."

"Then stay the course, Captain Ramsay, and bring us into shore."

The keel of their skiff carved into sandy shore. Ian and Ramsay jumped into the barreling surf, and, each manning a side, dragged the small vessel further ashore. Then Ian reached up, placed his hands at Jo's waist and swung her into his arms.

He smiled at Ramsay as he passed by. "Ye can carry the abbot."

"Don't even think about it, blacksmith. A simple hand down will suffice."

Jo laughed, her bright mismatched eyes beaming with pleasure. "Are ye sure ye wouldn't rather be cradling the abbot right now."

"I heard that!"

Ian threw his head back with laughter. Then he shifted his gaze forward, taking in the sloping shore and jutting rocks, which bordered the expansive meadow of sea grass, swaying and shivering in the breeze.

"What's this?" he said aloud, looking beyond the meadow to the row of cottages that belonged to his family. Ropes of sea grass woven with prime roses were strung from poles that rose up around three large trencher tables set in rows.

Jo beamed. "They must be preparing for a celebration."

"Aye, but what is the occasion?" He turned about, walking backwards up the slope with Jo still in his arms. He called to the abbot, who was, indeed, walking on his own two legs, although Ian noticed he did appear to be little unsteady. "Is today a feast day?"

The abbot tilted to one side, but Ramsay caught his arm and helped him straighten. "Not of which I'm aware."

"I know," Jo burst out excitedly. "Mayhap yer brother, Alec, had a vison of our homecoming, and they put together a gathering to celebrate."

Ian lifted his shoulders and picked up his pace. "There is only one way to find out." He set her down and threw his head back and whooped to the sky. Then, seizing her hand, he rushed forward, pulling her along behind him.

The cottage doorways swung open almost at the same time. Jack and Bella; Quinn and Catarina; Rory and Alex; and Alec and Joanie all stepped out. After a moment passed, their faces brightened with recognition and they poured from their cottages, rushing to greet their youngest brother.

Ian charged forward and greeted each of his brothers in turn, lifting them high off the ground and squeezing them until they each begged for release. To their, strong and beautiful wives, he bowed first, then kissed each one on the cheek before turning to his bride.

"Everyone, this is my Jo." He grinned. "I mean, this is my wife, Jo. Jo, this is everyone!"

Jo smiled graciously. "Ian has told me so much about ye all that I feel like we're old friends, not new acquaintances."

Bella came forward. "We're neither old friends nor acquaintances. We are sisters!"

Tears flooded Jo's eyes as she opened her arms wide. "I've always dreamed of having sisters." The MacVie wives came together and embraced. Ian's heart swelled at the sight.

Then a din that could match that of an army on the move suddenly rent the air as a choir of laughter and squeals reached their ears. Led by Moira, the eldest of Jack's lassies, the MacVie children thundered toward them.

"The bigger girls and that wee lass there with the long blond braid belong to Jack and me," Bella said, her pale green eyes shining amid her olive skin made darker by the Island sun.

Alex grabbed Ian and Jo's arms and turned them about. "That rascal with the black hair and showy, good looks like his father is mine," she said, winking at Rory.

"The black hair is the only feature ye can credit me for. He's yer son through and through," Rory shot back.

Laughing, Catarina, came forward, her hands at rest on her son's shoulders. "Do ye remember, Uncle Ian."

The lad smiled. "Of course, I do."

Ian scooped him up in his arms. "Nicholas, yer almost as tall as me! Keep on growing and I won't be able to do this for much longer." Ian turned to Jo. "This is yer Aunt Josselyn."

"Aunt Jo, if ye please," she said laughing. Jo beamed as Catarina and Quinn's eldest child reached for her, giving her a big hug.

"Thank ye for such a fine welcome," she beamed.

Ian set the lad back on the ground, and he raced off down the shore to throw rocks with some of the other children.

"Over by the waves, do ye see that wild thing with tangled black hair, that's our youngest. Her name is Freya," Catarina said, her face shining with pride.

Jo smiled. "Such spirit! I love her already!"

Ian put his arm around Jo's waist and led her to where Alec and Joanie were standing together. "Now, the last time I saw ye, Joanie, yer belly was a wee bit bigger."

Joanie blushed. "Indeed, it was." Then she pointed behind her.

Ian hunkered down and looked behind Joanie. Clinging to her legs, was a wee lass with straight, glistening black hair and eyes as black as her father's. She did not smile, nor did she shrink away. Instead, she looked at him with an intelligence far beyond her five years. "What's yer name, lass."

"Abagail."

"I'm yer Uncle Ian."

She nodded her head. "I ken."

"Did yer da tell ye it was me?"

She shook her head.

"Then how did ye know?"

She shrugged. "I've seen ye before."

He raised a brow at her. "When?"

A secretive smile upturned her lips. "Don't worry. I won't tell anyone where the treasure is hidden."

His eyes flashed wide. Then he pressed a kiss to her cheek. "Ye take after yer father, I see."

At this, Abagail's face broke into a fierce grin. Ian ruffled her hair before straightening and meeting Alec's gaze. "So, my wife was wondering if ye had a vision of our coming?"

Alec smiled. "Ye completely took us both by surprise," he said, motioning toward Matthew.

Matthew came forward, then, and Ian turned to Jo. "This is Alec and Joanie's adopted son, Matthew. He, too, has the Sight."

When Jo met the young man's gaze, her smiled faltered, but only for an instant, then it spread wider than Ian had ever seen it. "Ye're like me," she cried and tapped under one of Matthew's eyes. "One brown eye." Then she tapped under the other. "And one blue."

Matthew beamed at her.

"So," Ian called out. "My wife and I want to know what we're celebrating!"

"Only the greatest news ye could ever hope to hear," Jack said. "What say ye all—should we tell him...or should we show him?"

"Show him," everyone shouted together.

"I want to lead the way!"

Ian turned around and whooped. "Florie, my sweet, wee lass!" He scooped Jack's adopted lassie into his arms and pretended to sway beneath her weight. "I ken ye've always been partial to me holding ye lass, but ye're getting so big."

She grinned fiercely. "Mayhap, one day, I will be the one to carry ye."

Laughing, he set Florie down and reached for Jo's hand. "All right then, leader. Show us the way."

Florie sprinted ahead, calling to the children playing in the surf to follow her.

"Where are we going," Jo asked breathlessly, her face flushed and beautiful.

"My guess is to visit, Rose. Her cottage is beyond the jetties."

They walked along the shore. Just as her cottage came into view, Rose swung the door wide and stepped outside.

Sucking in a sharp breath, Ian sank to his knees.

His chest tightened.

A well of emotion too great to contain rushed up his throat. "Rose," he gasped and dropped his head in the sand and let go the flood.

Jo squatted down beside him. "Ian, what is it? Look at me?"

He could hear the sudden fear in her voice. He looked up and swiped at the tears streaming down his face. "'Tis Rose."

"Ian," Rose cried, suddenly spying her youngest brother. She dropped the basket of bannock she held in her hands and waddled toward him.

Ian sprinted forward. "Rose!" He dropped to his knees and placed his hands on her swollen belly. He had no words. His heart felt as if it might burst from his chest.

"Oh, stop crying," Rose chided. "Or ye'll make me cry, and then I'll never stop."

Taking a deep breath, Ian swiped his eyes again and stood up. His voice was choked when he called Jo to his side.

"This is my sister, Rose." Then he once more pressed his hand to her rounded belly. "And this is her soon-to-be sweet, wee bairn."

"My brother is not always such a sap," Rose said, reaching to embrace Jo.

"Babies are always the best news," Jo said brightly.

Rose nodded and smiled, rubbing her own stomach. "This is a blessing that I thought I would never know again." Rose's red curls flew in front of her face, and she lost her balance. Ian grabbed her, and she burst out laughing. "Ye should have seen me on the ship, teetering and tottering. 'Tis why we had to come home."

"We arrived just yesterday."

Ian turned and once more had to swallow the emotion rushing to the fore as he pulled Rose's husband, Tristan, into his arms. "Thank ye," was all Ian could think to say.

Tristan laughed. "It was no trouble. There is nothing I enjoy more than trying for a babe with my beautiful wife."

Ian took a deep breath before glaring at his brothers. "Ye should have just told me."

"And miss the opportunity of seeing ye blubber like the rest of us," Rory laughed. "Never!"

They made their way back to the line of cottages where Ramsay and the abbot awaited them patiently.

The MacVie men hurried forward to greet the abbot.

Smiling, the abbot embraced each of the brothers in turn, and then Ramsay came forward. "We stayed back so ye could have time together as a family," the blacksmith explained.

Ian shook his head. "But ye both are family."

Jack came forward then. "Abbot, I am grateful and happy to see ye, but I must ask—What the blazes are ye doing here?"

The abbot smiled and gave a little shrug. "I thought all of ye," he said, looking pointedly at Rory and Alex, who stood arm and arm with their daughter, "could use the company of a holy man."

Ian met his eldest brother's gaze. "The abbot has been unmasked, in a manner of speaking."

"That's right, lads. I'm now a wanted man."

Quinn drew close, his brow furrowed. "But how can that be?"

The abbot put his arm around Quinn's shoulders. "'Tis a tale to be told with good food and plenty of ale. Suffice it to say, that I am no longer the *secret* leader of the Scottish rebellion." The abbot's voice took on a more serious note. I am only a danger to my fellow monks now, and my agents."

"What about ye," Jack asked Ian. "Were ye caught as well?"

Ian smiled and shook his head. "Nay, I am still the only un-wanted MacVie."

Jo slid her hand in his. "That's not entirely true," she said, her voice low and sultry.

Laughing, Ian scooped her into his arms and started toward the beautifully decorated tables. "I thought this was a celebration!" he called.

Everyone rushed forward to finish the preparations. When all three trencher tables were filled with food and family, the Abbot Matthew stood and held his tankard high. "Scotland's coffers are full. Our king can now come out of hiding. Our beloved sister is going to be a mother again. The MacVies are all together for the first time....well, in a long time, and I am here to enjoy it all. *Alba gu bràth*, my dear friends!"

The MacVie siblings, their adoring spouses, and their exquisite children raised their cups high. "*Alba gu bràth*!

The End

THE DEVIL IN PLAID

A Standalone Scottish Medieval Romance

"Beautifully-written and vividly-imagined, The Devil in Plaid is an impossible-to-put-down read." ~ Amazon reviewer

An excerpt from The Devil in Plaid
JAMIE MACLEOD WAS ON his way home after a three-day hunting trek across the Urram Hills. Chasing after stags in the mud had more than tested his endurance and patience.

Dirt and grime streaked his legs, arms, face, and hair. Several surprises had delayed their homecoming, mudslides, flooding, a band of foolhardy tinkers. But the most surprising of all—and surely the most ill-fated—was the newest delay.

He crossed his arms over his chest as he gazed down at two women he'd never seen before. One was petite and wore a fine cloak of rich blue velvet. Her raven black waves glinted in the sun. Wide, sky-blue, terror-filled eyes locked with his. She was startlingly beautiful with skin as white and pure as milk. The other woman, clad in simple homespun wool, stood tall with broad shoulders and full curves. Her blonde hair lay in a thick braid over one shoulder. She stared up at him with eyes that mirrored her lady's, wide and full of fear.

"Who are ye?" he growled.

The women drew closer together, clasping each other's hands, but they did not answer.

"Judging by the fear and that glimmer of animosity I detect in both yer gazes, I'm willing to bet ye're MacDonnell lassies." Then his eyes settled on the petite beauty in the rich cloak. "And judging by the fineness of yer garment, I can only assume ye must be the Lady MacDonnell herself."

The black-haired beauty straightened her shoulders. Steel entered her gaze. Giving her chin a haughty lift, she said, "I am the daughter of Laird MacDonnell, so ye'd best be letting us on our way or..."

The woman's voice quivered before it trailed off as Jamie withdrew his broad sword from the scabbard strapped to his back. "Or what?" he said, his voice deadly soft.

With the tip of the blade pointed down, he let his weapon drop. It drove into the ravine floor. The women reached for each other and stepped back. An instant later, he jumped to the ground in front of them, forcing shrill screams from their lips. They clung to each other as he approached, freeing his sword from the earth when he passed by.

He kept his eyes trained on the lady. He needed to find out why the Lady of Clan MacDonnell—newly betrothed to the son of the most powerful clan in the region—was standing in a ditch on his land.

He stopped in front of her, holding his blade loosely in his hand. "Why are ye here?"

The lady met his gaze, her eyes unwavering. Still, she did not answer. His gaze dropped to her small hand, gripping so tightly to her maid's arm that her knuckles shone white. He glanced at her maid who trembled while she eyed his men on the ridge above.

Jamie circled around them. "I suggest ye answer me, or I will make my own conclusions." He stopped in front of her and drew close. "Mayhap, ye're unhappy with the soft puppy to whom yer betrothed, and ye came here to find a real man."

"My betrothal is none of yer concern," she bit out. He could tell she was grappling for courage.

He leaned closer still. "Ah, but 'tis very much my business, and why do ye think that is?"

Her eyes darted around nervously, but she offered no answer.

"Because ye're on my land," he snarled.

Her eyes widened. She clung closer to her maid.

Slowly, he returned his blade to its scabbard. Then he reached out and took hold of a lock of her black hair, stroking his thumb across the soft waves. She smelled of lavender and honey. "I suppose I could ransom ye."

She drew a sharp breath, then snaked her hand out and jerked her hair free from his grasp. Blue iridescent eyes widened as he drew even closer. Her bottom lip trembled, drawing his gaze to her full mouth.

She swallowed hard. "The dozen head of cattle ye stole a fortnight ago should be ransom enough." The fear in her eyes belied the strength of her tone.

He cocked a brow at her. "I was merely taking back what was already mine." Without looking back, he motioned for his men to jump down from the ridge. The loud thud of each of his warriors jumping to the ground sounded behind him, a chorus of his Highland brethren, which further widened the women's eyes and caused their feet to scurry back. They cringed with terror, and as well they should.

For centuries, their clans had feuded, always on the brink of war. And the only thing worse than a MacDonnell man in Jamie's mind was a MacDonnell woman. They were notoriously spoiled, fork-tongued vipers. "Ye still have not answered my question. Don't make me ask ye again. What are ye doing on my land?"

Her chin lifted, and for a moment, a flash of defiant strength shaped her delicate features. "This land is ours."

Jamie grabbed her by the shoulders and lifted her off the ground until they were eye to eye. "Ye don't want to make me angry."

A SHIVER RAKED UP FIONA'S spine as she hung, suspended in the air, staring into amber eyes, burning hot with fury. If the wild, hairy, monster of a man snarling at her wasn't yet angry, she did not want to know his true rage.

"The soil ye're standing on has long belonged to Clan MacLeod. Now," he hissed. "I am going to ask ye again. What are ye doing on my land?"

"Yer men attacked my escort."

His eyes widened for a moment, just a flash, but she had glimpsed his surprise.

"I gave no such orders."

"Be that as it may," she snapped, forgetting her fear. "MacLeod warriors attacked us on the open road."

Fresh anger flashed across his face the instant before he set her down. She grabbed Esme's hand and backed away, eyeing the enemy. Tension filled his shoulders. She noticed his fists clenching and unclenching at his sides.

He closed the distance between them in one mighty step. "If ye were attacked, then it was because ye were trespassing on MacLeod land. The land from the road to ravine is ours, given as a dowry from yer clan nearly half a century ago," he growled.

Her heart pounded. She swallowed hard, wishing Alasdair and her men would suddenly appear on the ridge and fire a dozen arrows into the devil's back. But they were nowhere in sight. The task of defending her clan fell on her shoulders alone. She took a deep breath and fought for courage. "That union was never consummated, which forfeits the dowry," she shot back, but inside her mind was screaming at her to stop talking.

At that moment, she needed to worry about survival not defending her clan's honor. She was alone with her maid in the woods inches from the MacLeod, the very man who haunted the dreams of every MacDonnell child.

He shook his head at her, giving her a look of disgust. "Yer grandmother ran off before the wedding. She was a faithless viper, a stranger to honor and decency."

"Decency?" Fiona blurted in outrage. Her grandmother had fled the betrothal because she feared for her very life, which Fiona was about to point out to the massive man glaring down at her when Esme grabbed her hand.

"This is not the time," Esme cautioned under her breath.

Fiona swallowed her protests. She tore her gaze away from the MacLeod's and looked beyond him at the fierce band of warriors—all as hairy and unkempt as their leader. Each man shot daggers from his eyes that cut through her fear to her very soul.

Esme was right. They were at the mercy of the enemy—an enemy known only for their cruelty.

She searched her mind for the words to make him go away when, suddenly, he turned on his heel and started to climb back up the ridge. His men followed.

Fiona glanced at Esme and lifted her shoulders in surprise. Mayhap, he was just going to leave them. *Please go*, she prayed.

"Are ye coming or do ye need my help to walk?" he called down to her when he reached the top.

"We will make our own way home," Fiona said in a rush before she started to turn her back to him.

"'Tis almost as if ye wish me to turn ye into a sack of grain and throw ye over my shoulder." His voice was deep and foreboding.

Fiona froze, knowing not to doubt his threat. She eyed the slope. "We will climb this ridge or die trying," she whispered to Esme who nodded firmly in reply.

Go to http://lilybaldwinromance to read
The Devil in Plaid.
Thank you for choosing the Highland Outlaws Series!
May you always feel the pulse of the Highlands in your heart.
Hugs,
Lily Baldwin

Made in the USA
Coppell, TX
11 April 2022

76404630R00152